LET'S
GET
QUIZZICAL

Also available by Kelly Ohlert
To Get to the Other Side

LET'S GET QUIZZICAL

A Novel

KELLY OHLERT

alcove
press

Published in the United States by Alcove Press, an imprint of The Quick Brown Fox & Company LLC.

Alcove Press and its logo are trademarks of The Quick Brown Fox & Company LLC.

Library of Congress Catalog-in-Publication data available upon request.

ISBN (paperback): 978-1-63910-505-2
ISBN (ebook): 978-1-63910-506-9

Cover illustration by Sarah Horgan

Printed in the United States.

www.alcovepress.com

Alcove Press
34 West 27th St., 10th Floor
New York, NY 10001

First Edition: October 2023

10 9 8 7 6 5 4 3 2 1

For my daughters, who are my everything.
But girls, put the book down.
You can't read it until you're older.

And if you're related to me . . . maybe skip
the second halves of Chapters Twenty-One and Thirty-Seven.

CHAPTER ONE
CHARLOTTE

"Pop!" I shout over the ear-splitting beeps of the smoke detector. I contort my body, trying to cover my ears, put down the drinks I've been balancing, and reach for the microwave at the same time. I pry that sucker open, and smoke pours out, filling the kitchen. An alarm in the living room adds its voice to the shrill chorus. Surround sound. Excellent. Just another Saturday at the Evans house.

"Pop! How long did you put the popcorn in for?"

"Four minutes! Why?" he yells. Sometimes I wonder if I'm experiencing the same reality as the people around me. The shrieking alarms didn't give it away?

"Who told you to put it in for four whole minutes?" I throw open the kitchen windows, then grab a towel and begin my dance solo across the room, fanning out the smoke.

"Orville!"

"Mr. Redenbacher also surely instructed that four minutes was for five hundred watts."

"Well, how much is ours?" he asks.

"It's because he left it unsupervised," Ma says. "You're supposed to supervise it. Listen for it to stop popping."

"I didn't know I was expected to babysit popcorn," Pop says.

Despite the ordeal, the alarm ceases its screeching, and the smoke clears out nicely. Visibility is getting to be less Grand Banks, Newfoundland, and more Hamilton, New Zealand—the number one and number ten foggiest places on earth, respectively, according to *WorldAtlas*. The air is practically breathable again.

Even though I moved out years ago, I still come to my parent's house most weekends to keep the tradition of watching family game shows alive. I've wanted to be a contestant ever since I started watching them with Gran at age four.

"Charlotte dear, we need more butter!" Ma shouts from the living room. I move aside some papers, to set down the popcorn bowl. My stomach twists, seeing it's another fresh stack of bills. I've got a running spreadsheet of Gran's medical expenses, but apparently it's going to need an update.

I risk another quick adventure in electromagnetic convection, to melt some butter.

"Over here." Gran sets aside her cross-stitch and holds up the enormous bowl of unburnt popcorn for me to christen with the melty goodness.

"What's this one going to say?" I ask, nodding toward her project.

She leans to the side, allowing me a better view of the start of a quote about honesty and transparency.

"Mother Teresa?" I ask.

She raises an eyebrow. "Very good. I still have to figure out where I'll put it."

We both scan the wall, already crowded with her work, most of which are stitched quotes.

"I'm sure you'll find a spot." I bring the bowl back to the kitchen and am tossing it with butter when there's a rogue beep from the smoke detector. I yelp and juggle the bowl, just barely keeping popcorn from raining down from the sky like edible confetti. At least popcorn makes a better confetti alternative than the gold, silk, and paper confetti made for a sultan's harem in 1895, which has since been outlawed for health concerns—although Pop's version of our snack may have qualified as being just as toxic.

I split everyone's popcorn into individual bowls and distribute them to Ma, Pop, Gran, and myself.

The familiar intro tune comes on, and I bust a move in my chair and hum along to it.

"Who's ready to *Brain Battle*?" Bobby Bailey, the long-time host of the show, asks in that chipper and suave voice he has. I'm going to miss him when he retires soon. His shoes will be difficult to fill. The studio audience roars, as is customary for the show, but it's more of a battle cry than a cheer.

Brain Battle is my favorite game show, which is saying something. Some of my most cherished memories are, oddly enough, sick days as a kid. I've tuned out the miserable-being-ill part and instead remember curling up on the couch with Gran. We'd spend hours snuggled together, basking in the warmth of a mountain of throw blankets and watching back-to-back episodes of every program on GSTV—the game show channel.

The lightning round begins, where the contestants individually answer questions to earn their spot on the team that competes in the second half of the show.

"This fictional volcano was instrumental in Tolkien's Middle-earth legendarium." Bobby Bailey raises an eyebrow before the cameras cut to the contestants keying in their answers.

"Mount Doom!" I shout at the screen.

"The correct answer is Mount Doom," Bobby Bailey says, and I beam in satisfaction.

"Well done, Charlotte," Ma says as I succeed at my sixth question in a row.

"When are you supposed to hear from the show again?" Dad asks.

We fall into an uncomfortable silence. Ever since I was old enough to audition for game shows, I've applied to every one I could find. I always pass the initial online test. I've even made it to the live interview rounds, where they coach us on energy level and on-screen mannerisms, but never any further.

I may be full of spunk in my family living room, but I lean toward being a bit more reserved out in public. Just in case a lack of enthusiasm was to blame, I've been practicing my jazz hands. Surely those would do the trick. My latest interview was only two weeks ago, and it was the big one: *Brain Battle*.

While I'd be happy with any game show, *Brain Battle* is the ultimate dream. A dream that, despite being close to fruition, may never come true if the whispers in the trivia chat groups and a recent news article are to be believed. Rumor has it *Brain Battle's* viewership has dropped. As labor costs rise, they're having trouble keeping up with production costs of the live format, rather than taping in batches. Concern that it won't be the same after Bobby's departure has only fueled those rumors.

"I might never hear from them. They don't reject you if you miss the cut. They either call you or they don't." The unspoken worry that I may never hear from *any* of them hangs in the air. With each week, month, and year that goes by, my dream dies a little, and with it, my motivation in other areas of my life. I metaphorically brush the thought away as I sweep the excess popcorn seasoning from my fingertips and onto the legs of my overalls.

"Well, I think that's a silly system," Ma says as the show cuts to commercials.

"Patience, sweet girl. It will happen," Gran says from her armchair. I walk over and give her a hug and check her oxygen tank.

"How are you feeling today, Gran?" I ask.

"Living the dream." That's why she's my favorite human. She's not even being dishonest about her feelings. She's the most positive person in the world. She fell ill a year ago with a mystery disease doctors haven't been able to put their finger on. Still, she treats every day as if it's the best, no matter how much pain she's in.

If she really felt like her day was terrible, she'd say it. Honesty is the single quality she values most, and she's full of quotes about it. I suspect she's always been an honest person, but she decided it was the hard and fast rule we'd all live by after the great scandal involving the man who is technically my grandfather.

Entire secret families don't exactly qualify as harmless lies. Supposedly, I have aunts and cousins out there that I've never met, but we don't talk about that, just like we don't talk about grandpa. Instead, we throw ourselves into honesty and integrity. If you're going to live by a core value, honesty seems like a good way to go, so I'm on board with it.

"The first novel written by this author was published posthumously in 2014, eighty-four years after it was first written."

"Laura Ingles Wilder!" Gran and I shout together.

"Jinx." I laugh and we bump fists gently.

"I haven't gotten a single answer today," Dad whines.

"That's nothing new," Gran and I say, again in unison, a broad grin splitting my face.

"Jinx again," Gran says, and Dad rolls his eyes.

Gran smiles and sinks back onto her chair, the lines on her face more prominent than ever. Oh Gran. She stays optimistic, even though we're all worried about her and about the cost of her care. Despite my parents and I all working hard and contributing to the costs, the money is getting short. If I could make it on a trivia show, I'd have a chance to win enough to get her the best care money can buy.

The show ends, and Gran is fading, her smiles seeming more forced and her breathing heavier. The music for the next show kicks in—a half-hour word-based show that was never our favorite.

"I think I'll take a quick nap before *It's Trivial*," she says, and the rest of us exchange worried looks. Mom subtly waves Pop and me to the other room while she gets Gran some painkillers and helps adjust her seat and fluff her pillow.

"I wish we knew what was wrong," I whisper to Pop once we've reached the kitchen and are out of earshot. I feel so helpless not knowing what to do to take care of her.

"I know, kiddo—me too." What lies unspoken is that we both know reaching a diagnosis means more testing, and second and third opinions, all of which costs money that we don't have. We were never rich, but we'd always been able to live comfortably until Gran got sick. It's incredible how quickly hospital bills can devastate finances. We'll come up with the funds somehow.

I pull the heating pad out of the cabinet and pop it in the microwave. It'll end up smelling like popcorn, but Gran will just say she likes her pain relief with a little seasoning anyway, or something like that.

Mom walks into the kitchen, carrying our empty bowls. "You can shut that off." She nods at the microwave. "She's already fallen asleep."

"That was fast," Pop says.

"She's been taking these power naps for the last week. She'll probably be wide awake again in fifteen minutes."

"Think she's okay?" I ask, not really knowing what I mean. Of course she isn't okay.

"She's a fighter." Mom's smile is tired, not quite reaching her eyes. Despite my being thirty, she still acts like she needs to protect me from hard truths. She doesn't lie, but she tells a truth that avoids answering the actual question.

"I guess we may as well make use of the time until she wakes up." I pull my laptop out of the bag hanging on the coatrack by the kitchen door.

Pop grabs the stack of bills off the counter and meets me at the kitchen table to crunch numbers, trying to twist them into a new shape that isn't quite so daunting. We spend our evening searching for salvation in a spreadsheet.

CHAPTER TWO
ELI

The pounding of feet against the belt of the treadmill slows its rhythm, fading to a stop, the upbeat music piping in through the room's speakers becoming more audible in its absence. Even when I'm not standing directly next to a running treadmill, it's always loud in here; the clanging of weights and whir of equipment a noisy background to my day. My last client of the afternoon steps off the track and onto the rubber floor of the gym. I hand him a towel from the nearby wooden bench.

"Great workout!" I high-five Ty.

He glares at me, bent over and still breathing hard after his cooldown. I chuckle. To be fair, I did run him hard today. "Let's go stretch before your muscles get as mad at me as the rest of you seems to be."

"Just because you can run those ridiculous intervals doesn't mean the rest of us can," he grumbles. Ty always gets grumpy with me when I push him, but he'll be over it in a couple minutes.

"And yet, you did. That limit is in your head, man."

"I still think you're using me to work out your own stress." While his workout was planned and purposeful, I can't argue with the need to destress and its impact on my own workouts lately.

"Yeah, yeah." I wave him off.

He reaches for his toes in a stretch. "For real, you doing alright?" Some clients like to keep things strictly business, but I have several I've been working with for years, Ty included. While I haven't dumped all my shit on him before, we've talked enough about life that he knows it isn't great for me right now, nor has it really ever been.

"You know how it is."

He frowns at my nonanswer, but leans into another stretch, and changes the topic, filling me in on his weekend plans as we head toward the locker rooms.

"I added a nine AM appointment for you tomorrow," Dave at reception says. "Someone new—asked for you by name."

I cringe, already knowing exactly who it is. I'd overheard one of our regulars giggling with her friend and suggestively recommending a session with me. I was well aware of the looks I drew from individuals attracted to men, but if they thought I was going to be sleeping with a client, they were going to be disappointed.

He laughs at my expression, "Looks like another one destined for a broken heart."

"I don't sleep with everyone who glances my way. That does not equate to breaking hearts." I should know. I'd broken one heart before, and that was more than enough guilt to live with.

"You coming out with us tonight?" he asks, breaking me from my thoughts.

Nia, one of the gym's other trainers, had said people were meeting for drinks, but a night out wasn't happening for me. I had to study, and alcohol was an unnecessary expense I wasn't splurging on.

"Not tonight."

Dave frowns, probably annoyed that I'm once again being antisocial. I do what I have to in order to get by.

"Will we see you on Thursday?"

"Yeah, I'll be there." The Thursday basketball games with the guys were one of the few social outings I managed these days. Pickup games at the park didn't cost a thing, and while time was a finite resource too, I needed those games to get out of the house for something other than work, before the weight of my responsibilities crushed me.

*　*　*

Once home, I fling my gym bag in the corner of my room, next to my scratched-up, hand-me-down dresser. I peel my shirt over my head, wincing at the soreness in my muscles. It was a long day on my feet. Even when I don't work out alongside my clients, I'm active all day. Today, I did several of the workouts, and I'm beat.

I shower, the heat soothing my aches. It's not as long as I'd like, but I don't want to jack up our water bill, and I have shit to do. I towel off and rub some muscle-relief lotion onto my shoulders. Then it's back to work, this time on the house.

I rock out to "Nine-to-Five," as I multitask my way through cooking dinner and running around the house, cleaning things whenever I can step away from the stove. I'm aware it's not exactly the anthem anyone would expect me to have, but that song is a jam. It's a favorite song that a high school ex introduced me to, and I still shamelessly enjoy it.

I take a step away from the stove, and a tile cracks under my feet. Damn it. Cooking, cleaning, and repair. I'm not Mary Fucking Poppins, and I can't keep up. The repairs on this house have become impossible, but it's my home, and it was there for me when my parents weren't.

I pull a load of laundry out of the dryer and set aside my father's work polo for him. He works two jobs, so I try to take care of the house we share.

My father is the king of doing the wrong things for the right reasons. He spent much of my teens behind bars, for theft and dealing drugs, but we're both determined that this time will be different. It has to be. Each time it isn't, the judges become less lenient. I'm afraid he's out of chances.

Dad gets home right as I pull dinner off the stove.

"Smells delicious." His eyes are ringed with an exhaustion that we don't talk about, but kills me to see. He's trying so damned hard. "Thanks, Eli."

We both sit at the table, allowing him a few minutes to relax while he eats. I pull out my laptop—so ancient its functionality is best suited for The Oregon Trail—to finish an assignment before my virtual course later this evening.

I'd barely finished high school when Dad got locked up the second time, but college was not an option then. Twelve years later and I've busted my ass with scholarship applications, though, and I'm taking courses to get my degree. College is one of my many projects to eventually get to a place where Dad and I can both work reasonable hours and not have a stack of bills to worry about.

"How are your classes coming?" he asks with genuine interest. I know he feels guilty for the path my life has gone down, but I don't blame him. I'm determined not to make the same mistakes he has. I didn't get off to the best start, and every minor misstep scares the shit out of me.

"Good. One more semester after this one."

"I'm proud of you," he says, and my heart splits open. That's another thing that's changed. He and I have gotten better at talking.

"Thanks, Dad."

He clears his throat. "I ran into Lucky today."

My muscles tense, and I'm rooted to the spot. Lucky was a friend of Dad's before. The type of friend not likely to help him stay on a good path.

"I said I hoped he was doing well and went on my way. If you see him around too, I didn't want you to worry." His shoulders slump. He's embarrassed to have to say things like this.

My muscles relax and I nod, not wanting to drag the conversation out and embarrass him any further.

He finishes his dinner, washes his plate, and disappears to shower before his next shift. I immerse myself in my homework, typing away at a paper. I should have had it done sooner, but damn if it isn't hard keeping all the balls in the air sometimes.

I finish the first draft at least and frown at the clock on the screen. Absorbed in my work, I hadn't noticed how much time has passed. Dad ought to be leaving for work, but it's been a while since I've heard movement from his room.

I knock on his door, but he doesn't answer, so I let myself in. He's dressed in his other work uniform but is sound asleep on his bed. I wish I could go to work for him, but I remind myself I'm contributing with my money from personal training, and finishing school is important so that we can break this cycle. We have to keep going so he never has to stoop to illegal means of keeping us afloat, and so I can avoid the temptation of what sometimes feels like the easier route too.

"Dad." I nudge him. He grunts and rolls over, and I sigh. "Dad," I repeat louder, giving him more of a shove. He jolts awake and looks at me.

"Sorry, I must have dozed off. What time is it?"

"Six forty," I answer.

"Shit." He bolts out of bed, fumbling among the discarded clothes littering the floor, in search of his hat.

"Here." I grab it from the top of his dresser and hand it to him. "You're wiped. You can't keep doing both these jobs." I feel guilty saying it because I know I'm not telling him anything he doesn't already know. The words have implications. The last thing I want is for him to take it as a suggestion he should turn to something else.

"I know. I'm working on a solution."

My heart leaps into my throat. That is exactly what I didn't want to hear.

"No, Dad. I am. It's not just school. I have other things I'm trying too. I'll figure it out."

"It's not your responsibility to figure it out," he shouts, thumping an open palm against the wall, frustrated with himself. He isn't a violent man, but it's a response I'm familiar with. Even though I'm an adult, he still feels like it's solely on him to pay for the house and all our other bills, as if I don't live here too.

"I'm not a kid anymore. It's on both of us." I don't mention that it fell on both of us even when I was still a kid, and for a time, on me alone. I know that's why he feels like it's all on him now.

Dad looks like he wants to say more, but he glances again at the clock. "We'll talk about it later." With that, he ties on his boots and bolts out the door.

I rub at my face in frustration before sitting down to finish the edits on my assignment. I have to focus on what I can control, before I lose it.

CHAPTER THREE
CHARLOTTE

I click my laptop shut, and Pop claps me on the shoulder.

"What happened to our party?" Gran calls from the other room.

I shake off the weight of our financial concerns, and we head back into the living room.

"We had to go get earplugs to tune out your snoring," I tease.

"Well, then we're even, after all that screeching you did as a toddler that you called singing."

Pop walks over to give Gran a high five.

"Brutal," I say, and she winks.

The phone rings before I can come up with a witty comeback. The screen displays an unprogrammed number. Probably a bill collector. I grimace.

"Oh, just answer it," Dad says, already reaching for his wallet.

"Hello?" I say.

"Hi, I'm looking for Charlotte Evans?"

"This is she."

"My name is Sarah. I'm the contestant coordinator for *Brain Battle*."

My heart shoots off faster than the Parker Solar Probe, ready to achieve its own record for fastest moving object. *No. It's not possible. Is it?* My hope soars, and I do my best to rein it in so I'm not completely obliterated if this call turns out to be nothing.

"Oh, hello," I say cautiously, zipping the conversational ball back her way so she can hurry and tell me why she's calling, before my heart explodes.

"Congratulations! You impressed us at your interview, and I'm calling to invite you to be a contestant."

My muscles seize in shock. I lose my grip on my phone. I lunge for it and bobble it in the air—a term I only know from extensive attempts to fill in the sports gap in my trivia knowledge—before it clatters to the floor. Seconds too late, I regain control of my limbs and scramble after it. *Oh god, what if I hung up? What if they never call back, and no one answers the line they called from? What if I blew it?*

My face heats and my hands shake so much it takes a few attempts to pick the phone up. On my knees on the carpet, one hand on Gran's chair, I put it back to my ear.

"Sarah?" I ask with desperation. "Are you still there?"

"Yes," she says, chuckling. "Everything all right over there?"

"Yes, I'm so sorry about that." I breathe a heavy sigh of relief and thank the cosmos and every possible deity that I haven't lost her call.

"Don't worry—you'd be surprised how often it happens."

I believe her, but I'm also confident no one wants this more than me. I can't imagine anyone else has devoted as many hours of their life to watching and cherishing game shows, studying, taking tests—everything. I cannot believe my dream is finally coming true!

"So, are you still interested?" she asks, a smile in her voice, something I can hear thanks to our ancestors using smiles not as a visual cue, but an aural one. When smiling, our facial muscles pull at our vocal chords in just the right way, to appear less threatening.

"Still interested?" I sputter, as if there could be an alternate reality where I might not be. That anyone could make it to this point and say no is laughable to me. "Of course I am! I mean, yes. Please! Thank you."

I'm not exhibiting my best professional interpersonal skills. I'm still shaking with excitement and nerves and other emotions that I lack the capacity to analyze at the moment. I need to survive this phone call so I can celebrate and maybe run a few victory laps around the block, Brandi Chastain style, to burn off some adrenaline. A laugh bubbles out of me. I don't think I've run since high school, at least, not any kind of long distance. No amount of enthusiasm is going to make me whip my top off for a jaunt up the street. The neighborhood watch would have a field day.

"I'm glad you're excited," she says. "It sounds like the team made a wonderful decision by selecting you. I always love when the contestants appreciate the show. It's such a unique opportunity. I wish I could go on it!"

That would be an impossibility for her, based on the rules for allowed contestants. No employees and no friends or family of employees either. I have read through enough rules pages for all the shows to make my eyes bleed. I've got *Brain Battle*'s memorized, along with all the laws regarding "Prohibited practices in contests of knowledge, skill, or chance." When I got my shot, I didn't want any risk of unknowingly breaking a rule and losing out on a prize. I'm determined to win and to do it fair and square.

Sarah goes over the details, including dates, attire, and where I can get a discounted hotel room. I try to put on a reasonable display of normality and communicating like a human being, rather than the Energizer Bunny, for the rest of our conversation.

The legal battle between Duracell and Energizer is one of my favorite bits of marketing trivia. Of all the things for two companies to fight over, they duke it out over pink bunnies. Interestingly enough, Duracell's bunny is sixteen years older than Energizer's, yet Energizer retains bunny rights in the United States.

"You'll be able to do that date, correct?" she confirms.

I hoard my vacation days like dragon's gold until the end of the year, every year, with this sole purpose in mind. I wasn't about to let something like a lack of vacation days throw a wrench in things. "Yes, that's perfect." Three weeks left to prepare.

I end the call with Sarah and stare down at my phone in disbelief. It hasn't quite sunken in that this is really happening. I look at each of my family members. Ma and Pop are agape. Gran is smiling like she knew it was going to happen all along. Gran's no psychic, but she always has this enchanting air about her, like anything could happen.

The silence hangs there for a moment while we stare at each other, letting it sink in.

"Pinch me," I suddenly insist. No one moves. "Pinch me! Hurry! I'm serious. Quick, someone pinch me, pinch me, *pinch me*!"

Finally, Dad moves and pinches my arm.

"Ouch!" I yelp. I look around again with wide eyes. "It's real!" I yell, and then we erupt in cheers.

Mom, Dad, and I leap about, hollering and hugging, and Gran does a little dance from her chair.

It's real. It's actually happening.

Mom pulls back from a hug, her hands on my shoulder. "When?" she asks.

I blink away the happy tears, grinning at her. "Three weeks," I answer. She smiles and Dad walks into the kitchen.

"We'd better get to work then," Ma says, nodding toward my bookbag, which is always on me and never without reading material. It's my traveling extension of my bookshelf where I keep trivia flashcards, maps, encyclopedias, sport almanacs, and pop-culture magazines. Anything that strikes me as good for studying.

"First we celebrate," Dad chides, holding up a bottle of champagne. "Then we study."

"Where'd the champagne come from?" I ask. My trivia brain immediately starts filling in the more complex answers, involving the Champagne region of France and a loophole in the Treaty of Versailles, allowing it to be made and named champagne in California as well.

"Gran insisted we hide some at the back of the fridge when you got the interview. Just in case."

I bend to give Gran another grateful hug. Pop goes to remove the cork, and Ma and I both lunge for him. "No!"

"Maybe you'd better let me do it, dear." Ma gently pries it from him. Pop frowns but can't argue, seeing that he has a knack for food- and beverage-related debacles, as evidenced by the earlier popcorn fiasco.

"To dreams coming true," Ma says.

The bubbly drink is fitting. I'm overjoyed, but underneath it, my nerves are slowly fizzing, and I know they will grow and overtake me in the coming weeks. All these years of dreaming culminate in this. What if I choke and get booted in the first round? Or I'm up against genius contestants and don't make it through?

Before the nerves can get the better of me, like I'm being squeezed by the world's most constrictive king snake, I laugh with my family, grateful this call came when I was with them, my favorite place to be.

* * *

Eli

The Michigan-weather roulette wheel dealt out warm weather for the day, perfect for some basketball. A cool breeze keeps the temperature comfortable, and a handful of kids shout and laugh on the nearby playground.

A few teens wander off to the small overgrown garden area, which I know from experience with a certain high school sweetheart makes for a great make-out spot. My hand slips as I realize that it's at least the third time this week my mind has wandered to her. She's never far from my mind, but this week she's been especially present in my memories. Something to unpack with my therapist if I ever find a way to afford one.

"Decided to have a social life after all?" Dave shoves the ball toward me.

"Pity game. You were so desperate for my attention." I throw it back to him. Dave's shot hits the rim. Raj tosses his bag to the side of the court and runs to snag the rebound.

"What's up?" Raj asks.

We take turns taking shots and giving each other shit as guys continue to arrive. There's a handful of regulars, and a couple randoms who show up as well. The way pickup games form ought to be studied. There are no posted times, no plan. We just show up, teams form like magic, and the game is on.

We're wrapping up our game as Olivia Newton John starts singing "Let's Get Physical," out of nowhere. Heads spin, looking for the source of the muffled sound, and Dave laughs. "You haven't changed that yet?"

"You're obsessed with me, Dave—when do I have time to undo all these pranks?" I jog over to the bag as the guys break off into conversation, and some head for their cars.

"Hello?" I grunt, primed to hang up on the unknown caller.

"Hi, my name is Sarah. I'm the contestant coordinator for *Brain Battle*. I'm looking for Eli Collins?"

I clutch the chain link fence to steady myself, because if this call is what I think it is, it's absolutely the type of conversation that could throw even me off-balance.

"Speaking," I say.

We needed a miracle. I'm afraid to hope that this might be it.

CHAPTER FOUR
CHARLOTTE

Three Weeks Later

I didn't expect the lights to be so hot. They missed that in the information packet and off-set orientation. I dab at the lines of sweat threatening to turn the sheath of makeup they plastered onto me into a river of tocopherol, dimethicone, and other ingredients I have memorized but wouldn't want to try pronouncing when tipsy at a bar trivia contest. If my nerves alone didn't generate enough heat to cause this cosmetic canal, these lights certainly do.

I mentally run down the instructions they gave me. Smile wide, stand tall. High energy, but don't overdo it. Don't make them regret picking me for the show, especially since they're desperate for viewers, even if they didn't mention that part. Most of all, don't blow this shot.

It's almost go time. My handler, Sarah, gives me a little wave as she walks out from the dressing rooms with the final contestant for our individual round in tow; a man with a strong build and confident saunter.

As she veers off along the slightly curved edge of the main stage, toward the semicircle of contestant pods, his face comes into view. I gasp in horror. His brown eyes widen under thick dark brows that I've always found attractive. This is not the first time I've seen him. Far from it. A day's stubble over his features, which have sharpened with age, only adds to the bad boy aura he's always carried.

Suddenly I'm seventeen again, alone under the bleachers, staring anxiously at my watch. My stomach twists, full of nerves. I can't believe I let him talk me into ditching classes. I've never been so much as a minute tardy. But it's Eli, and the mere thought of him gives me butterflies. With each passing minute, my hope dwindles, anger, shame, and embarrassment taking its place.

The lights and sounds of the TV set come crashing back, and I see spots in my vision, clouding out the unmistakable figure of Eli Collins.

On the most important day of my life, when it's imperative I focus solely on answering questions, he finally makes an appearance. I haven't seen him in twelve years, and it's been thirteen since the day he threw me under the bus. Thirteen years since the boy who is now the man in front of me broke my heart. I want to leap over my podium and *throttle* him.

Eli's smug smile disappears, and he freezes in place.

"Eli?" Sarah asks, questioning his sudden statue impression. She notices I'm the object that appears to have given him the Medusa treatment and glances between us. I narrow my eyes at him, and my chest heaves with fuming breaths. Why today of all days? I can't believe this is happening. Then again, the fact that unicorns don't exist didn't stop Scotland from making it their national animal. Anything is possible.

"Charlotte?" Sarah asks. Her eyes flick back and forth between us with worry. I may have turned him to stone, but I've wept over him too much in the past. He'll have to de-petrify himself or rely on his friends to chase the pigeons away.

"Do we have a problem?" Sarah continues. "We're a little low on time here. If there's an issue, I need to know now."

Eli's sexy brows furrow, pleading, and he waits for me to respond.

"No problem," I say through gritted teeth. There's definitely a problem, but there's no way I'm letting Eli ruin this for me. He already stole and shattered my heart; he's not stealing my chance to help Gran too. With any luck, he'll get knocked out in the lightning round, and I'll never have to see him again. Although, if he's anything like he was in high school, he's earned his place here, even if no one would have expected it from him. I twist my clenched shoulders around to loosen up.

"Places!" a crew member calls. Most of the competitors are a revolving door on the show, so they don't waste much time on crew introductions. "We're on in three, two, one!"

Bobby Bailey steps out and opens the show in his usual manner. He's full of charisma, even if age has stolen some of the pep from his step. His presence commands my attention, reminding me exactly where I am, and that this is all that matters. Eli who? *Eli the lying, abandoning jerk, that's who. We're not thinking about that right now.*

As instructed, I shout along with the crowd, and try to let myself get lost in the moment. I'm drenched in sweat and really looking forward to all the flak my family will give me for my enormous pit stains. Must. Keep. Arms. Down.

There's something tangible about the vibe in the room. The energy courses through and infects me. My eyes widen, my skin prickles, and my heart jumps. I'm living this moment, with the crowd roaring around me. The edges of my mouth feel like they might crack with how wide I'm smiling.

The cameras are everywhere. I actually did it. I'm finally on my favorite game show. Seven-year-old me would pee her pants in excitement if she knew. And five-year-old me. And nine-year-old . . . heck, thirty-year-old me might.

Bobby has completed his rundown on the rules of the first round: ten contestants are asked up to ten multiple-choice questions. Get an answer wrong, and you're eliminated. The last two contestants standing become a team for the second round. It's also a game of speed. In the event of a tie, first to enter the answer is used to determine a winner. We don't get an introduction unless we make it to the partners round, only a quick camera pan. I smile and wave when it passes over me and wonder what my family is thinking, especially Gran. I know they're huddled around the TV, watching now. I can picture Ma wringing her hands, and Pop pacing around the room, Gran tuning them out, her eyes glued to the screen.

I try to pin down the adrenaline coursing through my veins as Bobby eyes us all to confirm we're ready for our first question. Time slows as I block out the audience cheers behind me. I pretend the thin panels shielding my view of the contestants on either side are instead thick walls surrounding me, and I focus solely on Bobby. My heart is still in my throat, but there's nothing to be done for that. All I can do is my best.

"Yona Harvey, Ta-Nehisi Coates, and Roxane Gay have all written stories contributing to the mythos of what comic book hero?"

I dive for my B button, knowing the answer to be Black Panther. The spotlight focuses back on Bobby as all the answers are locked in and he announces that one contestant is out of the game. I feel bad for them, but at least they'll have a good movie to enjoy when the question inevitably haunts them, just like I'm still haunted by that time in seventh grade when I forgot to ask for a definition in the spelling bee, and spelled *maze* instead of *maize*.

Bobby moves on to the second and third questions, and no other competitors get knocked out. Question four is a geography question, and three others have their hopes dashed. The podiums they put us at have panels between them, so the winners don't know who they're being paired with until the start of the second round. Eli briefly slips into my mind again, and while I try not to wish ill will on people as a habit, I hope he's one of the four that has gone.

With six of us left, I only have to beat four more. I wipe my sweaty palms on my jeans. I'm going to be as dry as the Atacama Desert by the time this is over.

Questions five and six, history and science, respectively, fool no one. Question seven asks about a gossip blogger, a common subject that trivia buffs tend to overlook. I send past-Charlotte a silent thank-you for scooping up the gossip magazines in the checkout line from time to time. It does me a lot of good, because as more contestants fail the question, it comes down to three of us fighting for two spots, with three questions remaining.

Bobby paces in front of us, asking rhetorical questions that we've been instructed not to answer so that the other contestants don't hear our voices and deduce who their remaining competitors are. My tongue suddenly doesn't feel like it fits in my mouth, which has gone chalky with nerves.

Bobby picks up his card. "Question eight," he says as if he's going to read it, and then stares into the camera for a lengthy, dramatic pause before saying, "will come when we return from the break." He gives the viewers a mischievous grin as it cuts away, as if anyone who has seen the show before hasn't seen him pull this act at least once, if not dozens of times.

I knew there would be pauses for commercials. Still, this extra time to overthink and get in my head is exactly what I do not need.

My mind hears itself thinking about how the extra time will make me overthink and wastes no time doing so. *Don't blow it. So many viewers. Final three. Pit stains. Eli. Eli lending me a pencil. Eli climbing through my window to study. Studying with Eli. Not studying with Eli. Eli's soft lips on mine. Eli insisting we ditch together and promising to meet me under the football stadium bleachers. My resistance to rule breaking. Eli no-showing. The school's security showing up instead. Eli refusing to speak to me ever again, not even bothering to break up with me.*

My heart squeezes and the bright lights of the set seem to flash and blur. Oh God, I cannot lose consciousness right now. I won't. No. Not going to happen. *Forget Eli.* He's only a blip, and he has probably been knocked out already. I need the prize money to keep affording the best care possible for Gran. Need to win. I grip the rounded edges of my podium with white knuckles.

"Welcome back to *Brain Battle!*" Bobby cheerfully announces to the raucous applause of the studio audience.

I sway a little. If Eli is a blip, he's less of the dictionary "minor deviation" and more of the Marvel Universe–altering variety.

I mold my features into what I hope is a smile and finger wave at the camera as it passes. It hovers over me for longer this time, since there's only three of us. It feels awkward to keep waving, so for what must be the first time in my life, I dip into a curtsy and immediately feel infinitely more out of place than with just the waving. I'm not even wearing a dress. Who curtsies in pants? Who curtsies at all?

I bet Eli didn't do something silly like curtsy. He probably smoldered at the camera and made people want to crawl through their televisions and jump his bones. Now I'm thinking about Eli again. And his bones. Oh hell.

"Question eight," Bobby says again. "What's the name of the anthemic dance near the beginning of *The Rocky Horror Picture Show*?"

I fumble to select Time Warp, and equally struggle with question nine, not because either question is harder, but because I've lost focus, and my mind is swimming. Neither of my remaining competitors fails on either question. It comes down to question ten. If the trend continues, and we all get it correct, it will come down to speed.

I wiggle my fingers over the buttons to keep the muscles ready to go. I can do this. I won't let my family down.

"Which company . . . (The lights are still flashing; I don't think they're supposed to be flashing) . . . uses the ticker symbol . . . (Is the ground spinning, or am I swaying? It is sweltering in here. Maybe I should have asked for some water on the break. *Focus on the question.*) ". . . CAKE, C-A–" I fall forward and only just catch myself on the podium in time to keep myself from tumbling to the ground. With sudden horror, I realize that in catching myself, I've selected choice B. I didn't even hear the end of the question, let alone the answer options, and I've already selected mine. I've blown it!

My stomach lurches, whether from the dizziness I was already experiencing or the terror that I've answered incorrectly, I'm not sure. I blink and force myself to focus on the question to assess the damage, and whether I can just let myself topple over now. The small screen on my podium flashes the question Bobby read aloud: "Which company uses the ticker symbol CAKE?" My eyes flick across the answer options and lock onto what I know is the correct answer—Cheesecake Factory Inc. My legs wobble in relief. By sheer luck, I selected the correct answer.

I zero in on Bobby. "The correct answer . . ." He pauses for dramatic effect. It's out of my hands now. I wish that made me feel better. ". . . is the Cheesecake Factory." I lean hard on the podium for support as Bobby finally speaks.

"Well, well, well, Braniacs," he says, using the term for the Brain Battle fandom, "all three of our knowledge warriors have answered correctly."

I don't need to hear him say it. I know I've made it through. I mashed that button as soon as the answers popped onto the screen, faster than I could have read them. I'm so overjoyed. At least, I think I am. I ought to be leaping into the air in celebration. I should be reeling from a massive hit of dopamine right about now, but instead my stomach is tight and twisty.

"To break the tie, let's take a look at the response times."

It doesn't feel right. What if I don't deserve to win? I don't know if I could have read the question and answered it faster than the others. It was pure luck, an accidental unfair advantage, and it feels dishonest.

"Which of our knowledge warriors had the fastest fingers? The speediest cerebellums! The most dexterous digits. The nimblest noggins—"

I remember Gran quoting C. S. Lewis noting the importance of doing the right thing, whether or not there's an audience. I'm on national TV. It feels like the whole country is watching, but there's no telling if the cameras were on me and saw me almost fall, or that anyone would be able to tell that's what happened. I can only remember once in my life that I've made the choice to tell a lie that I knew would eat at me. It was for Eli, and it backfired.

No one would know. I've been raised to believe that a lie of omission is no better than an outright lie, but I'm on new ground here. The show is live and can't retape a new question and won't want to face legality concerns with changing the questions after they've been answered, even if I gave up my chance by calling attention to it. I haven't cheated. Accidentally pressing a button isn't against the rules.

"The response times are in, and we have our two winners!"

The display on my podium flashes in front of me.

Congratulations! You are moving on to the team stage.

I did it! I mean, I'd pretty much known I was moving on with my slipup-turned-expedient-answer, but seeing it in writing makes it real. Progressing to the next round is a dream come true, even if I'm still uneasy about the way I came by it.

"Contestants three and seven, congratulations! You will be moving on to the next round."

I look up and see the camera trained on me and others trained on the other podiums, catching our reactions. My audition notes and training kick in, and I remember to play it up. I was already internally screaming, but I jump up and down and do a celebratory wiggle within the confined space of my contestant cubicle.

"More from our new teams, after the break!"

Sarah charges toward me. She glances in the other direction, probably to make sure my new teammate can't see me.

"Let's move!" She grabs my arm and pulls me off set with her, then hustles me to a side room.

"Wait here, and stay ready. We'll come get you in a few minutes for your 'meet the contestants' scene, then we'll have another quick break before we move on to the team round," she says, and shuts the door in my face. The whole thing is over so fast, I don't have a chance to mention my slip with the button, taking the choice out of my hands.

The knot in my stomach tightens. This is not ideal. Not only is there a decent chance Eli is in another one of these rooms right now, but I also feel like I've been dishonest. I wish I could call Gran and have her tell me what to do, but I wasn't allowed to bring my phone to set. I don't have long before they call me out there. What would Gran do? I need that printed on a bracelet.

Honesty is important, but I think she'd tell me to focus on what I can control. I shouldn't waste the opportunity I've been given by freaking out. I need to take this time to get myself calmed the heck down. I could screech in relief when I catch sight of a basket of water bottles in the corner of the room.

I take a sip from one. The trickle of the cool liquid down my throat has a soothing effect on the rest of me. As the water goes down, so do my nerves. This isn't anything I can't handle. I throw back the rest of the bottle in fear they'll come retrieve me before I've managed to rehydrate.

The room is so plain, it looks more like a dated conference room than a piece of Hollywood. It's almost like the doorway was a wormhole transporting me away from my TV dream and back to the real world. Goose bumps rise on my arms, and I shiver.

It's striking me all over again that I'm really on the set of the show I've watched since I was a kid. On the other side of that door is a bright-lights fantasy world that has somehow let me in. It isn't just another failed interview; I'm a contestant on *Brain Battle*.

There's a knock on the door, followed immediately by a man with a makeup apron coming to touch up my look before I have to go back out there. I consider it an act of kindness that he doesn't comment on how sweaty and disgusting I am. He simply beautifies me and accents my features, then slips out of the room. He isn't gone for more than a minute before Sarah reappears.

"Okay Charlotte, time to meet your teammate. You ready?" she asks.

No. "Yes."

Sarah escorts me to the side of the set, and they cue Bobby to talk.

"Welcome back, folks. It's time to meet this week's new team"—he hesitates and turns to stare directly into the camera—"and for them to meet each other. Please bring out our knowledge warriors!"

The audience roars and chants right on cue, and Sarah gives me a little shove. On the other side of the set, a tall figure steps out with a casual gait that borders on smug.

Eli.

CHAPTER FIVE

ELI

Of course it would be Charlotte. She walks toward me in tailored gray slacks that are tight around her waist and flow around her ankles, giving her the appearance of floating across the set.

Charlie has always been confident, the self-assured way she carries herself giving her a regal air despite her often casual appearance. She shone. I could never shake the feeling that she was way too good for me. It only ever made me want her more. Apparently, nothing's changed.

She's got a pink top on, with a knotted pearl necklace. They even let her go on set with her signature messy bun. It wouldn't surprise me if they'd styled her hair and she'd gotten so caught up in the show that she'd tossed it in a bun without thinking, and the crew had given up. It'd be a very Charlie thing to do.

There's no mistaking the moment she catches sight of me. Her graceful stride stalls, and she nearly trips. When she looks back up, her eyes are on mine, and they're full of fire.

We meet in the middle, where a small X marks the floor. There, we've been instructed—and knew from watching the show—to pause and shake hands before moving to marks on either side of Bobby for interviews.

I pause at the handshake mark and extend my hand. Charlie looks at it, and then at me, before stepping back to her interview mark without shaking my hand. All right, I deserve that. I suppose it would have been too much to hope for her to make this easy on me.

I've spent years wondering if I made the right decision with Charlie and regretting the outcome either way. Another shot with her after a sudden reappearance in my life would be a dream come true, on *any* other day. I can't have this kind of distraction today. Winning is an imperative. Dad's overtired eyes haunt me every time I blink. I can't let Charlie get in my head now.

Bobby raises an eyebrow, but he's no rookie when it comes to hosting, and he doesn't miss a beat. "Uh-oh, looks like our new team is off to a rough start. As a reminder to our viewers, the individual round podiums ensure that our knowledge warriors haven't gotten to see their competition and teammate-to-be until now, but you two seem to know each other! Let's see if we can get to the bottom of this."

Bobby turns to me. "Tell us about yourself."

"My name is Eli Collins. I'm from East Lansing, Michigan, and I'm a personal trainer," I say, mustering as much enthusiasm as I can, given the "I will eat your face off in a ruthless and not at all sexual way" glare that Charlotte is shooting me.

"And you, young lady?" Bobby asks her.

She douses the fire in her eyes and smiles sweetly at Bobby, tilting her head and peeking at him through her lashes. "Hi, Bobby! It's such a pleasure to finally meet you! I've always been a huge fan of the show. I've watched it since I was five and have seen all the hosts." A blush spreads over her cheeks, and she holds a hand in front of her mouth, then stage-whispers loudly enough to ensure her microphone would pick it up: "But you're the best."

Is she flirting? If I didn't know better, I'd almost think she was trying to make me jealous, and damn it if a bit of envy creeps in. I wish that attention was on me. My muscles tense. I take advantage of the camera being on Charlie to work my jaw and force the muscles to loosen.

I had never wanted to let Charlie go, but when we dated, my life was a supernova explosion ready to turn into a black hole. It didn't take long for me to realize that I was dragging her down with me. In the thirteen years since, I've thought of her often, even breaking off other relationships when the memory of being with Charlie was more enticing than the reality of anyone else. Hell, I'd thought of her several times even in the past few weeks.

"Thank you. It's great to have you here." Bobby turns to Charlie next. "Tell us about yourself."

"My name is Charlotte Evans. I'm from Kalamazoo, Michigan, and I'm a research analyst."

"Now Charlotte, that was quite the snub back there. Have you and Eli met before?"

"You could say that." Her eyes flick to mine.

"I take it you're not fond of each other."

"We've had our ups and downs," she says. Her tone is casual, but there's an echo of hurt in her voice too, and my heart squeezes with guilt. I put that wound there, and it's haunted me for years. The collection of decisions I made, cornering myself into breaking us, are my biggest regret.

I need to focus, but there's that look on her face, just like the one she gave me when I ignored her after she covered for me. Damn it. My mind will be all over if I don't let her know she isn't nothing to me, like I led her to believe. Not with the evidence of her hurt still lingering on her face.

"But no, I wouldn't say we're each other's biggest fans," she adds.

Even if it might mean breaking her all over again, she has to know. Maybe then the Charlie part of my brain will shut up for five minutes so I can save my dad and me from years of living paycheck to paycheck.

"Speak for yourself," I interrupt. Bobby and Charlie turn on me.

"What is that supposed to mean?" she demands. The audience gasps at her reaction. I'd forgotten about the audience, but their synchronized inhalation draws my attention. I squint past the bright stage lights, to see so many faces watching the exchange with interest. Charlotte blinks, seemingly remembering where she is as well. "I mean, excuse me?"

"Things didn't end well between us, but I've always cared for Charlotte, more than she could possibly know." I meet her eyes and silently beg her to please hear and understand my words. Instead of softening, her nostrils flare. This is a side of Charlie I have never seen. She was never one to let her temper get the best of her.

Bobby looks to her for a response. In the corner of my eye, I can see the director hovering to the side of one of the cameras, hanging nervously on our every word, ready to cut to commercial. Charlie grits her teeth, "I guess we remember things a little differently," she says.

Apparently deciding that we're too close to exploding, the director signals to Bobby.

"We'll be right back for our team round, where Eli and Charlotte will take on returning champions Kayleigh and Carlos!"

The signal light changes to indicate that we're no longer live, and Sarah rushes forward. A tall, thin man with gaunt features tugs at his jacket as he strides toward us in long, slow strides that lack the urgency a commercial break ought to require. His eyes narrow as he glances between us. I dislike him immediately.

"We've got three minutes," he says, voice dripping with eerie calm. "Explain yourselves." He looks at Charlie and me, and when neither of us jumps to answer, he turns to Sarah.

"I'm sorry," she squeaks, then gestures frantically at Charlie and me. They told me it wouldn't be a problem!" The way her shoulders fold in and she subtly but noticeably leans away leads me to believe her dealings with him generally fall into the category of unpleasant.

"You knew?" Clint's face creases in anger, his deep voice as cold as stone.

"Not really. They just looked at each other funny and—"

"Fix it." He stares down his nose at Sarah for a long second before turning on his heels and marching off stage.

Sarah releases a shaky breath. "It's too late to make a change. Whatever is going on between you two, you need to hold it together for half an hour to film this show. Then you can do whatever the hell you want to each other. Please. There's a lot riding on this. More than you know."

Charlie nods. I nod. For good measure, Sarah nods back.

"One minute. Get to your marks." She shoves us both to our team podium, opposite the previous episode's winners, who are talking amiably.

"You care about me?" Charlie hisses in a rush. "What is that supposed to mean? I've been waiting for this chance my whole life. I can't believe you'd say something like that just to mess with me."

"Thirty seconds!" Someone yells.

"I wasn't messing with you," I whisper back. Sarah cuts us a worried glance.

"Three, two—"

"Welcome back to *Brain Battle*!" Bobby continues his spiel of introducing the returning champions on their second week at the show, but I tune him out, continuing my hurried conversation with Charlie.

"You have a funny way of showing it," she says.

"I know. I'm sorry. After the taping let's talk. I'll—"

"Shut up!" she hisses.

Not wanting to piss her off further, I go silent, probably much to the relief of the sound techs.

"Okay, teams. You know the drill! Are you ready to play?" Bobby asks.

If only I'd had an hour to talk this out with her. In one hour, I could have explained. I doubt she would've been happy, but she'd at least have some explanation and time to get over it, enough for us to be civil on the show.

She threatened that I wasn't going to ruin this for her. That's one thing we can agree on. I can't ruin it for myself either. I have my own reasons for needing the show. As much as this is a chance to reconcile with Charlie, there's only one thing I need more than that chance: to win. The money from winning just one episode could go a long way to digging my dad and me out of our hole of debt. Probably three episodes could get us out of it. We could keep our house from foreclosure and buy time until I can finish my degree and find a better-paying job to keep us stable without him having to resort to any of his "plans."

As much as this is not the ideal time to run into Charlie, I hope she can pull it together. I need her help. I *know* she's up to the challenge of winning this show. Despite my circumstances, I'd been a good student, but not as good as Charlie.

We'd both been in an honors algebra class, and though I'd paid attention, it wasn't clicking. I'd quietly visited the teacher during office hours for extra help, but I still wasn't grasping the concepts. I'd confessed my struggles to Charlie one day, and we'd spent an afternoon reviewing. I'm not sure how she'd explained it differently, but a lock tumbled in my brain, and I aced every test in class afterward. It was such a drastic change that the teacher had suspected me of cheating.

Charlie is brilliant. Barring the tension between us, there's no one I'd rather have as my teammate with the stakes so high.

As the returning champions, Carlos and Kayleigh get the first question, which Carlos answers with ease. They high-five each other.

"Eli and Charlotte, what country has the largest border with France?" Bobby asks.

"Spain," I say.

"That's not our answer!" Charlie yells.

Bobby glances at the judges' table, and they signal that we can change the answer. We're allowed to converse, and her narrowed eyes make it very clear that I will not be answering without consulting her again.

"I know you like to hear yourself talk," she mutters quietly, "but try checking with me first. We are a team, remember?"

Off camera, Sarah points frantically at her collar to remind us microphones are picking up everything we say. Next to her, Clint glowers. Charlie is not going to let this grudge die easily.

"All right, what do you think it is?" I ask.

"Ten seconds," Bobby says.

"You're forgetting about French Guiana. The answer is Brazil," she says.

My jaw falls open. "Oh." She's right. I nod, and she faces Billy.

"Our answer is Brazil."

"That's correct!" Billy says. There is some halfhearted protest from Carlos on the opposing team, that we got to change our answer, but it's quickly dismissed. They consult each other and get their next answer right as well.

"Where were the arena chants for the 2010 movie *Tron Legacy* recorded?" Billy asks.

Oh shit. It's like they had someone dive into our past to write these questions just to set me up. On the bright side, I know the answer, so at least for this question I don't have to stress about trying to win. On the other hand, well . . . I reflexively lean away from Charlotte just as she turns on me, eyes full of flame again. I'm not sure when she acquired this look, but I wish it weren't directed at me. At least she learned to be angry with me. Our senior year, whenever we saw each other, her lips would tremble, or her eyes would water. Normally proud, she'd duck her head and avoid meeting my eyes. It wrenched my gut. I'll work with the anger. It hurts less than seeing her pain.

Charlotte barks out a humorless laugh. "You know, I never got around to seeing that one. I had plans to once, but they fell through."

Seeing that she wasn't about to slap me, I stand a little straighter. "Some jerk probably made a big mistake and stood you up," I said.

She hesitated, probably expecting a defense, not for me to insult myself. She clears her throat. "If that's the case, then he's had a long time to make up for it. It doesn't seem to me like he regrets it."

I block out the show and focus on Charlotte. Her lips are pressed into a firm line. As I stare at her, her face relaxes just enough that they part the slightest bit. The subtle hint of vulnerability gives me hope. She might not be willing to take me back, but maybe someday I could earn her forgiveness. Maybe I could start that here, before the next question comes.

"Maybe he thought she was better off."

Her lips slam together again, but this time to hold back a tremble. She clenches her fists the way she does when she's fighting tears. This isn't the time or the place. I shouldn't be doing this to her on live TV, but she might not ever speak to me again. I already know the answer, so I can spare the couple of seconds.

"Ten seconds?" Bobby says, the statement coming out as more of a question. In all the years the show has been on the air, I don't recall ever seeing contestants completely ignoring it for their own conversations, like this. The studio is going to hate us.

"Comic-Con," Charlie and I snap at him in unison, our eyes never leaving each other's.

"Do you still think I was better off?" she asks me.

"That's correct," Bobby says with far less enthusiasm. He keeps watching Clint for direction. Clint's glare could conjure up a thunderstorm in the room. All other eyes are still on us.

"I hope not. I'd like a chance to prove that things could be different."

Time stops. I've thrown my heart out there for her to do what she wants with it. I fully expect her to trample it. Or pick it up and throw it. I don't know what I even want her to say. That she doesn't hate me would be a start. Probably only seconds pass, but it feels like forever.

Finally, Bobby throws to a commercial.

"Damn it, Eli," Charlie says as the crew storms over. "We need to focus on the game."

"I know," I say.

"I don't think you do. I need the prize money." The desperation in her voice instantly has me worried. I want to leap to her rescue, but I need her help to save myself too.

"I get it—so do I."

"This stops. No more messing with each other's heads. Our priority is the game. We can deal with"—she waves her hands around between us—"whatever that was after the show is over."

"Truce?" I ask.

"Truce," she says. This may not last more than the next half hour, but it feels like I've gained enormous ground. I can already tell I'm going to crash after this taping is over. It feels as though I'm wearing a lead vest, like for X-rays at the dentist, only heavier. Osmium vest. The breaths aren't coming in right. It's a far more emotional day than I was anticipating.

"So, not to put myself in the middle of whatever this is, but I'm literally begging you two to get your shit together. Clint's a scary dude, and he looks like he's about ready to wring my neck. Are we good?" Sarah asks.

"We're fine," Charlie says.

Sarah hugs her clipboard tight to her chest and nods at Clint before rushing off stage.

Bobby rubs at his temples. "I need a raise," he mumbles, and an instant later, as the on-air light flicks on, his charm returns, and he asks a question of the opposing team. It's the first question that they get wrong, giving us an opportunity to steal the points.

"Within five percent, what percentage of the Earth's population resides in the Northern Hemisphere?" Bobby repeats.

Charlie doesn't know the answer and looks to me. I grin and try to sprinkle some of my bad-boy charm in there for good measure.

"Ninety," I answer, my eyes on her.

She flushes at the attention, and my blood rushes too, knowing I can still have that effect on her. She tips her head in acknowledgment. The rest of the questions fly by, and adrenaline courses through my veins at the speed of the game.

With each question we answer successfully, I dare to hope a little more, imagining telling my dad that the house is paid off; him coming home from work at a single job, happy and well rested.

Some of the questions Charlie knows, some I do, some both of us. Kayleigh and Carlos are no joke, though. It's still anyone's game. It's a miracle that Charlie hasn't broken the skin on her arms and bled everywhere with all the nervous scratching she's doing. It reminds me of a study session for our chemistry final, junior year. She'd eventually let me kiss her stress away. I wish I could do that now.

As nervous as she is, her competitive drive takes over. She moves from nods of agreement to high-fives when we get a question right. The jolt of contact sends a rush of pleasure and sensory memories rushing through me.

Kayleigh and Carlos miss another question, giving us a chance to gain a bigger lead, but neither of us knows the answer. My heart races, and my eyes keep flicking to the score board as if the score will change on me if I look away for too long.

We miss a question next, and both swear under our breaths. Charlotte chances a shy smile at the moment of camaraderie. Her nervous fidgeting moves her closer to me. We've made it to the final round, and we're down by one. Our only chance to win is if the other team screws up their question, and then we answer their question and our own correctly.

"At eleven hours and five minutes, the longest tennis match in history took place June twenty-second through June twenty-fourth, 2010, between what two players?"

Charlotte's hand shoots out and grabs mine, squeezing like she's down to the dregs of the toothpaste tube and doesn't have a spare. Her eyes are locked onto Carlos and Kayleigh, and I don't think she's even aware she's done it. I freeze, terrified any small movement I make could cause her to realize she's holding my hand and send her running and screaming out of the studio. Charlotte Evans is holding my hand. I never thought I'd again see the day. What's more, I know the answer to the question.

"They don't know it," she whispers. "They don't know it! Tell me you know it. Please, please tell me you do."

"I do," I say, and she sags in relief.

"Thank God, you brilliant asshole."

All we can do is wait and hope they don't manage to come up with the right answer despite being unsure. Trying to read their lips is more than my anxious stomach can handle, and Charlie is squeezing my hand hard enough for it to be painful, so I search the room for a distraction. I notice the camera that's usually focused on us is angled slightly lower. It looks like it's focused on our hands. That will get her family talking.

"John Isner," Kayleigh finally says, and my heart drops. Something in my demeanor clues Charlie in that this is correct, because she eyes me, and her face crumples. "And Kevin Anderson."

I lean forward so sharply that, with our hands still adjoined, I pull Charlie forward too. I can't believe it. John Isner holds both the first and second record for longest matches at Wimbledon, but the match against Kevin Anderson is the second longest. They've gotten it *wrong*.

Bobby starts his short walk across the set toward us.

"John Isner and Nicolas Mahut!" I shout before he can repeat the question.

Charlie sucks in a breath and holds it, but I know I'm right.

"That is correct!" Bobby says.

Charlotte emits a close-mouthed scream and squeezes my hand again. She glances down, and a moment of surprise registers in her eyes at the sight of our clasped hands, but she doesn't pull away.

"It all comes down to this," Bobby says. *Get to the damn question, Bobby.* We could actually do this. I could get my dad and myself out of the debt swamp we're in and have a chance to do more. This is a real possibility. Our competitors no longer have any say. My heart pounds against my chest with the force of Mjölnir (Thor's hammer to the un-savvy.)

43

"Which star is closest to the sun?"

Fuck. I'm not good with astronomy. The Latin names don't stick in my brain. Charlie releases my hand and pats it. I meet her eyes and she grins. She knows the answer. I nod for her to go ahead. I have nothing to contribute. I count my lucky *stars* to have her on my team.

"Proxima Centauri." The Latin-derived words flow smoothly off her tongue.

Bobby checks the card, and my pounding heart skips a beat. "Congratulations, Charlotte and Eli! You have won this week's episode of *Brain Battle*!" I don't hear the rest. Confetti falls over us.

Charlie jumps toward me, arms outstretched, and I lift and spin her, pulling her into a hug.

"We did it!" she squeals, tears streaming down her face.

"We did it!" I agree. I want to talk to her more, but now that I know I'll have another chance to see her next week, it feels less urgent. I have to get to a phone. I have to tell Dad. He didn't even know about the show. I didn't tell him I was leaving the state and spending my minimal savings on a plane ticket, since the show only pays for returning competitors. It was a gamble that had paid off. I hadn't wanted to get his hopes up or have him talk me out of it, but now that I'd be getting the prize money, I couldn't wait to call and tell him. We just have to make it on our own a little longer. In the orientation, they said it can take two to three months after your final episode for the checks to be sent.

Eventually the chaos fades, and I make it to the room where they stored our things, and get my phone back. I'm just about to call him when Charlotte bursts in behind me.

"Eli?" Her mouth and nose twitch like she's just inhaled a large dose of black pepper and is fighting a sneeze. That doesn't bode well. I drop my arms to my sides. Whatever this conversation is going to be, I'm not sure I'm ready for it. I want to bask in our win a while longer before finding out my fate with her. "We did it!"

"Yeah, we did." I grin.

Her smile fades to a more neutral expression. "I'm thrilled about the win and thankful for you kicking butt out there, but also I'm still pissed at you, and it's freaking confusing."

I'm processing this when, seconds later, the door swings in again. Clint walks in, his face contorting into a scowl that is borderline murderous.

"We need to talk," he says.

CHAPTER SIX

CHARLOTTE

Clint Mariano has a gaunt face with eyes that sink back into the sockets, leaving them ringed with dark shadows that make him look like he walked straight out of a Tim Burton cartoon. He's a bit creepy, so his insistence on an audience with us rattles me.

"Would one of you like to explain what that was out there?" Clint asks. I recognize him from an article I've seen, speculating who Bobby's replacement would be. Clint produces the show but is supposedly gunning to host it as well.

"I was under the impression that it was a trivia show," Eli says, leaning against the wall. Damn if this doesn't take me straight back to high school. The cool guy and his cool-guy lean. I've always had a weakness for it.

The pose is purposefully casual, his version of a pissing contest with Clint. I can't imagine what Eli is thinking, feeling a need to stand up to the show's producer. Clint turns his back to shut the door behind him, and I take the opportunity to stomp on Eli's foot, to let him know just what I think of his ill-timed decision to dick-measure against the man who currently holds the key to both our financial futures.

Eli holds his palms up in front of him and gives an innocent shrug. That had better mean he's going to stand down.

Before he can say something else that's reckless, I interject. "What Eli means is, we got a little carried away early on, but I think the end of the show went nicely."

"Is that what you think?" Clint leans in far closer to my face than seems necessary.

I can feel my shoulders shrink and fold under his looming. In my peripheral vision, Eli takes in the way Clint is getting in my face. His jaw sets, and he plants his feet wide, like he's bracing to throw a punch. He always was protective. I attempt to plead with him with my eyes to keep his cool. Now is not the time, with tens of thousands of dollars on the line. Eli closes his eyes. When he opens them again, he says, "We're sorry, sir. We were taken off guard by running into each other unexpectedly. We hadn't seen each other in twelve years."

"Do you two realize that you have to remain a team for at least one more episode?"

"Yes," we both answer.

"Good, because we have your scores from the auditions. You two competed well today. You have a shot for a long run on the show, but that doesn't have to happen if you two make fools of yourselves and leave us having to cut to commercial all the time."

Did he just threaten to manipulate the contest? The only way I could think for him to do that, based on what he'd said, would be to stack the questions in our weak categories. Can he even do that? Is it legal? I thought I had the laws memorized, but I'm not sure changing the questions qualifies as lawbreaking since we're still genuinely answering them. Of course he can get away with it. I should have expected it. As Warren Buffet warned, and Gran is so fond of quoting, I should know better than to expect the expensive gift of honesty from cheap people.

Gran. I have to do it for her care. Grinding my teeth, I force a tight smile. "We hear you loud and clear."

"Excellent," Clint says. "We'll see you next week. Sarah will assist with your arrangements."

Clint leaves, and Eli and I are alone again.

"What the hell were you thinking?" I whisper-yell, pissed off but not wanting to attract more attention after the conversation we just had.

"That guy was an asshole," Eli says, and I want to throttle him. Maybe kiss him a little. Mostly throttle him.

"Then you should have felt right at home because so are you!" I say.

"Ouch. You wound me m'lady." He raises one of those sexy thick eyebrows. Damn it, why are his eyebrows still so sexy? That's not supposed to be a thing!

"Hey," he whispers, his hand grazing my elbow. "We won."

We still have so much to talk about, but I smile. "Yeah, we did. Can you believe it?"

"With you on my team, I was never worried," he says. It's a total lie. I saw worry on his face at more than one point during the game. Flattery won't get him into my flared trousers. Oof, that sounded so dorky, even in my head.

"Can you lose the man-candy act for just a minute?" I ask.

"I'm candy now, am I?" he asks.

"Be serious. This is a huge deal!"

"You're making it too easy," he says.

I rewind the conversation in my mind. Huge. I grimace. I did walk into that one. If I roll my eyes any harder, they'll pop right out. I'm trying to be real with him for one minute, and all he's got is awful pickup lines.

I scowl at him. I don't have to talk to him. I don't have to deal with him at all until we're back on set next week. Who I do need to talk to is my family. They were all watching. Even with the tape delay, they've seen it now. I hate that they can't be here to celebrate with me. We can finally get Gran the care that she needs. We were going to do anything for her, no matter what, but now we actually have the money for it and won't have to keep pinching pennies and stressing out.

Money aside, Gran has always been so supportive of this dream I've been chasing, and the little girl in me can't wait to tell her all about it.

I envision the three of them crouched around the TV for the final question, Ma and Pop gripping the edges of their seats, Gran smiling like she already knows we've got those last two in the bag. I can picture Ma and Pop springing out of their chairs to celebrate, and Gran settling back in hers with the most peaceful smile. I'm so overcome with the emotion of it that my eyes well with tears.

"Shit, Charlie." Eli runs over and crouches in front of me. He takes my hands into his. The smugness is gone, and his forehead crinkles with worry. "I'm sorry—I'm being a dick. I know this is a big deal."

"You have no idea," I say. Everyone would want to suddenly win this kind of money, but he doesn't know what it means to me.

"I think I do," he mutters, casting his eyes down, and that tense jaw is back. There's a story there, but it's been a long day, and I don't have the energy to hear it. I nod my acknowledgment and stare at our hands, folded together.

"Don't think just because you helped me win, we're suddenly cool," I say.

He grimaces. "Look, about that—"

"Why don't we just leave the past in the past for now," I say, cutting him off before he can make excuses. Thirteen years ago, I fell in love. Thirteen years ago, I had my heart broken. I've had my fair share of dates, and even some boyfriends, since then, but I haven't gone out on a limb and compromised my morals ever again. I haven't fallen so hard again either.

A lot has changed. Whether Eli has some excuse he considers valid or not, I just don't want to hear it. It's not that I can't have an adult conversation and am willing to let some foolish misunderstanding ruin something great. It's that I know how easy it would be to fall for him again, and to be that vulnerable with him . . . I shiver. He hurt me too much before. I'm not prepared to open myself up to that.

I'm not sure I've ever gotten over Eli. The last thing I want is to dredge up all these emotions. "I can be civil. I'd be willing to get a drink with you when the show is said and done, but for now I think it's best if we stay focused. Today's prize money will do a lot for me—for my family—and not to be greedy, but we can use all we can get. I want to make the most out of our chance here."

He frowns, but eventually he says, "Okay, I can do that." He's letting me take the lead, which thaws my heart toward him, but only by about one degree. No amount of tap water will thaw that sucker out that quickly without my emotions turning rancid. If he wants another chance, he's going to have to pop me in the fridge and wait it out the old-fashioned way.

"Did you catch that threat earlier?" I ask.

"It was hard to miss." He scowls and shakes his head.

"Do you know what kind of questions you got wrong on the tests? It sounds like they may target those."

"Not off the top of my head, but I'm sure I can remember if I think about it."

"I know mine were sports," I say. "No matter how much I try, I cannot remember sports statistics."

"I'm good in some sports, but not across the board," he admits.

"Let me know if you think of your other categories. I'll do my best to study up in the next week. Here, give me your phone."

Eli hands it over. My finger hesitates over the add contact button. The last time I did this with him, it was for a study group, and it quickly evolved into something more. I can't let that happen again. In this case, communication is a necessary evil. I send myself a text, hoping it's a move I don't end up regretting. I hand him back the phone, and after he takes it, he stares at me. I feel myself blush under the weight of it, wondering what he sees. Does he still see the naive seventeen-year-old he took advantage of, or does he see the woman that won't let that happen to her again? Do my features look different to him? Does he like the way I've changed over time, or do I still look like the same Charlotte?

Eli's once patchy stubble is now thick and full. Despite presenting himself as such a hard ass in school, he'd had rounded features back then. They've since sharpened. He's all grown up and looks like he'd know exactly what to do with me if I let him. Not that I was going to, but a little fantasy can't hurt.

Eli is still staring at me as I crash back to earth after my daydream. "What?" I finally insist. "You're staring, and it's getting super weird."

"Kalamazoo isn't all that far from East Lansing. We could always study together."

Go out of our way to spend more time together than we have to? Certainly not. I definitely don't want to do that. Right? I want to. Holy shit, I want to. Wanting to seems like it's the precise reason I shouldn't do it.

"If we're studying together, we'll be looking at the same materials. We'd cover more ground separately." The excuse sounds weak, even to me.

"We can still read through different materials, and we've got the same goal, so we won't distract each other."

"I don't know . . ." I trail off. It's pointless, though. I'm sold. This broken heart can't stay away. Mad or not, the temptation to be near him again is too strong.

"Come on, Charlie." Eli turns on the smolder, and that's so not even fair.

"Fine," I say.

He grins and runs a hand over his stubble, tracing that chiseled jawline of his. I squeeze my knees together to soothe the budding sensation there. *We won't distract each other.* Somehow, I seriously doubt that.

CHAPTER SEVEN
ELI

"Have a good shift," I call to Dad as he heads out the door. The prize money won't come for a few months yet, so he can't cut back until then, but I have a feeling he won't be falling asleep between shifts anymore. He's still tired, but the bags under his eyes don't stand out quite as much as they used to, and he's standing straighter. He seems to have hope again. There's a light at the end of the tunnel.

Yesterday, I walked into the house and said, "We're going to be all right." He looked at me, brows wrinkled in confusion. Once I explained, he folded me in his arms. We didn't talk much beyond that, but for once in our miserable lives, it feels like something is going right.

The money would only go so far. It isn't "quit a job permanently" money. Even once we receive it, once the government takes their cut, he will probably only be able to scale back on his hours. Still, I'm close to finishing my degree, so hopefully I can find something where I can earn more in the next year. If I could win another episode or two and bring home a significant amount of money, maybe we could get the house paid off and pay back taxes, and finally breathe easy.

Dad's truck rattles and clangs down the street, and I turn my attention back to getting ready for Charlie's arrival. I set out a pile of books, magazines, and my laptop in the living room, for studying. The house is clean. It never gets to be a mess. We're home so little that we don't have time to trash it. We don't always have time to scrub it floor to ceiling either, but despite the messy bachelor stereotype, we keep it at a good middle ground.

I do a quick run-through with the vacuum, keeping a close eye on the clock. Charlie was never late or early to a date or class back in high school. She had an uncanny ability to arrive precisely on time. I suspect she arrives early and waits around to walk in the moment she's supposed to.

Sure enough, at nine sharp, there's a rap on the door. Charlie stands there in loose-fitting overalls over a tight white tank top, which leaves tantalizing pieces of the sides of her stomach exposed. I swallow the natural salivation that's occurring at the sight. She bites her plump lips, painted cherry red. Lipstick for a study day. Interesting.

I finally drag my gaze from her lips and clear my throat. "Hey."

"Hey, yourself. No smooth lines today?"

"The last ones didn't go over so well. I thought I'd better keep it simple." She tilts her head to the side and studies me before allowing herself what I think is an approving smile. Charlie may have fallen for the Eli charm back in high school, but as a grown woman, she holds some serious grudges against me. Our chemistry is clearly still here, but it's going to take more than a perfectly executed smolder to win her over.

"Are you going to let me in?" she asks.

Yes, Eli. Quit mooning over her and let her in the house. "Oh, right. Sorry. Come on in."

I hold the door, and she steps through, fixating on the floor. I expect her to look around, take things in, pass judgments. The way she glues her eyes to the carpet is strange. It's almost like she's trying so hard not to form any assessments that she's afraid to look at anything. Guess she still doesn't think much of the high school fuckup that fooled her into thinking he could be more, only to let her down.

I'd offer her a tour, but it would feel weird to show her Dad's room. The kitchen and living room are essentially one room, and the bathroom is clearly visible. There isn't much to show, but modest trimmings in a house that smells like bleach and lemon. Suddenly I feel self-conscious and wish I had something to show off. Maybe we should have met at a library.

"Where do you want to sit?" she asks, looking up enough to glance between the table and the couch.

"We're in for a long day. The couch will be more comfortable," I say.

We walk over to the couch, and her hair catches on the strap of her messenger bag as she pulls it over her head.

"Here, I got it." I untangle the clasp on the messenger bag from her bun and step back.

"Thanks," she mutters, her cheeks glowing pink.

"Sure."

We both sit, slow and awkward. She holds herself up on the couch, rather than sinking into it. She's so stiff I'm not sure she's even putting her full weight on it.

"So," she says.

"So," I echo. This is going great. She's probably wondering what the hell happened to the charmer she knew in high school. I can't even begin a conversation with her. "Where do you want to start?"

"I picked up a bunch of sports almanacs from the library," she says.

"Cool. I thought I'd start with scrolling through old celebrity news blogs. I think pop culture was my biggest weakness."

"Sounds like a plan." She digs out her almanacs, puts on her oversized glasses, and finally settles into the couch as she starts reading.

She's driven over an hour to be here with me, and we say all of two sentences to each other before beginning to read silently. My gut churns.

"Do you want a water or something?" It's the only thing I can think to say, and if we sit in complete silence for the next several hours without getting rid of some tension, the discomfort will shred me.

"That would be nice, thank you." She doesn't glance up from her reading.

Frowning, I slink to the kitchen and pull out two glasses. Her full lips move, silently reading from the almanac. Thick strands of loose hair hang in front of her face. It's got to be distracting. I want to brush them aside and tuck them behind her ears. I want her to look up at me with those doe eyes of hers, from behind those goofy glasses, and see me for who I am. Maybe I'm an asshole, but it's for the right reasons. I want that to be enough for her. I want to taste those full lips and feel the pressure of them against mine.

Water splatters over the floor. "Shit!" I set the glass down on the counter, sloshing more water over the side in my haste.

"Everything all right in there?" she asks.

Yes, I'm just a total creep who got so caught up in staring at you, I became oblivious to the world around me and forgot what I was doing. "All good."

She accepts the water with a smile and a quiet thank-you.

I take the seat on the opposite side of the couch, careful not to push my luck on proximity. Nearness to her sounds dangerous, and I'm trying to remember that she hates me.

"I see you never learned to read in your head," I say, using the observation as an icebreaker.

She smirks, eyes trained on the page. "You always did give me a hard time about that. I try not to, but I forget. I can't help it."

"You shouldn't stop. I teased you because it's endearing."

Charlie doesn't respond, but color tinges her cheeks before she becomes engrossed in her reading again. Her lips continue to move, whether or not she does it on purpose. I smile to myself and dive into my own studies.

We work quietly together for hours, with only quick comments about water refills or an interesting fact to break the silence. The comment about her mouthing the words only broke the tension enough to make it bearable. An awkward air still hangs between us. I'm dying to explain myself, but she laid a clear ground rule that we weren't going to discuss the past. Still, my eyes keep straying from my page and onto her. Hopefully, she can't feel me constantly watching her. I'm not getting a lot done.

Around twelve thirty, Charlotte tucks a bookmark in to mark her page and closes it. "I'm hungry."

I close my book in kind. "Me too. I could run and pick something up," I suggest. Charlotte grimaces. Yeah, it probably would feel a little weird to leave her here alone. "We could go somewhere?" I don't really have the expendable cash for a restaurant. Fast food could be as cheap as groceries, but dining out is another story.

"No, I don't want to take too long. I have to work the rest of the week and can't drive out here every day, so I want to get as much studying done as I can. I can study at home too, but I know that my family will pop in and distract me."

"That doesn't leave us with a lot of options. We've got some cold cuts in the fridge, or I can make a mean PB&J," I say.

"Peanut butter and jelly it is."

Charlotte excuses herself to the restroom while I make the sandwiches. I'm just stacking the smothered slices on top of each other when she sits at the table.

Without the books to use as an excuse for our lack of conversation, the silence looms thick and bounces off the walls. There's nothing but sticky chewing and doing our best to look anywhere but at each other. Finally, I can't take it anymore.

"I know you said you don't want to talk about the past, but this is painful. I'm not trying to pick a fight, but I want to clear the air. I'm hoping we can make a good run on the show. It'd be a lot easier if we could get rid of the elephant crowding the room."

She purses her lips and studies her simple sandwich like it holds the secrets to the universe. "Intrusive pachyderm or not, I don't think that's a good idea."

I tense and throw my hands up. "You can't honestly tell me this is comfortable. And I think there'd be less risk of us exploding at each other on live TV if we get things out of our systems now."

Charlie bites her lip. She's doing so much staring into space I'm going to have to dig out eye drops for her soon. At long last, she takes the last bite of her sandwich and meets my eyes.

"Fine. I'm listening."

Finally. But shit, now that she's listening, I don't know what to say. For years I've wondered what I'd say if I ever saw her again, and wished things could have turned out differently. Now I have a chance to turn things around, and my mind is blank. I guess it's best to start with an apology.

"I'm sorry," I say. There. Simple and sincere.

She looks at me and shifts her head forward as if I might be saying something else and she just can't hear it.

"What, that's it? That's the big talk you wanted to have? Sorry for what? Do you even know what you did wrong?"

Her nostrils flare again, and she braces her palms on the table like she's going to push away from it and walk right out the door.

Maybe simple and sincere was a bit misguided. "No. I mean, yes. I mean, what I'm trying to say is, I'm sorry for blowing you off that day. That wasn't my intent. I was on my way to the bleachers to meet you."

"You just—what? Changed your mind? You convinced me to ditch. You know how out of character that was for me. You know how much I didn't want to, and you talked me into it, then left me alone to get caught. I . . . ugh!"

She stands up and paces the kitchen, clearly not done, but needing a minute to find her words. "I almost got a detention. I lost my perfect attendance award."

I can't believe that's honestly what has her so angry. A high school award seems a trivial thing to hate me for. "You're upset about the award?"

Charlie closes her eyes and takes in a deep breath. Not a good sign. I need an instruction manual for this conversation. "It's not about the damn award! That was just a"—she waves her hand around—"side effect. You know how important integrity is to my family. You've seen my gran's cross-stitched sayings all over our house. I lied to leave class to be with you, then got caught. I destroyed my family's trust in me and lost their respect, something it's taken me years to earn back. On top of that, I covered for you. They knew I wouldn't just do that on my own without prompting, so I lied again, to cover for you. What is the thank-you I get? You never speaking to me. You never even bothered to break up with me!"

If that's the case, then we're *technically* still dating. A smirk sneaks out and I rush to cover it before she notices. A piece of me is tempted to say, "Can we just kiss and make up?" But even lacking an instruction manual, I know that wouldn't go over well. I may not be as smooth as I pretend to be, but I'm not completely oblivious.

Her eyes start to water, and it's like a knife to my gut. "I'm so sorry. So, so, sorry."

"You never told me why. The things I did that day went against who I am as a person. I did them for you because I loved you. I must have done something wrong, and all these years I've had to live with that. I've tried to forget you. I've tried so damn hard, but every now and then, a quiet voice tells me I'm not good enough and that I'm doing something wrong—*everything* wrong, because there must be something wrong with me for you to just abandon me like that. I've had to wonder for years what happened."

"You didn't do anything wrong."

She shakes her head and wipes at a tear. I take a second to grab tissues from the bathroom, and bring them to her, before I try again.

"I didn't mean to mess things up for you at school or make you change who you were for me."

She sputters out a weak laugh. "Do you honestly think I give a damn about the attendance, or even lying for you?"

"I—" I stammer out, but I'm at a loss. She just said she was upset about both of those—so kind of?

"Eli. I wasn't thrilled about either of those things, but I only point them out because it's easier than facing the real pain. You just vanished from my life. You treated me like I was a ghost. Did I mean nothing to you? You completely ignored me, and to this day I don't understand what happened. Every day at school, watching you looking right through me was unbearable. It hurt, Eli. It hurt so fucking much. It still does."

I'm regretting starting this conversation. I want to hold her and wipe away her tears, but I'm certain that wouldn't go over well, and I don't know how to fix it. My stomach knots, knowing I've made things worse, forcing her to relive the past in this conversation. I have to find a way to make her understand why I walked away.

"I know. I'm so sorry. What I did was wrong. I was trying to protect you."

"By abandoning me?" she shouts, wiping away a stray tear and shaking her head furiously.

My frustration builds and I blow out a breath. "I didn't say I handled it well! I let you take the fall for me. I was on probation, and I was going to get expelled if I got caught skipping class again. I was a selfish fuckup, there's no denying that. Even *I* knew I was a fuckup. That's why I stopped talking to you."

Charlie heaves in deep breaths. Her eyes dart back and forth, focusing on each of my eyes in turn, unable to settle. "I don't follow."

"I was on my way around the side of the bleachers to meet you when I saw the dean coming. I was a coward, and I hid. I didn't want to go down my dad's shitty path. I needed to stay in school. I felt awful doing it, but I let you shoulder the blame. I'd already screwed things up for you, and I knew if I stayed with you, I'd only keep messing up your life. I was on the road to nowhere, and I didn't want to take you with me. You were so smart and beautiful. I knew you could do big things for yourself, and I couldn't stand ruining that."

"You couldn't have just told me that?"

"I was seventeen. I chickened out. You know you would have told me it didn't matter. You would have fought for me, and if you pushed, I wouldn't have had the self-discipline to argue. I'd have let you," I say.

She fumbles with the loose strands around her face. Twisting them into little frustrated braids. "It could have worked. You seem to have turned out fine. Maybe I could have helped, but you didn't give me that chance. What was so horrible about your life that you shut me out completely?"

My stomach lurches. I guess we're really going into this, no stones left unturned. I'm just glad Dad isn't here. I can't talk about him when he's around. "You know how my mother was never around? She took every cent my dad had, and disappeared. His job wasn't paying the bills, and he started resorting to desperate measures to keep us afloat. Stealing, dealing drugs. Around the time you and I started dating, it caught up with him, and he got thrown in jail."

I watch her carefully for a reaction. She doesn't scowl or show surprise; rather she's uncertain and intent. Concerned. Concern is better than anger. I've never told anyone about this before. It's a relief not to have it all on my shoulders.

"But . . . who took care of you?"

"Nobody seemed to notice I was alone. I guess people assumed my mother was still there, even though I hadn't seen her in years. It wasn't like I was little. I was seventeen." Seventeen and completely unprepared to have to take care of a house and myself.

"You were alone?" she asks, her voice suddenly small.

I nod. My chest aches.

"I'm sorry," she mutters.

I puff out some air in disbelief that this has somehow turned to her being the one to say that, as if she is to blame for anything here. I shrug. There's not much more to say about it, really. It is what it is.

Her shoulders slump, and she stuffs another bite in her mouth, like it's a means of changing the topic. I eat too so she doesn't end up waiting for me. A neighbor's lawnmower sputters to life, its muted sound adding white noise to our lack of conversation.

"We should get back to studying," she says. I pick at her words, looking for the hidden meaning between them. They're quiet and gentle, free from her earlier venom. The argument has passed. She still won't meet my eyes. Either she pities me, or she's accepting but not forgiving. "Need to make the most of our day."

Maybe today doesn't have to be our only study day. She said she can't keep driving here, but there's no reason I couldn't go to her. Driving back and forth would be a challenge, but if she'd have me . . .

The dropped subject and return to studying feels like an olive branch, in its own way. If I make an offer, the worst that can happen is she says no, and then we're in no worse a place than now.

"You know, I convinced my clients to do virtual coaching sessions while I'm on the show. I figured I'd need extra studying time and wasn't sure if I'd need to stay in LA during the week. I still have to work, but I could work from Kalamazoo." I let my suggestion settle in.

She frowns at me. "That's a lot of time together. I have a better understanding of what happened back then, but that doesn't mean I excuse it. You broke my heart. One conversation doesn't solve that, Eli."

"Understood." I bury my face in my book, attempting to focus and not dwell on her rejection. I know it's well deserved.

We study in silence for a few minutes before she slams her book down and huffs, "What is your plan? You would drive all that way every day?" she asks, both angry and doubtful.

Apparently, she's just as distracted as I am, and isn't having much luck fighting what's between us, still lingering beneath the surface. I press my lips together to avoid a smile that will only piss her off further.

We both know I can't afford a hotel, and gas isn't cheap. My offer is contingent on her letting me stay with her. A tentative truce, with her thinking about forgiving me, is not exactly "get an invite to stay the night" territory.

Before I can answer, she starts rationalizing. "We both need this win. Really need this win. Strategically, studying together makes sense."

I nod, not about to say anything to deter her when she's doing all the convincing for me.

She pulls at her hair to tighten her bun, and nudges her glasses further up her nose before letting out another frustrated huff.

"It's logical," she says.

I nod again.

"You're not saying anything."

I shake my head.

"Smart."

I nod.

Charlie chews at her lip. I don't know how they still look so full and kissable with all the gnawing she does. It's a wonder they aren't nibbled to shreds. I need a bribe to tip the scales. Time to bring out the big guns.

"I'll bring snickerdoodles."

She lets out a little moan. She's always had a weakness for snickerdoodles. She mentioned they were her favorite when we started dating, and while Dad was still around and I wasn't so badly trying to keep my head above water, I looked up a recipe and made them for her a few times.

"That's just playing dirty," she says.

"No, I—"

"Stop," she interrupts. "I know I set myself up with that one. Stop right there before you say something ridiculous and make me change my mind."

"Change your mind?" Hope was an emotion I rarely felt, but she was bringing it out in me.

"Yes." She lets out a long heavy sigh, dragging it out to ensure I understand what a concession this is for her to make. "Eli, would you like to stay at my place for the week?"

I jump right in before her threatened mind change can come to fruition. "Yes, I'd be—"

She holds up a finger and I pause to let her finish. "In my spare bedroom. Platonically."

I laugh and hold my hands up in defense. "That'd be great."

I remember sitting next to her on her bed, our shoulders and legs pressed together, books open across our laps. Both of us pointing to a line of text at the same time. Our eyes meeting as our hands brushed. Her lips parting.

She swallows. Is she remembering the same? "I'm serious. This is just studying. I'm still mad at you."

"I know. I promise to be on my best behavior."

She narrows her eyes at me. "That's not saying much. Scoundrel."

Maybe she's right.

CHAPTER EIGHT
CHARLOTTE

Eli Collins is coming to my house. My house. Eli Collins. And I'm totally not freaking out about it at all. Standing in my closet, wearing a combination of five outfits that I can't decide between, after burning the shit out of my breakfast is perfectly normal.

He's coming here to study all day today, then stay the night. Again, that's fine and not stressful at all. Then, he'll work from my house while I'm at the office for the day.

Yeah, this is definitely freak-out mode.

Maybe I understand his reasons better, but I still don't excuse the way he treated me. I was head over heels for him, and he just stopped speaking to me. His opinion on my house and my looks means nothing. Nada. Zip, zilch, zero. And yet . . .

My phone rings, and the screen lights up with Eli's name. Guess he never got the millennial memo that we text instead of calling, whenever possible. Is he not coming anymore? I work my way toward forgiving him just enough to invite him here, and he ghosts me again. That would figure.

I mentally brace for his rejection once again and then pick up the phone.

"Hello?"

"Hey, Charlotte," he says with that smooth voice of his, and I'm not sure if I should be still/preemptively mad at him, or if I want to swoon over hearing him say my name again.

"What's going on?"

"I was on my way, but there's a slight problem." My heart drops. I should have known better than to let this man back into my life any more than I had to. I shut my closet door, since it no longer matters what I'm wearing, and shouldn't have in the first place.

"I see," I say through gritted teeth.

"Don't hang up. It's not like that. I'm fifteen minutes away and my car broke down."

"Oh." I unclench a little. Maybe I shouldn't keep jumping to conclusions with him.

"I need to call a mechanic," he continues, "but I wanted to call you first. I'm trying not to mess this up, and I didn't want you to worry when I wasn't on time."

Worry? Who, me? A twinge of guilt pricks my stomach. "Do you need me to come pick you up?"

"Do you mind?" he asks without his usual cockiness. The softness in his voice sounds almost insecure.

"Of course not. Text me a location, I'm on my way."

Before I can get caught up in second-guessing my outfit again, I yank off my top and switch to one I'm pretty sure goes with the pants I'm wearing, and hope for the best. I slide across the hardwood to the door in my socks, Tom Cruise style, but with the notable addition of pants. I throw on my shoes and grab my keys and am out the door.

When I pull up behind him on the shoulder of the highway, he's watching the tow-truck driver hook his car up, his face marred with worry lines, his posture rigid. He got very good at his cool bad-boy demeanor in high school. It's strange and concerning to see him so off-balance yet again this week. When he catches sight of me, his face smooths.

"Eli." I drape myself against the side of my car, super casual and probably super sexy, going for levity.

His mouth quirks up in that smirk of his, and *Charlotte! You. Are. Mad. At. Him. Still.*

"Fancy meeting you here." I say, and he does that thing where he presses his hand to his upper lip and rubs at his cheeks, covering up a laugh.

"Excuse me, are you laughing at me?"

"Of course not—I wouldn't laugh at my rescuer." He's totally laughing.

I narrow my eyes.

"You, um—" he points at his nose. I lift my hand to the place he indicated and feel something cottony. My eyebrows shoot skyward in horror as my other hand flies to my face to also pat my nose, because my brain won't accept this reality until both hands have confirmed my nightmare. I was so focused on the outfit, and then on getting here to help, I ran out the door with a pore strip on. Even worse, I greeted him while attempting a sexy pose with a pore strip on.

Damn it all to hell! I don't even know why I was trying to look sexy, since I'm *mad* and not at all interested in him.

"One moment, please." I duck into my car and glower at my reflection in the rearview mirror. "I am an intelligent woman," I mouth. That man just fries my brain. I yank it off in one quick, painful movement. "Ow!"

I survey myself in the mirror, making sure I haven't left anything else embarrassingly out of place. My nose is a brilliant Crayola orange red, one of eight retired colors, but at least I have clean pores and the strip is gone. I compose myself to face him in my new unintentional Rudolph cosplay.

"Anyway. Sorry about the car."

"It was bound to happen eventually, but I was hoping it would last a little longer. Give me two minutes to get the car squared away and then we can get out of here?"

I nod, and his eyes dip, scanning my body, before he turns back to the tow-truck driver, and I can't even complain, because my eyes zero right in on his ass as he saunters away.

* * *

"You go ahead and help yourself to whatever. The guest room is over there."

I excuse myself for a quick restroom run before returning to the living room. No Eli. He had a green duffel in his hand when he walked in, so he must be unpacking. The door to the guest room is mostly closed, but I catch movement through the opening. Shoulder muscles tense above some mouthwatering back dimples as Eli changes his shirt.

Compose yourself, Charlotte! Abandonment. Ignoring. General assholery. How much did I really care about those things again? Fuck the snickerdoodles, I want a taste of that.

He pulls his shirt down, snug over his chest, and I hastily move to the couch and try to look busy, not like the spying Drooly McDroolerson I actually am right now. He walks out, and grins at me. "Diving in already?"

"Might as well." I'm proud of how cool and collected I sound. At least I am until I realize I'm holding the book upside down. He doesn't comment, but as he digs his stuff out of his backpack, his smile is a little too knowing.

We study for a bit on opposite sides of the couch, and I'm annoyed to find that I'm not seething with rage. When I look at him, rather than animosity, there's a curiosity to get to know adult Eli better, and a bit of the giddy butterflies I used to get when I was around him.

"What are you studying?" I ask him.

"Celebrity gossip still. Apparently, Lady Gaga is godmother to Elton John's kids."

"Interesting."

"Indeed. You still on sports?" he asks.

"Yep. Did you know sheep counting is an official sport in Australia? Or that the world record for consecutive pushups is"—she squints at the page—"holy guacamole, ten thousand five hundred and seven."

"Ouch." He rubs his biceps sympathetically. "I think I'd fall a hundred or so short of that."

I laugh and roll my eyes at him. This feels way too easy. Damn his good looks and easy charm. I need to be careful with my heart. He may have my understanding, but certainly not my trust. I'm still working on the forgiveness part. I just need my lustful body to get with the program.

Every couple pages or so of reading, my eyes slide up to watch him, a subtle adjustment, like a deer that creeps forward hoping slow and careful enough steps won't catch the attention of its predator. On something like my fifth snoop, Eli's smirk is back.

"Did you lose something over here?" he asks. "Or if you want a picture to hang onto for when I'm not staying in the other room, all you have to do is ask."

I roll my eyes, hiding the fact that yeah, I kind of do want one. After I got home yesterday, I almost braved a deep dive into my storage crawl space for my high school yearbook, until I remembered I'm thirty now, and pining over a seventeen-year-old's picture, even if he's also thirty now, would be creepy and gross. Also, reliving high school photos and seeing all the yearbook signatures would be so cringy. It's best left lost to history, like the Amber Room at the Catherine Palace, a collection of Amber panels, sometimes referred to as the eighth wonder of the world. They were stolen from Russia by Nazis, but failed to resurface after the war, leading treasure hunters to search for them, and in some cases die under questionable circumstances in the process.

Mercifully, he lets the subject drop and doesn't continue to embarrass me. After a few more hours of study, with a brief interlude for lunch, it's three o'clock, and my eyes feel like they're bleeding.

"Want to take a break?" he asks.

"Yes," I admit. "But I also want to learn all these things to make sure we win this week."

"I know—me too. But if you're burnt out, you're not going to remember it anyway."

"Fair point." I yawn.

"We need to switch gears. Why don't we role-play?"

I fight back the blush at the onslaught of mental images of Eli and myself in compromising positions, and I raise an eyebrow at him. "If you think I'm going to dress up and play doctor with you, you're in for a disappointment."

"I mean, sexy librarian seems like it'd be more fitting for the current situation," he says.

"Not happening." I'm wishing that I could hire the construction crew of Instacon in India, or Mini Sky City in China, some of the fastest construction projects in history, to build a wall around my heart and keep this man from taking up residency there, where he might do immeasurable damage.

He laughs. "Relax. I just meant we should quiz each other. Half of it is knowing the trivia, but half of it is making sure we don't freeze under the pressure, right? We should mimic the conditions of the show."

Not a bad idea. I probably would have panicked more over the lights and cameras and being on the spot with the questions if I hadn't been so distracted by the fact that Eli freaking Collins had appeared out of nowhere.

"All right, I'm in." I toss my book aside and sit up straight, facing him, legs crossed.

He clears his throat. "I'm Bobby Bailey, and welcome to *Brain Battle*!" he says in a horrible and over-the-top impression.

"That's your Bobby Bailey impression? That's terrible. You sound nothing like him!"

His mouth drops in feigned offense. "Excuse me? I sound just like him."

"You gave him a British accent."

He frowns. "Okay, maybe it could use a little work. Could you do any better?"

"You have to scoop up to words more. Like some kind of speech slide whistle." I straighten and take a deep breath. "Welcome back! Let's meet today's knowledge warriors!"

"Okay, you win. That was pretty good."

"Thank you," I tip an imaginary hat to him.

"Moving on," he says. "Charlotte, are you ready for your question?"

"This isn't working. I don't feel nearly as stressed out as on camera."

"I could stream it on Instagram or something," he suggests.

"You absolutely will not!" I shout, but my skyrocketing heart rate was unnecessary. I already know he's not on the 'gram. I checked.

"Well, I just don't feel like you're taking this seriously." He folds his arms.

"I'm not quite feeling the atmosphere. Those lights were like miniature suns."

"Twenty-seven million degrees feels like a bit of an exaggeration."

"Miniature red giants then," I retort.

"Miniature giants? Now you're just being oxymoronic."

"*The point is,* I'm not sweating nearly enough."

He smirks and slowly shakes his head. *"Babe, I could make you sweat."* The words flood my brain in his voice as clearly as if he'd actually said them. While I'm busy squeezing my thighs together for relief, he's smiling innocently. He obviously saw the perfect opening but bit his tongue. He's left his player act behind and is joking around with me. It feels so natural, my guard keeps dropping. Clearly the patrols I've set around my heart are sleeping on the job. I wonder if there's any Yeoman warders available to take over. Those folks in their red coats and poofy hats, and with their constant vigilance wouldn't let me down.

"Not sweaty enough? That can be fixed," he finally adds, but not with the sexual implications I was expecting. He takes off toward the bathroom, returning a moment later with, of all things, my hairdryer.

"What are you doing?" I ask.

He flashes me a grin, then turns away to plug it in. Next thing I know, he's shining the painfully bright light of his phone's flashlight in my eyes and is blasting my face with hot air from the blow-dryer.

His mouth moves, and I hear garbled sounds, but nothing I can decipher.

"What?" I shout over the noise of the dryer.

He again says something, louder, but all I can make out are the vowel sounds.

"This is significantly louder than the show," I yell.

Eli clicks off the blow-dryer. "Now you're just being difficult."

"It never bothered you before," I say, throwing in a bit of a flirtatious lilt. His mouth quirks to the side, and he goes silent for a moment, considering. I think back too. Snuggled up next to him on his bed, wanting so badly to kiss him breathless, but incentivizing both of us with kisses to study instead. We passed our classes, and still got to the kissing eventually, so it was a good kind of stubborn.

He's staring at me like I might have the power to harness the sun, but I'm no Helios nor Māui. "Charlie, I . . ." he trails off.

I bite my lip, waiting for the end of that sentence. I don't know where it's going, but from the way his chest heaves with a deep breath, and that intense look he's giving me, it looks like it would be an adventure.

An adventure that will have to wait, apparently, because his phone rings with a notification. The moment, so full of anticipation, dissipates. We both shift awkwardly, breaking eye contact. There's an ache in my chest at the lost opportunity.

A day of competition, a day and a half of studying, and one real conversation can't be enough to rekindle what we lost. I'm not sure what I want from him or what I wanted him to say. I'm too confused by our situation to guide this. I need him to take a step so I can see how I react in the moment.

As analytical as I am, a natural on-the-spot reaction seems the only way to figure out what I want without letting myself overthink it. I did a surfing simulator at a waterpark once. Before I got on, they didn't ask me which foot I thought I should put forward; they stood behind me and gave me a small, even shove, to see which foot I naturally threw forward. Don't think, just do.

He turns away, unplugging the hair dryer to return it to the bathroom. He's only going a few feet, and he's coming right back, and yet the site of him walking away makes me itch.

CHAPTER NINE

ELI

A prolonged day of studying winds down, and Charlotte and I are in a strange limbo. We're both doing a lot of checking each other out. Neither of us is being subtle about it, but neither of us is acknowledging it either. I don't know what that means.

My bit with the hair dryer, goofy as it was, worked to loosen her up. For a minute, things were comfortable, relaxed, fun. I wanted to kiss her—to tell her just how much I still cared. I wanted to beg her to let us start over, but then the damn phone went off, and any courage I felt disappeared.

If I want a shot at this, first I need forgiveness. I'm probably going to wind up battling my way through the friend zone first. We've got a game to win. Teammates and friends first, maybe more later.

I check the notification to see an emailed estimate from the mechanic. The thought of another large expense makes me feel sick. I don't know if I can afford to repair it or if I'll have to sell it for parts and get by with only Dad's truck.

The unexpected bill puts more pressure on our already dire situation. Here I am, teasing Charlie like we're back in high school, while my Dad busts his ass at work, not knowing our hole has gotten deeper. It instantly puts me in a mood and renews my focus.

"I think I'm going to call it a night," she says, hours later.

It's late. I suspect way later than she usually goes to bed, but neither of us knew how to approach the awkwardness of sleeping under the same roof. Is it weird if I'm awake while she's in bed? I didn't want to go to bed before her, but there's only one bathroom, so I can't get ready at the same time as her, and fuck, why am I so awkward?

"Yeah, I probably should too."

We both retreat to our individual rooms. I'm supposed to change, but I'm not exactly a pajama guy. I usually sleep in my boxers, so there isn't anything for me to change into, but I'm not about to strip before using the bathroom. I throw on a pair of workout shorts and grab my toothbrush. Her bedroom door opens at the same time as mine.

"Oh," she says.

"You go ahead," I say.

"You're the guest."

Great, now it feels like I'm on the clock to use the bathroom. I piss and brush my teeth in record time, then knock on her door.

"All yours," I say when she opens it.

"Okay." Neither of us move. For two intelligent people, normally adept at conversation, we're not impressing anyone with our wit now. Charlie breaks the silence with a laugh. "This is kind of weird, huh?"

I smile back, "Yeah. I'm glad you let me stay, though." She's so close. I wish I could pull her to me. A hug could be enough. Just feeling her in my arms could sustain me and relieve some of the tension I've felt since receiving the quote this afternoon.

"I'm glad too." She gently lifts my arm from the doorframe where I'm leaning, and ducks under it and off toward the bathroom.

"Good night, Charlotte."
"Good night, Eli.

*   *   *

It is not a good night. Either she keeps it hotter than the stage in this damn house, or the knowledge that she's sleeping just on the other side of this wall has me sweating. The clock radio she has on her guest room nightstand reads five thirty, and I groan. It's been one of those nights where I likely drifted off at some point, but I sure as hell don't remember sleeping.

The sheets look like the Tasmanian devil plowed through them; The Looney Tunes one, not the real-life marsupial. I stare at the clock a while longer, willing myself to sleep, until at six AM an alarm sounds on the other side of the wall, and I can abandon this failed mission.

I'm going to have to get used to this fast if I'm going to stay here and get enough sleep to be a functioning human for the show later this week. I pull on my shorts and a T-shirt, and head to the kitchen to root around in the cabinets for coffee.

"Good morning!" Charlotte shouts from the other room, and she moves past the doorway in a blur. Someone doesn't want me to see her bedhead. "I'm just going to jump in the shower."

"I could—" I start.

"No, you may not join me," she adds, already knowing where I was going. I hadn't actually expected her to agree.

After we've both dressed and had a quick breakfast, she hovers by the door, and my eyes are glued to the way her pencil skirt hugs her hips. "You sure you're going to be all right here all day?" she asks.

We've talked about this. I offered to try and find other places to hang out during the day, but I can't do physical training from the library or coffee shop. Still, I don't want her to feel obligated.

"I'm good, but if you're uncomfortable, I can go. Please don't feel pressured."

"No, I'm not uncomfortable. I just feel guilty leaving you alone," she says.

"Don't. I'll see you tonight so we can study more. Just a few days until the next show."

After she leaves, I survey the living room: my office for the day. She gave me permission to move things around for my sessions, so I carefully do some rearranging, moving a reclining chair to the side and pushing the coffee table against the couch to open up floor space.

It's tempting to snoop through the house, but she's shown me a lot of trust, letting me stay here, and I won't betray that by digging through her things. It doesn't feel like snooping to look at what's displayed in the open, though.

She has an entire wall of bookshelves, and when she was going in and out of her room earlier, I saw even more in there. Some fiction, a lot of nonfiction. Atlases and maps. Stacks of magazines. It's clearly no coincidence she's on the show. She studies this stuff all the time.

We used to watch game shows together when we were dating, and she always talked about being a contestant one day. Apparently, that dream stuck. If she hadn't appeared in my thoughts on a regular basis, I probably wouldn't have thought to apply either. If I hadn't still been regretting my choices, it never would have crossed my mind to try a game show when I was looking for something, anything, to help our financial situation.

I get my shitty laptop set up for my virtual training session with my first client, Leslie. She's a badass woman who told me she already knows she's fine as hell and doesn't want to change a thing about how she looks, but is done having people open jars for her, so we're strength training and working up to power lifting.

"Hey, Leslie," I say when she appears on screen.

"Hi, Eli, how's it going?"

"Living the dream. Thanks again for doing a virtual session this week." I hadn't gotten much pushback. Most of my clients were glad for the chance to learn in-home workouts they could do when they're not able to get to the gym.

"No problem!"

We go through our workout. I planned ahead, with living room modifications, and it goes pretty well. I wouldn't do it all the time, but it's manageable for my time on the show.

"Great job! You crushed it today. Let's stretch it out." I guide her through some arm stretches, then bend into a downward dog–like pose to stretch out calves. While bent over, with my head toward the camera, I hear the lock tumble behind me, followed by a feminine shriek.

"Who are you? What are you doing in my daughter's house?" The door slams behind me before I've even managed to stand and turn around.

On screen, Leslie has toppled out of her pose, laughing. "We were just about done anyway. I can finish stretching on my own. You go deal with whatever that was."

"Thanks." My face heats as I click out of the call. By the time I get the door open again, Mrs. Evans has retreated to her car and appears to already have Charlie on the phone. She cowers behind the vehicle, like some robber or murderer broke into her daughter's house and decided to drop and do some yoga before getting on with their lawless hooliganry.

"There's a butt—I mean, there's a man. I mean, there's a man butt in your house."

While I'm aware my ass was facing her and sticking in the air when she walked in, I am more than a floating butt. I am a full human here. Eyes up top, Mrs. Evans.

"Sorry, Mrs. Evans—I didn't mean to scare you."

"Eli?" she asks, lowering the phone from her ear.

"Yes, ma'am," I say.

"I knew you were on the show with Charlotte, and you two were studying together, but I didn't realize you were staying at her house." Her eyes narrow in a way that makes me certain she's convinced I'm here for only the most nefarious of purposes and will defile her daughter, if I haven't already.

"It was the only way we could study together through the week. With work, there wouldn't be enough time to drive back and forth."

She folds her arms. She tries to stare down her nose at me, which doesn't exactly work because I'm a solid foot taller than her. It still manages to be intimidating, though, because first interactions with the parents of the person you're head over heels for is always a good way to suddenly feel like a child. Also, the last time I remember seeing her, she was throwing seventeen-year-old me out of her daughter's bedroom after I got caught sneaking in the window, so that doesn't help. Maybe getting caught isn't the right expression. Charlotte had been excited for about two minutes, and then the guilt over sneaking had gnawed at her enough that she'd announced my presence. She's never had a dishonest bone in her body.

"What are your intentions with my daughter?"

"My intentions?" I ask, and she only raises an eyebrow in return. It's a fair question, but not one I know how to answer. I guess, to win a game show with her a few more times, and over the course of that, hopefully win her over enough to let me have another shot. With the show winnings—even if it's just the first episode—my life is more on track. Combined with a job and school, maybe I could feel like I was enough. That feels too impossible to say, though.

"To win *Brain Battle* and see where things go," I say.

"Things?" She makes a face like she's just eaten putrid garbage. Apparently, that wasn't the right thing to say. Time to backpedal, except there's a small voice coming from somewhere, like an ant has gained abilities for human speech and begun shouting at us.

Mrs. Evans and I both glance at the phone in her hands, each of us having forgotten Charlie was still there. I'm suddenly incredibly glad I didn't share my feelings for her when asked about my intentions.

"Young lady, would you like to explain why a man whose plan is to—and I quote—'see where things go' has moved in with you for an indeterminate amount of time?"

Mrs. Evans listens to Charlie, with the phone pressed to her ear.

"That may be, but I found him in a rather compromising position," Mrs. Evans says.

"Hey, I was working!"

"By sticking your bottom in the air on camera for a woman?"

"My 'bottom' was facing away from the camera, and I was just leading a client through stretches at the end of her strength training."

"I'm sure."

"What would be so wrong with it if I'd been doing something else? I'm making money," I say, getting all worked up defending myself over a would-be career I don't even have. Meeting the parents is not a strength of mine.

"Ma!" Charlie yells loud enough that even I can hear.

"Oh, all right, I'll just grab the pan and leave," Mrs. Evans says. She hangs up with Charlie and pushes past me into the kitchen. When she returns, she stares me down. "Behave yourself," she says before getting in her car and driving away.

When I get back inside, my phone buzzes on the table.

It's Charlie: *What did you do?*

CHAPTER TEN
CHARLOTTE

I pull into my driveway, wishing that studying was still in my plans for the evening. Focusing at work all day was a challenge. I couldn't even focus on the word *focus*, without my mind running off on tangents.

Ford Focus, a car in production since 1998. The predecessors were Ford Escort in Europe, North America, and Argentina; and Ford Laser in Asia and Oceania.

Focus: a 2015 movie starring Will Smith and Margot Robbie, directed by Glenn Ficarra.

Focus can be achieved through the Pomodoro Technique of concentration.

Down the rabbit hole I go. My priority is the show, and I don't want to do anything else but prepare for it. A voice at the back of my mind suggests that time with Eli is definitely a factor, but that is not a voice I plan on listening to.

My study plans were derailed, however, by Eli's ass somehow ending up in front of my mother.

I burst through the door, ready to chew him out, but I falter as I'm momentarily disoriented. The furniture is shuffled around, which I gave him permission to do, but something else is different. I sniff. Is that . . . lemony freshness?

"Did you clean?" I ask.

He hesitates, studying my face. "Maybe?"

"I don't think that's a very confusing question. You did, or you didn't."

"Since we're studying in the evenings, and I invaded your territory, I thought it might be a nice gesture. The look on your face is making me second-guess that. Too weird?"

Cracks in the foundation. I clutch at my chest, as if to keep them from splitting further. My wall must stay strong.

"It isn't weird, but stop trying to butter me up. You can't bribe your way to forgiveness."

"Are you saying there's something else I should be doing to get there instead?"

I sigh. I'm not much of a sigher, but Eli sure is bringing them out of me. My damned trivia brain starts hurling memorized quotes at me. Mel Robbins suggests forgiveness for the sake of your own peace, whether or not it is deserved. Eli is trying. Would it be so terrible to forgive him and grant myself the peace of being able to focus on preparing for the next episode?

Ghandi teaches that forgiveness requires strength. I am strong. Forgiving him doesn't mean caving in. It doesn't mean I have to open myself up to him again completely. It doesn't have to equate to vulnerability.

He's still watching me, waiting for a response.

"I'm working on it." I sigh, and briefly squeeze his hand.

He hesitates, then says, "Okay. Should we get to studying then?"

"I'd love to, but unfortunately, your ass got us into trouble, and now we're expected for spaghetti night."

His jaw hangs a bit. "My ass?"

"Yes. Ma went on a tirade about your ass that I didn't quite follow, and then demanded that you come over for spaghetti night. What happened with that, by the way? Do I even want to know?"

"I was stretching!"

"Well, she was rather insistent. If I fought it, she'd show up here instead, and we wouldn't be able to get rid of her. This way, we eat a quick dinner, we're in, we're out, we can come back here and study."

"Fine," he grumbles.

*　*　*

The first thing I do is give Gran a kiss on the forehead. In the chaos of prep and travel for the show, I haven't visited her or talked to her as often as I usually do.

"There's my girl," she says. "And Eli! If it isn't the Danny to her Sandy. Wasn't expecting to see you again, young man."

Eli's eyes widen at the comparison, and he grins. At least Gran doesn't appear to be holding a grudge.

"Gran!" I scold.

"What? I call 'em like I see 'em." She winks at him. "Fair warning: we're having cavatappi and meatball, not spaghetti as promised."

"Pop did the shopping?" I ask.

"Yep," Gran replies.

I help Gran to the kitchen. Eli clears his throat and extends his hand out to Pop. "Nice to see you again, Mr. Evans."

"Nice to see you using the front door this time," Pop says. My cheeks flame, and I'm pretty sure he's giving Eli's hand an unnecessarily tight shake. "I understand you gave my wife quite a scare this morning."

"I'm a personal trainer, sir. I was doing a virtual workout with a client. I was guiding her through a cool-down stretch when Mrs. Evans walked in. I didn't mean to alarm her."

"So, Eli, where have been all these years?" Ma interjects. Her tone is clipped, with an implication that he never should have left me. This is spiraling.

Eli opens his mouth to speak, but I cut in, attempting to spare him from further grilling.

"He still lives in East Lansing. Just up the road from our old house." Pop had gotten a job offer in the Kalamazoo area just after I'd left for college. No longer needing to stay put so I wouldn't have to move away from friends, my parents had relocated, and it had worked out for me to get a job near them after I graduated.

We fill up our plates, and I continue to thwart the tense checkup conversations my parents keep trying to start.

"Quit harassing the boy," Gran says as we dig into our food. "They need to practice. Put on a game show."

Reluctantly, Ma turns the TV to GSTV. If we can't study, at least we have this.

Brain Battle isn't on, but *Quizlings*—another trivia show—is. Before the show starts, Ma pulls me into the other room.

"Gran had a doctor's appointment today," she says.

"Anything new?" I ask.

"No, but some of the treatments they're suggesting we try out are a bit more complicated. They're recommending we consider a part-time nurse."

I grimace. "Any idea how much that will cost?"

"No. They gave me some numbers to call, but I haven't had a chance to yet. I'll email you the numbers, once they come in, so you can add it to the budget, but I wanted to give you a heads-up."

"Thanks." We both head back to the kitchen before we're missed, and take our seats to eat and join the trivia.

"The Panama Canal!" everyone shouts, in response to the first question.

We shovel a few forkfuls, not wanting to be caught with a mouthful when it's time to answer a question. There is zero conversation happening in between questions. With our history, the conversation over Gran's care, and the pressure of the show, the atmosphere is rife with tension, and a little bit of competition, though I'm not sure what everyone is trying to prove to whom.

"The Hubble Telescope," Pop and Eli say while my brain fumbles for the answer. I would have been able to come up with it eventually.

"The Hundred Acre Wood!" Ma, Gran, and I shout.

Then the questions get harder. The family gets fewer correct answers, with most being answered by Eli and me, and everyone starts to loosen up in each other's presence. What starts out feeling like a competition turns fun, and we laugh around forkfuls of food.

I try to soak in every minute with my family, because if we end up winning this week's episode, the show is putting us up in a hotel for the week, rather than having us keep flying back and forth. If we go on a run, it might be a while before I get to see them again. Even if they gave us a hard time tonight, I love them.

Eli survives my parents' inquisition without complaint, and my heart thaws a little more. We catch each other's eyes, telling private jokes before answering questions together. We're starting to feel like a team.

CHAPTER ELEVEN
CHARLOTTE

Eli and I sit across from each other in the boarding area at the airport, ready to head to LA for our second episode.

"What seat are you in?" Given the last-minute nature of our booking, neither of us was able to preselect a seat assignment.

"27E. Damn middle seat. You?" he asks.

"No way, I'm 27D!" Maybe that came out sounding a little more excited than it should have, given we spent the week together. *Dial it in, Charlotte.* "I just mean, you never know what you're going to get with seatmates. At least I know you don't smell like BO and aren't going to hack up a lung on me or anything."

Yeah, he's not buying that for a second. His eyes are trained on his boarding pass, but he's got that damned knowing grin.

"Okay, fine, I'm glad I'm sitting next to you. Happy?" I huff.

"I didn't say anything," he says.

"You didn't have to. It was the smirk."

"Some people find it charming," he says.

This time he doesn't bother with the smirk. Just a deadpan stare. Damn it. Sometimes an inability to lie is so inconvenient.

"It's adorable. Stop gloating. Ass."

He chuckles, and the gate attendant calls our boarding group.

"Shall we?" he asks, and we join the line. As he zones out, looking around the terminal, I take the opportunity to drink him in. We made a pact to both wear comfy clothes for the five-hour flight. I spent a half hour digging through my cozy clothes before landing on what deep down I knew I'd go with all along: the yoga pants that make my ass look fantastic.

He opted for sweatpants. Sweatpants that show a clear outline of a certain appendage when he walks. Hopefully no one notices any drool slipping out the sides of my mouth when I forget I'm not supposed to stare at it, because damn.

"Hey, we can trade seats," I say as we get to our row. "You need the leg room more than I do."

He hesitates, like he's about to argue, but he knows me well enough to realize that even if he declines, I'll insist he take it anyway. "Thank you, I appreciate it."

A week ago, I probably wouldn't have offered, out of spite, but it's amazing how much can change in a few days. The first day at his house, we had our blow-up and decision to call a truce. Then we moved to my house.

It was as if, as the week progressed, we moved in concentric circles, slowly spiraling toward each other. The first day we tiptoed around with lots of *"Oh no, you go first,"* and *"I'm fine, how are you?"* and *"I don't know—whatever you'd like."*

Then conversations became natural. We said what we meant, even if it was blunt. The distance between us on the couch shrank, and we put less effort into hiding stolen glances, even if we didn't admit to catching each other stealing them.

I haven't forgotten our history, and I still don't trust him. He's going to have to earn that. But when I reach for the fury I held toward him a week ago, I can't find it. It's just . . . gone.

We watch the safety presentation in silence. As we taxi to the runway, my heart jumps. I press back into the seat, just to feel something solid there. I close my eyes and will my breathing to slow.

"Are you okay?" he asks.

"Mm-hmm," I answer on a deep inhalation. I've flown enough in my life and have researched the physics and engineering enough that it doesn't scare me in general. Logically, I know that flying by airplane is currently considered the safest mode of transportation. I'm fine once I'm in the air . . . unless there's turbulence.

"Shit, are you afraid of flying?" he asks. I'm one of the estimated thirty-five to forty percent of individuals who experience some form of anxiety when flying, but I don't fall into the category of the two to five percent who truly suffer aerophobia.

"Not so much the flying as the takeoff and landing." I'm not about to hyperventilate on him, but my body does have a physical reaction to the nerves that I fight to control.

The engines whir and we pick up speed. My hand flies to his and squeezes. *In. Out. In. Out. Breathe.*

His hand squeezes back, grounding me, even as the plane leaves the ground. My stomach lurches with the lift. I zero in on the sensation of his hand in mine.

"You're all right." He whispers. "I've got you." His thumb gently rubs the back of my hand. I give him a small nod, still keeping my eyes closed, and focusing on breathing. I'm eased by his words, even if on an intellectual level I know there isn't a damn thing he can do if we crash.

Finally, the plane levels out, and my stomach settles with it. I take one last deep breath, then open my eyes and smile at him. "Thanks."

"No problem. Better now?" he asks.

"Yeah."

"You're still crushing my hand."

I loosen my grip and lift his hand to inspect it for damage.

He laughs. "Don't worry—nothing broken. I'm sure I'll regain feeling in my fingers soon."

My face heats, "I'm sorry. I didn't realize I was squeezing so hard."

"All good. You ready for more studying?" He grimaces.

It's my turn to laugh at his just-bit-a-lemon expression. "You don't look like you are."

"Honestly, my brain is fried. It's overstuffed. Nothing I read right now is going to stick."

Thank God he said it, because I don't have five hours of studying in me. I've been preparing for this for years, and we've studied all week.

"Same," I admit.

"Do you feel ready?" he asks.

"I'm not sure it's the kind of thing I'd ever feel ready for, but ready as I'll ever be. I'm stuffed with more knowledge than I was last week, and we pulled it off then." There are so many factors that can contribute to whether we win or lose. We could be a hundred times more knowledgeable than we are right now, and just get the wrong questions. There have been few times in my life when I've felt like I have so little control, and so desperately need things to go in my favor. The way Eli's muscles strain, I know he's worrying about the same. We both need this money. We're both feeling the pressure of the high stakes.

"We've got this. Thank you for working so hard to win. I need it, and there's no one I'd rather go through this with than you." He winces as he says it. I'd been charmed by the words, but the accompanying expression worries me. Why tell me he wants another chance if he doesn't?

Pushing my unease aside, I smile back. "Me too."

"Yeah right." He ducks his head in a self-deprecating way.

"I mean it. The past is the past. I'm not sure that I trust you yet, or how long it will take me to get there, but there's no more grudge. I forgive you."

His brown eyes meet mine and flicker as he searches my face. *It's true*, I silently tell him. *I don't trust you with my heart, but I don't hate you either.*

"Anything to drink?" a stewardess asks, nudging her cart alongside us. I almost order my usual in-flight ginger ale, but the show isn't until tomorrow, and we'll have plenty of time to sober up and avoid hangovers once we land, and I could use some alcohol to take the edge off my flight jitters. I glance at Eli to make sure this isn't a solo party, and he turns on his full-blown smolder, directed right at me. Flynn Rider can't hold a candle to Eli's smolder. My leg trembles and he grins, like he knows exactly what kind of effect he has on me. Yeah, I'm going to need a drink now, whether he joins me or not.

"I'll have a mimosa, please," I say.

"Make it two," Eli adds.

We receive our drinks, and the stewardess moves on. "What are we toasting?" Eli asks.

"To winning?" I ask.

"And fresh starts," Eli says.

"To winning and fresh starts." I raise my glass.

"Cheers." We gently tap our plastic cups, because the flimsy plastic doesn't exactly clink.

"Oh, I have snacks too." I root around in my bag and pull out Twizzlers and cheddar & sour cream Pringles. "Your favorites, right?"

He grins and grabs the Pringles. "They are. I can't believe you remember that."

I blush and shrug. "It's no big deal." I want to tell him that of course I remember. I remember every second I spent with him. I remember every detail about the people who are important to me, and he was always important.

When the conversation dips, I put on *Sweet Home Alabama*. He puts on the news, but about five minutes in, I catch him abandoning all pretense of watching his own screen and openly watching mine.

"It's a great movie," I say. Watching it on his own TV might be the more practical option, but then he'd have to fast-forward or rewatch the beginning. I offer him an earbud, flushing at the swoony Jim and Pam vibes it gives me.

He caves and accepts the earbud, which seemed like a great choice before I was watching it with my former high school sweetheart. As the movie progresses, and the former flame reappears and they fall for each other again, we both shift around. The tiny space between our seats widens by what few centimeters it can, and things get awkward. We both drink a lot more to deal with the discomfort, and then we're both wasted. Or at least I'm wasted, and I think he is too?

The little air conditioner above me slurps as I twist it off, then back on again. "Is this thing on all the way? It's hot in here. It wasn't this hot in here before, was it?"

"It's definitely gotten hotter," Eli agrees. His eyes are hard on me as he says it, and another surge of heat washes over me. Is the mile high club really a thing? The bathrooms are miniscule. I feel like it's only a thing for people who can fly by themselves on a private jet, but I'm tempted to drag him into that sardine can with me to find out. Maybe I should order some water.

Eli fiddles with his air conditioner, coming to the same conclusion I did, that those little things are not effective enough in these tiny spaces. We settle into our seats and both move to use our shared armrest at the same time.

"Sorry." He pulls his arm back into his lap.

"Don't be." I meet his eyes, and the world spins. I'm not sure if it's Eli that's making me light-headed or the alcohol.

"Okay." His voice sounds as dry as mine feels as he settles his arm against mine. Little ripples of energy spark along my arm where we're touching. I wish I could feel his skin against mine—damn fabric. I realize belatedly I'm wearing a sweater and sit upright to take it off. I fling my arm back in the small space, to pull out of the sleeve, and my fist makes contact.

Eli lets out a pained grunt and doubles over.

"Oh my god, I'm so sorry!" I shriek, and an attendant shoots me a look from a few rows up. The mortification at punching him in the groin sobers me fast.

"I'll be all right—just give me a minute," he wheezes, still doubled over.

I bite at my lip and watch him fight through the pain. After a minute, he straightens and gives me a tight smile. "If you wanted to touch me, you could have just asked."

I roll my eyes, but his tactic to make me feel less guilty works. "Maybe later," I say flirtatiously, and his eyebrows shoot skyward.

I sit forward to attempt sweater removal once again, and Eli lifts his knees protectively. "Here, let me help you."

"Okay." My voice is soft, as I turn away from him and carefully roll my shoulders back to allow him access. Eli's hands move achingly slowly, grazing my cheek to brush my hair aside. His hands slide down my neck and catch the neckline of the sweater. He glides them down the edges of the fabric, over my shoulder, and is careful to pull the fabric away so he isn't publicly fondling me.

I send past-Charlotte a quick thank-you for putting on a thick bra that doesn't show just how hard my nipples get at the nearness of his hands running down the length of my body. He pulls the sweater gently back and peels it down my arms. My skin alights with fire. We're both fully clothed and haven't so much as kissed, yet I'm so turned on I might combust. The heady combination of the liquid courage and the sensual act of removing my sweater has us teetering on the edge of a very public make-out session. I don't envy the poor soul in the window seat on the other side of me.

"That's better," I whisper, settling back and again laying my arm alongside his. This time we're skin to skin, and there's no hiding the way my hair is on end and the goose bumps that ripple my flesh despite the heat. I swallow hard, even though my mouth is dry. I lick my lips to wet them, and Eli's eyes widen. My gaze catches his lips, and an unseen thread pulls me toward him with such force, I'm outnumbered in the tug-of-war ten to one. We both lean in, and then the grandpa next to me clears his throat loudly.

"Excuse me. I need to use the restroom," he says.

The thread of tension is cut and vanishes in an instant.

"Right." I shake my head to clear away the fog and the feeling of how badly I wanted to kiss Eli. So much for not trusting him with my heart.

We stand, and the man edges past. Once we're again seated, we fold our hands in our own laps. Suddenly we're like any two unknown passengers, stuck next to each other, who go to great lengths to tuck in on themselves and avoid touching their seatmates.

"So," Eli says.

"That was—" I begin.

"It's probably best that—" he says.

"Oh." My tone is flat, and the edges of my mouth droop in disappointment. Even if the vibe was lost, I'd been ready to ask if he wanted to try that again.

His eyes widen. "No, I wanted to. I meant, with the alcohol—"

"Excuse me," the man from our row says again, returning from his restroom break. We again do the shuffle to let him through. When we sit down, this time the moment is completely lost.

"Two hours to go," Eli mutters.

The alcohol has caught up with me. I've lost the giddy thrill of it, and now my eyelids are heavy. I've spent the week tossing and turning, thinking about Eli being in the other room. Sleep has been limited, and when I did manage it, it was interrupted by my own spasms of pleasure from dreaming about him. I'm a mess.

"Charlotte?" he asks.

"I'm just so tired," I say.

"Rest, then. We're ready."

I lay my head back on the seat, twisting around uncomfortably in the small space.

"Here," Eli whispers, lifting the armrest between us. "May I?" he asks, holding an arm out.

If I hadn't sent him enough signals already, letting him put an arm around me now would seal it. I ought to be sure. I ought to think this through and figure out what exactly I want from him. But I'm too drunk and tired to care. I nod sleepily, fighting to blink my heavy eyelids.

He folds his arm around me, and I lay my head on his chest, finally caving to the exhaustion and letting myself fall asleep.

* * *

Two hours later, Eli gently nudges me awake. I pull myself upright and wipe my cheek dry. Horrifyingly, there's a wet spot staining his shirt, where my head was laying. Fantastic. Not only did I use him as a pillow, but he didn't wake me when I drooled on him.

I gesture toward his chest. "Sorry." My cheeks flame with simultaneous mortification and swooning.

"No worries. We're almost there. They just made the announcement to buckle up for descent."

I can't even blame the sudden decrease in altitude for the way my heart jumps into my throat.

CHAPTER TWELVE
ELI

We're ready. We've got this.

Sarah escorts us to our holding room until the first half of the show determines the team we'll be playing against.

"Have you two seen all the buzz on social media this week?" Sarah asks. She's practically skipping into the room.

I trade glances with Charlie, and she shrugs.

"No," I say. "What buzz?"

"The *Brain Battle* fandom is wild about you two! The show's chat boards were full of chatter about the sparks between you two last week."

"Sparks?" Charlie asks.

It may have only been one week, but with all the travel and changes between Charlie and I, it feels like so much longer. Centuries have passed. Kingdoms have risen and fallen. Wrongs have been righted, chances have been taken, and Charlie drooled on my chest.

I shouldn't be as excited about that last one as I am. In the past I've looked around planes, and when I've seen someone who isn't reading, watching anything, sleeping, messing around on a device, or talking to anyone, they're just staring ahead of them, I've thought, "Wow, what kind of person sits on a plane and stares at the headrest in front of them for hours on end?"

The last two hours of that flight, I did just that. I didn't dare move to put a movie on and risk waking her. After years of missing her and wishing things were different, she was asleep in my arms, and I could not have cared less about a patch of drool.

I kept glancing down and wanting to rest my head atop hers; place a soft kiss on her hair. If only we were an actual couple and I had the freedom to do that. Instead, I was the newly forgiven asshole from the past, with whom she'd tentatively allowed an alliance bordering on friendship.

"Um, yeah." Sarah frowns at us in turn, looking at us like we're both completely dense. "The onscreen arguments that Clint was ready to toss you off the show for. Did you forget?"

"No," Charlie answers.

Kind of. Not entirely, since we spent the week focused on our weak categories in case he made good on his threat, but really, we would have been doing that anyway. Or maybe not. Maybe his threat was the push we needed to work together this week. Maybe I owe that corporate asshole a thank-you card for getting me so much face time.

"And then the handhold!" Sarah squeals. "I didn't catch that live, but a fan posted the video, and it's been going around, and then someone made a meme on it, and half the people adding text to the meme probably don't have a clue what it's from at this point, but you two are all over. People didn't know what to make of you, but they want more. I'll bet we have record numbers tonight, and he was actually mad at you for it. Ha!" She pushes open the door and lets us into the room.

"Okay, there's water and snacks on the counter. That door over there is the restroom. You've got . . . thirty-two minutes until you're on. Someone will give you a five-minute warning and walk you to set. Later!" She flits out the door without bothering to ask if there's anything else we need.

"I thought the camera had caught the handhold, but I wasn't sure," I say.

"Oh, I knew it did. I heard about it from my parents and Gran right away." Charlie's cheeks burn a pretty pink. Of course, her parents did. No wonder they'd given me the third degree. "I hadn't known the video was circulating, the fandom was talking about us, or that we're apparently a meme. I was so absorbed in studying this week, I didn't go on social media at all."

"I don't go on social media ever," I say. This is not exactly true. I do an occasional social media search . . . mostly checking in on her over the years as I wondered where she was and kicked myself for never reaching out.

"Oh, come on." She folds her arms over her chest and glares down her nose at me in a shocking resemblance to the way her mother had.

I take it as the challenge it is and step closer to her to meet it. "Just because I'm pretty doesn't mean I'm vain enough to fish for likes."

"That's not all they're used for." She matches my step forward, further closing the gap between us.

"Maybe not, but it's a pretty big part of it." One more step closer. Any more, and we'll be nose to nose.

It doesn't stop Charlie. She tilts her face toward mine, so her lips are only an inch away. "You seem to know a lot for someone who doesn't use them."

"What can I say?" I whisper, "I'm well informed."

Charlie laughs and steps away before it can go any further. "All right, mister—keep it in your pants. We've got a game to play."

We quiz each other as a warm-up. The whole point of our nearness this week was to study for the show, with the intent of winning and progressing to another round. While we worked though, my attention was more on being with Charlotte, and I think hers was more on being with me too, despite the issues with my car.

Now that we're here, the reality of the game is impossible to ignore, and my nerves have come into play.

*   *   *

"It's time to welcome back last week's winners. Please give a warm welcome to—" Our names are drowned out by the live audience's cheers. My palms are already slick with sweat, and my heart rate is sky high. With the exclusion of the individual round, we only have to make it through half an episode, and the time flies.

"Question four," Bobby says. The questions are fast and furious, and Charlie and I are in the zone. We've got this.

We have none of last week's communication issues. With a glance, I know if she has the answer, and she knows if I do. If we both know it, we consult each other before either of us responds. We can't miss. We've answered every single question correctly, and none of last week's tension is there. We've spent a whole week getting comfortable with each other again.

I pick her up and spin her around in celebration of another question answered correctly. Our poor competitors look miserable. As we near the end of the episode, they've only missed a couple questions, but we stole the points and are well ahead. On another week they might have stood a chance, but just like in high school debates during speech class, Charlie and I are the dream team.

The whole show goes by in a blur. When it comes down to the last questions, our answers don't matter because we have such a strong lead, but Charlie leans into my arms, and looks up at me, slowly mouthing, "Paprika," with a wide smile. It takes all I have not to bend down and kiss her then and there. When her gaze drops to my lips, I'm pretty sure she wants it too, but there's no way our first kiss since our reconciliation is happening on stage.

"That's correct," Bobby announces.

The studio audience erupts, and a storm of multicolored confetti rains down on us. We've won a second week. I have a valid excuse to spend seven more days with Charlie. At home, my dad, who swapped shifts so he could watch, can see that things really are changing.

I brush confetti away from my face. As Bobby closes out the show, our prize money flashes in red on a screen above us. As soon as this money comes through, he can be done working way too many hours at two jobs. Finally, he can have some rest, and I can have the peace of mind that he isn't going to do something to cover our debts that lands him in jail again.

Neither will I. As much as I didn't want to admit it, I was just as afraid that if things got any worse, I'd fall into the same patterns and end up following in his footsteps.

The celebration is loud and chaotic, but in the center of it is Charlie, grinning at me. I can afford to finish school, and I can allow myself to earn her trust. I know that poverty is often systemic and nothing to be ashamed of, but I feared who I'd become, driven by necessity. Without poverty nipping at my heels, I'm confident I can be the man she deserves, or at least I can try.

I pull her into a tight hug. Her arms squeeze me, and she shakes with relieved laughter. When we pull back, I wipe away her tears of joy. The lights that indicate we're live switch out, and they call the end of the show. Around us the excitement of our win fades, and the crew moves in to clean up.

Sarah hands the losing team off to another crew member to escort out, then walks over to us, beaming.

"You two were great!"

"Thanks," Charlie says. "It wasn't as stressful this time. It was fun!"

I nod my agreement but can't help wondering if the stress from last time was more from being on the show or from my sudden appearance. Maybe a mix of both.

"You two can head to the holding room. If you wait just a few minutes, I can get your details for this week. You're still planning on staying, correct?

"Yes, we are," Charlie says.

"Great! I've gotta do some things real quick, and I think Clint wants to talk to you again. Sit tight."

The door clicks shut behind Sarah, and I turn to Charlie. Not only will we have more money coming in, but I get to spend another whole week with her, free from any obligations other than staying on our toes for the show. If she had changed her mind, though, I'd have gone back to Michigan too. I'm fully prepared to follow her around like a lost puppy.

She watches me with wide eyes, and all of a sudden a giggle bubbles out of her before she slaps a hand over her mouth.

"You okay?" I ask.

"Oh yeah, I'm great," she says in a way that implies that the opposite is true.

"You look like you're freaking out. Why are you freaking out?"

"I'm not freaking out, I'm just . . . you know what? I think I'm going to see if I can find that meme."

A deliberate subject change, but I'll let her have it. I pull out my phone to look for it as well, not that I even know where to start, and my attention snags on a text from my dad:

I think we're going to have to sell your car.

Shit. I'd filled him in on what had happened, and given him the mechanic's quote, but we'd yet to decide what to do. If he'd texted that earlier today, even knowing we had a shot at more prize money, something else must have happened.

I open up the text thread and read on. He congratulated us on our win, but prior to that is the explanation.

It's raining. A chunk of the ceiling caved in where that drip was, and my bedroom is now Niagara Falls.

Double shit.

"What happened?" Charlie asks.

"Nothing," I mutter. "Did you decide?"

"I thought we were being honest with each other," she says gently. "What is it?"

I sigh. She's right, though choosing not to burden her with my problems doesn't feel like dishonesty. Then again, if I want us to have a chance, then she should be the person that I unburden myself to. For years I've kept stuff like this to myself, only ever telling Dad the things he needed to know, to try and keep him from stressing. Having someone to share it with would be nice.

"My dad texted earlier. The roof is leaking. We'll be fine—it's just another thing. You know? It's a good thing we won this week and have a chance to keep going."

She folds her mouth in that mix of a comforting smile along with a grimace, because she's trying to soothe, but it's also not something to smile about. "I know. I'm relieved about the prize money too. If we can keep this up . . . it's big. Thank you again. You were great."

"So were you," I say, and pull her toward me for a hug that feels as natural as breathing, and I can't believe that this is my reality after one week. I want to hold her forever.

The door bangs open without a knock, and Charlie and I spring apart.

Clint looms in the doorway, as creepy as ever. I don't like him and instinctually shift to put myself between him and Charlie. I can practically hear her eyes rolling behind me, but whatever: at least this dude won't be laying a finger on her.

Clint raises an eyebrow at the way he caught us and my territorial behavior.

"That's . . . a change," he says. Was he watching the show? Maybe from last week, but anyone who saw the two of us out there today would not be surprised to have walked in on us hugging. If anything, he ought to be surprised we weren't doing more, or maybe that's just my overactive imagination wishfully thinking.

"Come to threaten us again?" I narrow my eyes at him. Fuck, does this guy get my hackles up.

Charlie clears her throat conspicuously behind me.

"No, actually." His voice is cold and smooth, and it gives me the fucking willies. He cannot get out of here soon enough.

"Come with me. Leave your things here." He nods toward our phones and hesitates just long enough to ensure we're complying, before walking out of the room. We follow him down the hall and to an office with his name on the door.

"Shut the door behind you," he instructs, taking a seat at his desk. He motions for us to sit in the two chairs opposite him, both of which are significantly smaller than his. "I have a proposition for the two of you."

Charlie's hand finds mine. "What do you mean?" she asks.

"We have the preliminary viewer numbers for the evening."

"And?" I ask.

"They're high," he says.

"And?" I repeat.

"Higher numbers mean more money for me. The marketing people tell me you two are quite popular with the fans, and that already tonight the chat boards are 'exploding.'" He hesitates on the last word and says it distastefully, as though it's not something he'd ever deign to say in that context.

I'm feeling like a bit of a broken record at this point, but the creep really needs to get to his point. "And?"

Charlie gives my hand a warning squeeze. What? All I've said is *and*. I'm behaving.

"*And,* Mr. Collins, I like money, and as you may have heard, I want to be the next host. I can't be the next host if there is no show. If you two are good for our numbers, I'd like to ensure you stay on a while longer. Obviously, this doesn't leave the room. You two keep doing your . . . charming routine. We supply you with the answers, you two keep taking home prize money. Everybody wins."

"Except the other innocent people who jumped through hoops to get on the show and who we'd be cheating out of their fair shot," Charlie says. "No, I won't do it."

My mind is reeling, running through scenarios. We're smart, but we missed several questions on the first episode. There's no guarantee we'll keep winning. Dad's earlier text, and images of him asleep between shifts, heavy bags under his eyes, assault my thoughts. It could be so easy. Instead of studying all week and still leaving things mostly to chance, all we have to do is memorize a few answers and secure a future for ourselves and our families.

I glance over at Charlie, and her eyes are full of flames and indignation that the producers would even consider asking. She didn't even hesitate to think it through. I know it's wrong. I know they shouldn't be suggesting this. I know it's illegal.

I also think we'd be naive to assume this doesn't already happen all the time. The fact that it's been suggested to us on our second week here, after getting threats last time, is a clear indicator this is status quo for them. If it's going to happen anyway, why shouldn't we benefit? It'd be one thing if we were both doing well financially, but we both really need this money.

"Charlotte—" I say. She whirls on me, and any growing seed that may have been sprouting in my mind that this was a real option shrivels in an instant. The absolute hurt on her face guts me. She's lied for me once before, and I treated her like absolute shit for it. I can't do it again. She opens her mouth to protest, but I shake my head. "No, you're right. Of course, you are. We can't do it. We won't."

Charlie's shoulder's slump in relief. Clint's gaze slowly wanders over us, studying our conviction on this. "Very well. You have no evidence this conversation ever took place. If you so much as think of speaking a word to anyone about this, I promise you will regret it." His voice oozes with fury. Clint is a man accustomed to getting his way, and he's not happy to have lost that today.

We leave and I'm relieved to have him gone, but as the reel of images of my worn-down father and his text continue their torturous loop in my mind, his offer sounds more tempting the longer I have to think about it.

Charlie squeezes my hand and shoots me a look of thanks. "Let's grab our stuff and get out of here," she says. The me of ten minutes ago was blowing noisemakers and leaping in the air he was so excited. Now, I barely register my own response. I seriously considered the offer. If she hadn't been there, I might have taken it. I can see it in her eyes that agreeing with her on this has earned me back some trust.

The problem is, I'm not sure I deserve it.

CHAPTER THIRTEEN
CHARLOTTE

If I had any doubts about the financial state of the show, I don't anymore. First, Clint's bribe and threat, and now . . . this. It's no wonder they offered to put us up for the week here, this is absolutely cheaper than our round-trip tickets would be.

The place they put us doesn't even have a name. The sign just reads "Hotel." Or "Motel." It looks like they started with hotel, but after some soul searching, knew deep down they were a motel. The result is some sneaky lettering to make it difficult to tell if the opening letter is an H, or an M. It's a *hmotel*. Or maybe it's a symbol for something else entirely, like the local extreme couponing gang. Or maybe it's just all the rust obscuring the original lettering. The point is, it's a dump.

"You okay?" Eli asks as we walk toward the front desk. "You look green."

"If you're going to tell me I look like shit, you should at least throw a fun fact in there."

"People originally said anything from 'white' or 'gray' to 'yellow around the gills,' but somehow green is what stuck," he says.

"Speaking of stuck, what's making me green is the used parking-lot condom that attached itself to the bottom of my shoe like it was in the barnacle Olympics." It's going to take some major mental gymnastics to talk myself into sleeping here.

"Checking in?" a tired looking twenty-something asks, poised to type and eyes fixed on the computer.

"Yes, please. Charlotte Evans and Eli Collins," I say.

She glances up and her eyes widen.

"Oh my god, that's right! The people from the show always stay here, but I didn't make the connection that you two would be."

"You're familiar with us?" Eli asks.

"Duh, you're in that meme. Can I get a picture of you two? Maybe I can get a second meme started. Can you do a meme-y pose?"

"I'm not sure that's a good . . . meme-y pose? I don't know . . . What?" I fumble with my words and glance at Eli for help.

"Just the room keys, please." Eli says.

The way he's so sure of himself in his response has me feeling brave.

"And do you by chance have adjoining rooms?" I ask.

The clerk raises her eyebrows and folds her lips in, like the moment we're out of her sight, she is going to text everyone she knows that I just asked that. Eli's eyebrows shoot up as well, and I hastily add, "To make it easier to study together."

Spoiler alert: studying together is more like an added bonus.

When Clint made his slime-bag offer earlier, I could tell Eli was wavering, and we need to talk about it. I was immediately pulled back to thirteen years earlier and saw him begging me to ditch with him, only to blow me off. That was the event that set the end of the relationship into motion and led to a lot of heart-break over his abandonment. It's not something I'm keen to relive.

Seventeen-year-old Eli would have agreed in a heartbeat. I'm in disbelief that Clint suggested something so wrong. I'm not sure what to do about it. Even though we declined, knowing they're doing this feels icky.

Eli grabs my suitcase for me before I have a chance to protest, and we march toward our rooms. I try not to take in the surroundings, choosing to remain as blissfully unaware about the state of the building as possible.

At least Eli's on my side. The Eli of today took one look at me and refused the offer. He'd held my hand and turned down the easy route, even with a fortune hanging in the balance. He's changed. He chose me. Between that and our earlier chemistry on the plane, I'm still not saying I'm planning to jump him. I'm not sure if I'm ready for that, but I'm literally leaving the door open to see what happens.

We enter our own rooms. I set my bag down on the old and hideously patterned maroon and green comforter and waste no time unlocking the door that connects us. It's only another few seconds before he pulls his open.

"We did it again." His grin is smug.

"Heck yeah, we did." I lean toward him, going for another hug. The average person spends an hour a month hugging. I'm baffled to be thinking it, but I'd like to spend a lot more of that time hugging Eli, and it has nothing to do with a hug's ability to reduce heart rate and blood pressure. Before I can get my arms around him, I worry that without the in-the-moment excitement of the show, we haven't reached a casual hug phase, and I regretfully abandon that mission. In the middle of the doorway, there's nothing I can grab to avoid looking like that's what I was going for all along, so I flip between going for it and pulling back. My body inches forward and back, like I'm some sort of glitching robot that keeps shutting down mid-hug.

Eli's smirk softens and he saves me from further embarrassment by folding me in his arms. Instant oxytocin. Warm Eli hugs are still pure heaven, but I'm also itching to talk about what happened, and this is the first chance we've had to talk without being overheard. I pull back and hover in the doorway.

"So, Clint . . ." I trail off. I'm still so mystified by it, I'm not sure where to begin.

"Fuck that guy." He shakes his head and sits on his bed.

It's like an unspoken invitation for me to sit as well, but what kind of message am I sending him if I sit on the bed? I don't want to send mixed signals, particularly not ones that imply that I'm ready for something I'm not. Lust has me ready to jump right into bed with him, but part of me knows that if I do, I'll lose all hope of protecting my heart from him.

Then again, I don't want to communicate I'm never ready for it either, which the chair feels like it'd do. Vulnerable heart or not, horny Charlotte is being very loud and insistent. I attempt to lean on the arm of the chair in the corner of the room, probably failing to look remotely natural.

"I know. What are we going to do about it?" I ask.

His thick eyebrows furrow. "What do you mean? We told them no. Did you change your mind?"

"No! Definitely not. I meant, what do we do now that we know they're rigging the show? It's wrong."

He tries to cover it, but I don't miss his quick flinch. "I know it's wrong. I'm aware of the rules."

"We have to report it, don't we?"

"I don't think we have any obligation there. We already did the right thing turning him down. We'll win on our own merit. That's what we do about it."

I leave my awkward perch and pace the room, trying to ignore the fact that my feet are sticking to the carpet. I need him to understand this. "If we stay silent, aren't we complicit? I don't know if I can live with myself, knowing this is going on and saying nothing. I've dreamed about coming on this show my whole life, and we both need this money."

Eli runs a hand through his hair and tugs at the ends in frustration. "I can't afford to blow this opportunity."

"I know. I understand that, but—"

"Do you?" Now pacing, his foot finds the same sticky spot mine did, and he shakes it free and lurches, gagging. "You can't know what it was like. I won't cheat, but I also don't think I can report this. I'll earn the money on my own, but I need it."

It probably was narrow-minded of me to say that I understood when I haven't lived his experience. I want to support him, but I also don't know about the lives of every other contestant the show is affecting.

I take his hands and stare deep in his eyes, begging him to understand. "How many people in similar situations have been swindled out of their shot?"

"I get that, but we're not the ones who screwed them. Clint and whoever else is involved did. What about his threat? If we tell anyone, he'll make sure we regret it."

I wave him off and step back. "He's bluffing."

"He gave me a bad vibe. I'm not sure we want to cross him." Eli scratches at his jawline, and I recognize it for the nervous fidget that it is. He's genuinely concerned.

"All the more reason it's important to stop him, then."

Eli studies me, then sighs. "You're serious about this, huh?"

"Aren't you?" My confidence flickers. I need to know he's changed. This is a deal breaker for me, just when I was starting to hope for what we might be.

"What do you suggest we do? Walk into the streets banging a drum and shouting that they rig the show?" It isn't sarcastic, more resigned. Tired. He doesn't want to take this stand. This isn't the enthusiasm I was hoping for, but he isn't refusing either. He needs the money like I do, and if we speak out, we aren't likely to get it. I want the best care for Gran. She's everything to me, but I've been working hard and getting her the best care I could as it was, and I'll continue to. She wouldn't want the money if we'd come by it dishonestly. I have a lifetime of evidence of that. I have to find another way to make it work. The money isn't worth much if I can't sleep at night.

"There's got to be a committee that tracks this stuff," I say.

"We don't have any proof," Eli responds.

"Damn it," I mutter. He's right. If we make noise, it might ruffle a few feathers, but it's likely to blow over quickly without any real ramifications. "Maybe that's where we start."

"What do you mean?"

"We find proof."

"What kind of proof?" he asks.

"I haven't worked that out yet." *Stay with me on this,* I silently plead. It's not a test, but it's not *not* a test. I'm using double negatives and saying they mean something different from the positive form; Eli definitely has me in knots. All I'm saying is that years of internalized heartbreak and mistrust don't go away overnight. I'm glad he told Clint no, but maybe it's not just proof that the show has been rigged that I'm looking for. Maybe I need more proof that Eli has changed too.

If ever there were a moment for his integrity to waver, this is it. There's so much at stake. If we can make it through this, it will be like a big sign in neon lights, confirming he's changed; confirming it's safe to trust him with my heart.

I suck in a breath and hold it.

He shuts his eyes and breathes in and out. He looks at me again and gives me one firm nod. "All right. I'm in."

CHAPTER FOURTEEN
ELI

The smile that erupts on her face is pure magic, and the awkward tension breaks as she throws her arms around me for another hug. I could get used to all this hugging. I breathe in her scent, like eucalyptus and paper.

She pulls back, readjusting her glasses. "Where, exactly, do we find evidence?"

The idea of calling out that asshole Clint and his cronies is appealing until you add in the other considerations. There's no guarantee we'll win again, but after two wins, we, or at least I, am feeling invincible. The money from the first two episodes is ours to keep whether we win or not, but if we expose the show, I can't feel confident we'll ever see that payout. The potential loss of that money is something neither of our families can afford. I don't like Clint's vague threats, and I don't trust him to keep the game fair. We're valuable to him, but we also pose a threat. We've got a fine line to walk, and we lack control over Clint. He decides just where that line is. I have to work with Charlotte on this, but also keep us in the game.

"First, we need a contingency." I sit back down, the better to avoid the sticky floor, and try not to think about the state of the sheets. Her eyes flick from the bed to the chair again, and I pat the space beside me. "We're not taking the answers, regardless. If we haven't found anything by the next episode, I think we should compete anyway. I know we probably won't get to keep our winnings if this comes to light, but if there's a chance at that, I want to try."

Charlotte sits, careful to leave space between us. She purses her lips and quirks them to the side, clearly weighing my words and the ethics of this plan. "Okay, I don't see anything wrong with that."

"In terms of finding evidence . . . we have no clue how long this has been happening or who is involved. We could talk to Sarah, but that's risky."

She's shaking her head before I even finish. "Too much of a gamble to go to her. Maybe we should start with other competitors who had a long run on the show?"

She crinkles her nose. Every time she does that, I want to sweep her up and kiss her.

"I wonder how far back this goes," she says.

"I'd bet a long time, but I think we should start with when Clint took over."

"Agreed. He creeps me out big-time." She pulls out her phone, frowning at the screen. "That's weird."

"What?"

"Nothing, just a strange email." She waves it off and continues to scroll and tap. "Aha! Eight years ago. Oof, that's a big window."

"We need to narrow it down."

"He probably came in cocky and wouldn't have thought he'd need extra measures like this. We should look at when the ratings started to dip."

I nod and she taps away at her screen some more. I lean over to look at the articles with her. Her cheeks turn pink, and she shifts. The bed dips, pulling me straight into her.

"Shit, I'm sorry." I stand and quickly back away. The last impression I want to give is that I was trying to make a move on her when I know she's not ready for that.

"I was just startled. It's okay." She chews at her lip before patting the bed beside her. "You can come back."

We look at the numbers together and discover they really started to drop about four years ago. Not exactly a small time span, but better than eight. We've cut our window in half.

"There was that one older blond lady who always looked like she had just walked out of a wind tunnel, and the college guy she got paired with. They made it through a few episodes," I say.

"Oh yeah! Man, she must have gone through an entire can of hairspray every day." Charlie laughs, and the stiff position she'd been in since moving to the bed relaxes a little. "The makeup team probably tried to tame it, only to find rock-solid locks shooting straight into the air. They'd have needed a chisel and would've had to carve it like wood."

"And she kept making these wild eyes at the guy she was partnered with."

"I'm sure she was shamelessly flirting off camera. What were their names?"

Neither of us remembers, so she looks for them while I do a search for the show's winners and make a list of everyone who ran three or more episodes. I make a fast-food run to the In-N-Out next door, and when I get back, we treat my bed like a picnic blanket and spread out our small feast while we look for contact information.

It's a lot of searching, and time passes without either of us having much luck. We find a few people on social media, but most of their private messages are closed. If we openly comment on a post of theirs, the show could figure out what we're doing. We send off a few email queries as well, and I decide to circle back to wind-tunnel woman. Cornelia Debutant. I'm clicking back through her social media when I catch something I hadn't before.

"She lives around here!"

When Charlie doesn't immediately respond, I find her sound asleep on her keyboard.

It's not the "she looks so peaceful" pose you see on TV or in the movies when someone falls asleep like this.

She had been lying on her stomach, working at her laptop, and faceplanted onto the keyboard. She is sprawled facedown, and if I don't move her or the computer, there is a legitimate risk of death by drool to the electronics.

"Charlotte." I nudge her, but she doesn't respond.

"Charlotte," I repeat louder with a sharper nudge. Still nothing. If I couldn't see her breathing, I'd be concerned. Woman sleeps like the dead. "Charlie!" I shout, and she inhales a loud snort that definitely could be heard through the thin walls of the shitty motel, if not shake them. She'd be so pissed if she knew I'd heard that.

Giving up, I slide the laptop out from under her, shut it, and move it to the nightstand in her room. I pull down the covers to make room for her. Then, I carry her to her bed, laughing at the keyboard indentations marring her cheeks.

She's beautiful. Brilliant. Honest. Kind. At least, when she's not pissed at me. I haven't exactly seen her at her best lately, but she's still Charlie. My heart thunders in my chest. I love her, and I'll be as patient as necessary to earn her trust. Wherever things go with the game show, there's one thing I know for certain: I want Charlie in my life. I only hope she decides she wants me too.

After pulling the blankets over her, I shut off the light and close the bedroom door.

I shoot off an email to Cornelia Debutant before I head to bed. But I lie awake for far too long.

CHAPTER FIFTEEN
CHARLOTTE

I sit at the small wooden table in the corner of my room and flip open my laptop to check my email. It's a procrastination tactic, as I continue avoiding Eli as long as I can this morning. I've showered, or rather taken a quick rinse, in the five seconds of warm water the hmotel appears to have allotted me. Even that seemed like a stretch for the system. It spewed water in bursts like a person who kept being told hilarious jokes with their mouth full.

I don't remember how last night ended, but I don't think I walked myself to bed. I suspect Eli carried me. I assume he put the laptop here as well. I know he's capable of sweet acts like that, but he's been cast as the villain in my life for so long, it's hard reconciling it with the Eli in my head.

Plus, I'm not a delicate sleeper. I snore. I drool. I am the worst. I was not popular at childhood sleepovers. My face heats to think that he bore witness to that.

The way my stomach jumps around with nerves, I could pull a Mary Toft and throw the medical community into turmoil, convincing prominent doctors I'm ready to give birth to a fluffle of rabbits.

I haven't received any responses to the emails I sent, but there is one unread email in my inbox; the one I'd seen yesterday but didn't want to open in front of Eli.

It's from Kenneth Stuckey, a name I've heard on rare occasions throughout my life. I've never met him nor corresponded with him before. I can't imagine why he'd be reaching out now.

Dear Charlotte,

My apologies for writing you out of the blue like this. I don't know if your grandmother has mentioned me or if you have any idea who I am. I'm not sure how you will react to what I have to say, but all I ask is that you hear me out and read this email in full.

I am your grandfather. Many years ago, I went out with your grandmother. She was an enchanting woman. But I had a family. I made some poor and reckless decisions that hurt a lot of people. When Martha told me she was pregnant, I realized what I'd done to my wife and children. I couldn't straddle that line and be a father to two families, and I wasn't willing to let go of the family I already had.

While I cannot regret the time spent with my family, I'm not proud of my actions. I've regretted all my life the way I abandoned your grandmother and that I've never had the chance to meet you and your mother. I've tried reaching out to your mother, but she's been unreceptive. I hope I still have a chance to make amends with you.

I'd be happy to answer any questions you have. I just want to get to know my granddaughter. I hope to hear from you soon.

I stare blankly at the screen, trying to process what I've just read. He abandoned Gran fifty-four years ago, and now, out of nowhere, he wants to connect? Something must have triggered it.

It's going to be something I have to sit with. I'm in no way prepared to respond to him now. I pull up my phone to see what else I've missed while I slept like a corpse through the night. There's more notifications than I've ever seen. I pull up a first from my friend Paula.

Girl, you're viral! Your name isn't with it, but this meme of you is everywhere! Who's the hottie?

The rest are the same. Whatever meme Sarah mentioned must have taken on new life after yesterday's episode. Everyone seems to have seen it. Everyone . . . including Kenneth? It's possible something else led him to reach out, but the timing of my appearance on the show and him initiating contact seems awfully convenient. A money grab? If so, he's barking up the wrong tree. The money from our wins will go a long way with Gran's bills, and I'm not taking a cent from that for my deadbeat grandpa that I never met. And it's not exactly a mega millions win either.

Having procrastinated long enough, I shut my laptop and put down the phone.

I bounce on my toes behind the adjoining door. I raise my hand to knock, and then pull it back.

Ugh. I just want to go back to bed. Viral fifteen minutes of fame, a conspiracy on the show, an estranged grandfather, and an Eli who probably saw me snore and appears to have carried me to bed.

I'm frozen to the spot. I can't chicken out all day, though, and of all those things, Eli is the one I feel most equipped to deal with. I lift my hand one more time, and the door swings open before my hand reaches it.

"How much longer were you planning to debate?" he asks. For the last week I've had to push aside the knee-jerk annoyance and panic I've felt when I've seen him, to remember that we're on good terms now. That he's okay. That we're okay. Today, those feelings are mysteriously absent.

"How did you know?"

"I heard your side open, then I could see the shadow of your feet under the crack at the bottom. I tried to be patient, but you've been standing there for fifteen minutes."

"I was just reciting the Gettysburg address. Remember, I memorized it for extra credit? I wasn't stalling or anything. Just going through the ole 'Four score and seven years ago' for funsies."

"Riiight."

My cheeks burn hotter. I probably look like a tomato at this point. "What happened last night?"

"You face-planted onto your laptop. I tried to wake you up, but you were so far gone that I was convinced Maleficent cursed you. I carried you back to your bed."

It's exactly as I'd feared. I'm going to die of embarrassment.

"Right. I'm just going to . . ." I trail off, easing the door shut.

"Oh no, you don't." He wedges himself in the doorframe. "It was, well, *cute* isn't the right word. *Endearing?*"

I bury my face in my hands. "Let's please change the subject. What is our plan for the day? I checked my email, but I don't have responses yet from anyone." Just Kenneth freaking Stuckey, who will not be getting a return email, at least not for a while.

"I haven't heard back from anyone either, but I do have a solid lead."

My heart jumps in my chest. "You do? That's awesome! Who? Can we go talk to them?"

"Cool those jets. I found some contact info for Cornelia. I'm waiting on a response, but I also saw that she's local. We can give her a day to respond, and if we don't hear anything, we take our chances and show up." He leans against the doorframe, smug with his game plan, and I'm disappointed that I missed watching the boy leaning against the lockers grow into this man. I wonder exactly when that jawline sharpened, when those muscles formed, and when that scruff grew in thick. It feels like I've missed a lifetime.

"That gives us today free," he says. "You can do whatever you want. Don't feel obligated to stay with me."

Cue the instant self-conscious palm sweat. I'm over here lamenting missing the past twelve years with him while he's trying to get rid of me.

"Did you have things you wanted to do on your own?"

"Why, Charlotte, that almost sounds like you'd be disappointed if I said yes."

I stare at the floor, hiding my face and the obvious proof that he's right. "No, you can do whatever."

His finger gently lifts my chin, making me meet his eyes. "There's nothing I want to do on my own. I want to spend the day with you."

"I'd like that." I smile back at him, and we spend a moment lost in each other's eyes. When it starts to get awkward, I clear my throat. "What's the plan, since we're not pestering Cornelia today?"

"That's the other thing I wanted to talk to you about. We still want to do the best we can on the show, but as long as we're here, I don't want to sit inside and study all week."

"Okay. What did you have in mind?"

"Museums," he suggests.

My inner geek commences backflips, something that my actual body is definitely not capable of, in spite of idolizing incredible gymnasts all my life and rewatching videos of Nadia

Comaneci's perfect ten, and Keri Strugg's second vault despite her injury. Although it still cracks me up that the name for the sport comes from the Greek word *gymnazein*, meaning "exercise naked."

Eli's suggestion is perfect—exactly how I'd wanted to spend the week. I'd researched what museums were out here as soon as we found out that staying was a possibility.

Eli grins too. He always played the bad boy, but it's no coincidence he ended up on the show. He was failing some classes when we first started dating, but it was mostly because of attendance. He sat next to me, and I noticed a failed test. He tried to hide it, so I asked for his help in another subject, so he wouldn't be embarrassed, before offering mine. Half the time our make-out sessions had been kicked off by mental sparring matches. Each of us responding to each other's courtship displays, only instead of ruffling feathers and dancing, we attracted each other by spouting random facts.

"And galleries," he adds, eyes wild and gleaming with possibilities.

"Yes, this is brilliant!" I grab my purse. As I'm tossing things into it so we can go, my phone vibrates, and a Los Angeles number pops up on my screen.

"Hello?"

"Hey, Charlotte, it's Sarah."

"Oh, hi, Sarah. What's up?"

"Have you been online at all today?"

"Only briefly. Why?" I glance up at where Eli's watching me curiously and still leaning. *Swoon.* I switch the phone to "Speaker," so he can hear. I've got nothing to hide.

"Everyone is talking about you. You two are everywhere, even more than last week. We want to milk the publicity while we can. We'd like to get you two together in the open as much as possible this week. You're in LA. Everyone's on the watch for people from TV. You've got enough buzz that someone is bound to post a photo or two."

"We'd been thinking about hitting a museum," I say.

"Perfect. I can tip off the paparazzi. Don't know if they'll actually show up or not, but they might. We have a car you can use that we loan out to staff and contestants, and we have some free passes. Just be as visible as you can."

I'd just been planning on the free places, but if the show was paying, we could go where we really wanted. My inner geek is cartwheeling.

"Thanks!" I say.

"All right, I've got to call Eli."

"No need, he's right here with me."

"Hi, Sarah," he says.

Ohhh." She draws it out, like she's certain we've been up to shenanigans of the bedroom variety. My rogue cheeks flush, even though nothing untoward has happened, and Eli smirks, noticing my reaction.

We finish the call with Sarah and pick up some breakfast burritos from a street vendor outside the hmotel. We devour them on a bench while we wait for the car Sarah sent to be dropped off.

"What exhibit are you most excited about?" Eli asks.

Roaming around museums is one of my favorite pastimes. I can't wait to spend the whole day at one with Eli. As stressful as the situation with the show is, this will be a nice respite from true studying and from whistleblower research. "The nature gardens for sure. Do you remember—"

"That time we went and weeded and planted at the butterfly garden for extra credit? It was unforgettable," he says.

It was hard work. We'd spent the whole day weeding invasive plants, and planting more of the kind the butterflies needed, but the magnificent insects passed through all day, their brilliant colors shining in the light. I was mesmerized.

When we'd first gotten to the garden to fix it up, Eli kept looking around. Too cool for school and wanting to protect his image, he was afraid other people would see him volunteering to make a butterfly garden, but then he relaxed. We spent the whole day side by side, talking and laughing and sweating.

"Unforgettable, huh?" I take another bite of my burrito, savoring the sweet and spicy flavors of the onions, peppers, and seasoning. "It was great. I've read so many books on lepidoptera since then. They're such amazing little creatures."

He grins at me. "I could listen to you talk about the subjects that make you excited all day."

I blush and look away, focused on the burrito—perfectly warm and colorful, and oozing cheese out the side. That's why we've always clicked so well. We understand each other's enthusiasm for different subjects. Even if we don't always share the same interests, we both understand just how exciting new information can be. It was nice to remember what made us work and that it hadn't all been in my head.

"The butterflies and the flowers were beautiful that day, but if I'm being honest, it wasn't those that made the day memorable."

I swallow my last bite, hard, and look up at him.

"It was always you. After they took Dad, I was on an island. With you was the only time I didn't feel alone. I remember every detail of every day I spent with you."

I look away and fold my wrapper over and over again until it's a square the size of my fingertip. This is a lot. I understand why he did what he did, and I forgive him, but it's an adjustment, even as I see glimpses of what made us feel right.

"I'm not sure what to say," I finally settle on.

"You don't have to say anything. I just thought you should know."

I smile over at him, and he laughs.

"What?" I ask.

"You've got some hot sauce—" He points at a spot on the side of his own mouth.

I grab a napkin and dab at my mouth. It comes back clean, and I frown over at Eli.

"Here, may I?" He reaches for the napkin.

I hand it to him, and he scoots closer on the bench. Leaning in, he gently dabs the napkin to the side of my mouth, opposite to where I'd been wiping. As he pulls his hand away, our gazes lock. My heart rate quickens, and my face flushes at the quiet intensity and his careful touch.

"That's better," he whispers.

Just then, a sleek black car pulls up to the curb in front of us.

"Nice! Driving in style." I'm surprised the show can afford a car like that to loan to contestants, given their financial issues. My confusion deepens when the driver makes no move to exit or hand over the keys.

Suddenly, there's a bang like a gunshot. I yelp, Eli dives in front of me, and I cling onto him. An enormous rusty hearse painted lemon yellow, with thick purple vertical stripes, sputters around the corner.

It rolls up behind the black car, emitting a howling slow screech as it comes to a stop.

No.

"You Eli and Charlotte?" the driver asks, leaning out the window. No, no, no.

"That's . . . us," Eli says reluctantly.

"She alright?" the driver asks, nodding at me. I realize I still have talons dug into Eli and have him propped up like a shield. Exactly like a shield, because oh my God he jumped in front of me. He literally tried to take a bullet for me. I don't know what to do with this information, but my face flushes and I feel a little dizzy. I loosen my grip.

"We thought we heard a gunshot," Eli says.

The man laughs. "Nope, just the car. Good luck." He tosses the keys, which Eli catches. Then, the man climbs into the passenger seat of the black car and zips out of sight.

We stare in silence at the monstrosity before us. This is more along the lines I would have anticipated, and if Sarah wanted us to draw attention, well, this is the thing to do it. There's even a large sticker on the back window. It's dangerous and inconvenient, reminiscent of Ricky Bobby's Fig Newton sticker, but I do love *Brain Battle*.

I haven't explored LA before, only going between the hmotel and the studio so far, so I spend the drive staring out the window, grinning at my surroundings. The car sputters, sparks, bangs, and jolts the whole way there, but miraculously we make it in one piece and park.

Eli and I walk together up the large steps to the Natural History Museum of Los Angeles. We enter the double doors and freeze in place.

CHAPTER SIXTEEN
ELI

My hand hovers behind the small of Charlie's back. I'm careful not to touch her. It's clear from the shrinking size of the barrier she puts between us, and the fewer subconscious scowls, that she's warming up to me. Still, I want her to be the one to initiate casual physical contact, even if it's just to lightly touch my hand. As she walks up the steps, I can't fight my natural inclination to brace to catch her should she slip, so I continue to let my protective hand hover.

Her gaze is past the huge columns that line the entryway, and onto the atrium behind it, where huge fossils stand.

A woman wielding a clipboard marches up to us and breaks our revery. "You two must be Charlotte and Eli?"

Charlie reacts first. "Yes, that's us."

"Wonderful. I'm Wanda, and I'll be your guide today. Sarah called ahead and set you up with passes and a guided tour."

I glance at Charlie, who looks at me with her lips drawn in and down in a "well, would you look at that?" kind of expression.

We'd expected tickets, but not a tour. Apparently bickering and flirting on national TV gets you some nice perks.

"Great, thank you," I say.

"My pleasure. Did you have anything specific you wanted to see, or should I just follow the typical tour route?"

"We have some things we're excited about, but I think we want to see it all, or at least, as much as we can," Charlie says.

"Don't feel like you have to stay with us the whole time. We can always explore on our own too," I say.

"It's no trouble. Right this way," Wanda says.

Charlie and I trail, just out of earshot, behind her.

"You trying to get rid of her already? You just want to ditch the tour and wreak havoc on the museum, don't you?" Charlie whispers. Her tone is playful, but I sense the skepticism behind it.

"No, I was just trying to be polite. We're both going to inundate her with questions, and the poor woman is bound to be exhausted by the third exhibit. I was just trying to give her an out," I whisper back, defensive.

"You sure you weren't pulling a Ferris Bueller?" Or an Eli Collins. It doesn't take a genius to figure out that she's remembering the fateful day I asked her to ditch with me. *I'm not the same guy,* I want to shout. *Take a chance on me just one more time.*

"Scout's honor. I'm interested in the guided tour for all that we wouldn't get from reading plaques."

Wanda takes us from room to room, and to her credit, shows no signs of the fatigue we'd expected from the barrage of questions we ask. Charlotte, keen on all things that fly, not just butterflies, shares her own fun facts in the hall of birds, like that the whistling swan can have as many as twenty-five thousand feathers.

As we stroll past the pigeons, Wanda adds some Hollywood flair to her interesting facts.

"Keeping the seagulls around for the filming of Alfred Hitchcock's film *The Birds* was quite the project," she says.

"I feel like anyone from a beach town would think that keeping them around is the opposite of a problem." I remember swarms of them from a summer day when Charlie had surprised me with a drive out to South Haven for the day. We'd gotten ice cream and been chased around by a whole flock of them.

She grins and nudges me, and I hope she's remembering the same.

"How did they do it?" she asks Wanda.

"They tied the birds to Tippi Hendren's clothes with nylon threads for the scene where she's attacked. It took an entire week to film. For the rest, they were fed a combination of wheat and whiskey to keep them from flying too much."

We both grimace.

"That's kind of terrible," Charlie says.

At one point I catch a flicker of a wince from Charlie when Wanda is talking. I'm certain it means Charlie has caught her in an inaccuracy but checks herself and politely nods along. She can be sweet and go along with things for other people, but if it had been me, she'd have been ready for a full debate on the topic, and we'd have both loved every second of it.

My favorite room is the dinosaurs. They've always been interesting to learn about because of how impossible it is for the human mind to grasp time and just how long ago they roamed the Earth. It's baffling to think that not only did the Tyrannosaurus rex and the stegosaurus roam the Earth at different times from each other, but that T. rex lived closer in time to humans than they did to stegosauruses. I love natural history museums for the dinosaur skeletons they specialize in. It fascinates me to see these massive bones and imagine what the dinosaurs were like.

"Eli," Wanda says, "since you liked the dinosaur exhibit, I think you're really going to love this last one."

We enter a long dark hallway with glass walls on one side. On the other side of the glass are brightly lit, clean rooms, their light a stark contrast to the dark walls and floors of the hallway. Inside the rooms are equipment, people in lab coats, and bones. I race to the window, and Charlie is not far behind.

There's pride in Wanda's voice as she adds, "Welcome to the Dino Lab, where our paleontologists are preparing newly discovered fossils."

"This is incredible," I say. When you're a kid, the museums are all about interaction, all the little activities you can do. Then when you're an adult, it's a lot of staring at objects. I love it anyway, but this is something entirely different. This is observing science at work. History in the making. She really did save the best for last. I grin at Charlotte, wanting to share this moment and my excitement with her. She reaches out and gives my hand a quick squeeze, and I know she gets it. "For a lot of years, I wanted to be a paleontologist when I grew up."

"Who didn't? Did you have one of those little paleontology kits to scrape and brush fossils out of?" Charlie asks.

"One." I don't need to add the rest. I would have loved more if we could have afforded it. "I've never actually seen the work done before, though. What are those machines? Tell me everything," I say.

Wanda happily obliges. After I've peppered her with all the questions I can think of, and Charlie has done the same, we remain side by side, entranced by the work of the paleontologists behind the glass.

"Well, that was the last stop on our tour. The gardens aren't part of it. I could add you to the nature walk this afternoon, but, Charlotte, based on the butterfly knowledge you mentioned earlier, I'm guessing you'll be familiar with most of the flora and fauna out there. Would you like me to stick around in case you have further questions?"

I give Charlie an "I told you so smirk," glad I gave Wanda this out at the beginning, though she might have said the same without it.

"I think we'll be good from here. Thank you so much for humoring us. I know we're probably a bit much," Charlie says.

Never apologize for taking up space, I want to tell her.

All the information we've taken in from Wanda has been great, but I've been dying for some alone time with Charlie, so we could talk and be us. I told her parents I wanted to see where things go, and Charlie seemed to agree. She said she forgave me, but it still feels like I'm on thin ice. Forgiveness by no means guarantees a future between us. If I only have this week with her, I want to soak in every minute of it.

"Not at all. I do lots of tours. It makes them a little more fun when I have people clearly interested in what I'm talking about, and who want to know more than the basics," Wanda says.

We say our goodbyes, and Wanda retreats, leaving Charlie and me to our own devices. We back away from the glass to let some other visitors have a chance for a better look, and continue watching in silence. I doubt this qualifies as a date, but if it does, it's been a great one. With time free from the watchful eyes of our guide this afternoon, it's only bound to get better.

My stomach growls.

"Your stomach is wambling." Charlie grins.

I wrap an arm around her, as we both head in the direction of the grill for a late lunch. "Definition and etymology?"

"'A rumble of the stomach,' of course. Also, 'feeling nauseous or stumbling around.' From the Middle English *wamlen* or Danish *vamle*: 'to become nauseated.'"

We snag a patio table to sit and eat.

"That was awesome," Charlotte says. It's so blunt and enthusiastic, I laugh.

"Yeah, it was. We haven't even gotten to the part you were looking forward to the most," I say.

"I know! Museums are the best." She hesitates, as if afraid to finish. I nod, encouraging her to continue. "I'm glad I got to experience this one with you."

"Me too," I say.

She shifts in her chair awkwardly and stuffs an absurdly large bite of sandwich in her mouth. Did she want to take the words back as soon as they were out?

"I just mean," she says around a bite, and now I know she's backpedaling, because talking with a mouthful is not in Charlotte's code. "Not everyone appreciates the info overload, and most people I go to things like this with get bored quickly and just power from exhibit to exhibit."

The words are barely discernable around her food. I'm about to reassure her, when her eyes pop, and she slams a palm on the table. Then she stands and points frantically at her throat. Jesus, in her rush to explain away a tender comment, she made herself choke on her damned sandwich.

"She's choking," I yell, drawing the eyes of the people at the tables around us. "She's choking!" I repeat louder, hoping the person next to me will be an EMT or something because I have a vague grasp of the Heimlich maneuver, but it's one area I'm not confident in.

I leap over the chair between us. My heart races in my chest, and I search the tables for a first responder springing to action, but none appears. Charlie is turning blue. She bends, heaving her body over the table, trying to dislodge the sandwich. No one is coming; it's going to have to be me.

Focus. I sift the information in my addled brain as I reach around her. This is entirely a different type of stress, where I have to recall information, than the show's. This is life and death. This is immediate consequences, and I struggle to wrestle the old instructions from the depths of storage in my mind.

Make a fist, thumb side in. *Check.* Place it just above the navel. There, somewhere around there anyway. I thrust inward, and nothing happens. I'm terrified I'm going to crack her ribs or something, but I know I have to thrust harder if it's going to have any effect.

A circle of onlookers has formed, but still no one steps forward to offer help, though at least one person seems to have their phone out, calling for help.

I pull my hands in again several times. *Please don't die, and please don't let me break you,* I chant to myself with each pull. Her face purples, and I know I'm running out of time. Heave, heave. *Come on, Charlie.*

CHAPTER SEVENTEEN
CHARLOTTE

Stars spot my vision. I'm going to die here. Eli pulls me against him, and nothing changes.

Oh god, oh god, I can't breathe.

He pulls me hard against him again, and finally a disgusting chunk of food flies across the patio. I gasp in sweet air, my breathing labored. Eli gently lowers me to a chair, where I sag like a ragdoll and rest my head on the table, trying to let my breathing even out.

He kneels next to me, and I see his worried face out of the corner of my eye. "Charlie, are you okay?"

I manage a nod, still catching my breath. He lets himself fall back and sits on the ground, running a hand through his hair. "You scared the hell out of me."

I scared the hell out of me too. Choking was not on my visit-to-the-museum bingo card. Add pseudodysphagia to my list of phobias. And all that because I was no longer even pretending to keep Eli at arm's length and was enjoying our time together. For some reason my technique to avoid that revelation had been to shove an entire sandwich in my mouth so I'd be too busy chewing to talk.

My breathing finally levels out, and though I'm still shaken up, I no longer feel like I'm about to keel over.

"Thank you." My voice comes out raspy and raw, and he clambers to stand and grab my water. I again nod my appreciation and take a sip. A few of the onlookers have gone back to their meals, but some linger.

Eli sinks into his seat and shakes his head. "Please don't ever do that to me again."

"You saved me," I say.

"I'd do it a million times more if I had to, but it's an experience I'd rather not repeat," he says. His eyes keep darting around, he's pale, and actually shaking.

He wasn't kidding. I really scared him. Would he be reacting this way to having held anyone's life in his hands? Probably. I find that I want his terror to be because it was specifically *me* he was afraid of losing. Given the way he's burned me in the past, investing myself this much in how Eli feels about me is a dangerous path to go down, yet I can't bring myself to heed my own warning. I want him to feel this way, and I want it to be all for me.

He smiles, albeit weakly. I want to hug him. Reassure him that I'm all right.

One of our onlookers finally approaches us. Odd timing given we've both settled down and are back to conversation, but she clears her throat to interrupt, nonetheless.

"Are you the brainy beaus?"

I look to Eli, and he shrugs.

"I don't think so?" I say, unsure.

"That team from *Brain Battle* everyone's talking about, right?" she says.

"Oh yeah, I guess that's us," I say.

"You two are adorable. I was shipping you from that first argument on the show! The way you went from bickering to holding hands in one episode was so adorable. Did the show stage that? Because you never really know what you can trust with TV shows like that. Like, is reality TV *really* reality TV? I don't think so, but I've never been on one so, like—"

"It wasn't staged," Eli interrupts before he's dealing with someone else keeling over from lack of breath, only this time from talking too much.

"Oh! I knew it! And the second episode? Fire! Can I get a picture?"

"Didn't you already take several?" Eli glares at her. He's not wrong, I definitely saw her taking pictures earlier, I think even while I was choking. He leans forward in a vaguely accusatory way. Her enthusiasm fades, and she shrinks away from him, lowering her eyes guiltily to the ground.

I elbow Eli, and he lets out a quiet "Oof."

"We'd be happy to take a photo," I say.

She claps and hands off her phone to someone nearby before joining us. Next thing we know, other people are joining in, asking for photos too.

"Geez," I mutter. "It's like the line to see the Easter Bunny at the mall."

"Mall Easter Bunnies are terrifying. Nobody is this excited to see a mall Easter Bunny." Eli shudders against my arm, and I giggle.

"Why though? They have the show once a week, and it's a total revolving door of contestants. There's no way all these people know us. I'll buy running into one or two, but this? I couldn't name a single person from a meme unless it's a screenshot of a celebrity from a show or a movie."

"They don't have a clue who we are. We're in LA. They saw the first one fangirling and didn't want to miss an opportunity to get a shot with a celebrity that they can brag about. They'll try to google us later," he says. "And the meme has gone around enough that it probably makes us look familiar, even if they can't put their finger on why."

It's all so surreal. We're being treated like celebrities, and we absolutely are not. It's kind of fun, but the line is getting out of control, and I just want to see the gardens.

Another couple wanders up for their turn with us. After we pose for the photo, they ask us to sign their backpack.

"Make sure you write your full name," the man says, with emphasis on the word *full*. Yep. No clue who we are. That's about enough. I notice some museum staff hovering nearby, keeping an eye on our crowd to make sure it doesn't get unruly, and shoot them a desperate look. They take mercy on us and make their way to the front of the line and start shooing people away. It reminds me how, in the 1870s, a Belgian village tried— and unsurprisingly failed—to train a clowder of thirty-seven mail cats to deliver letters. I wish I could have borne witness to that experiment.

"All right, let's let these fine folks get back to their tour." Thankfully, the crowd, clueless as to who we are, and not all that eager for their turn with us, listens and dissipates.

Our food has long since gone cold, not that either of us has much of an appetite left.

"You know what would make me feel better?" If I don't say or do something, we both might stay frozen there forever, struggling to move on from the near-death incident we just faced, and become the latest additions to the museum's fossil collection.

"Butterflies?" he asks.

"Butterflies," I agree, so we clean up our lunches and make our way out of the main museum and around to the gardens.

As we walk, I catch him eyeing my hand. Tough guy Eli wants to hold my hand. Maybe I only notice it because I'm watching him too.

Holding his hand could be nice. What would be the harm in a little hand-holding? We already did on the show, and I squeezed his while we were in the museum earlier. Why fight it?

I walk closer to him and twist my hand so it'll be easier to grab. I leave it to him to make the move, but I let it lightly bump against his as we walk. He takes it with zero hesitation, as though he'd been starving for my touch.

As we walk, I breathe in deep, inhaling the flowers' sweet scent. Each time we pause by the pond or the dry creek bed, I resist the urge to lean my arm against his and lay a head on his shoulder. After all the chaos of the day, having the peaceful exploration of this beautiful area with him is healing. I occasionally catch one of our earlier onlookers watching us from a distance, but thankfully they don't push beyond that.

"Are we going to talk about it?" Eli asks as we enter the butterfly pavilion. We find ourselves surrounded by brilliant greenery and the stunning sight of colorful wings everywhere.

"About what? Our newfound fame? My near-death experience?" I ask.

"More so what caused the near-death experience. The fact that you used chewing as an excuse to avoid further conversation."

"You noticed that, huh?"

He blows out an exasperated laugh and rubs his neck with his free hand. "Charlie, I notice everything about you." My whole body goes fizzy and light before he continues. "But, you're avoiding again."

I bite my lip. "Do we have to?"

"We don't have to do anything you don't want to. But I think it's important. I've spent years away from you, with you knowing

I was a jerk, but not knowing why. I want to do better this time around, and that means talking. I think we've been doing all right so far."

He was right. Lies of omission were no better than outright lies. "I said I was glad I was here with you. Then I freaked out."

He smiles and takes my other hand in his, so we're facing each other on the bench, with hands joined in our laps. "Why did you freak out?"

I swallow hard and duck my head, but I can picture Gran's gentle face folded into her stern mask. It was always more comical than terrifying, but I complied with it, nonetheless. I know she'd be urging me forward, telling me to be honest with him.

"You really hurt me last time. I'm afraid of that happening again. When you didn't immediately say you were glad to be here with me too, I was afraid the way I'm enjoying this was one-sided, and I was embarrassing myself . . . like I am now." I want to attach myself to one of these branches and wrap myself into a chrysalis to hide. Right here with the butterflies would be a wonderful place to shroud myself from the world.

Eli nudges my chin, lifting my face up toward his, and looks in my eyes. His cocky smirk is there, but his eyes are sincere, and maybe even a little watery. "It isn't one-sided. I'm enjoying this. I'm sorry for the past, and I'll never stop being sorry. You don't have to worry about that happening again, I promise."

I want to believe it. I want to believe it so bad because he's everything I loved about Eli back then, and so much more. He's brilliant, and underneath the attitude that he shows everyone else, and sometimes me, he's incredibly sweet, and now he's my literal hero too. I never expected to see him again, let alone be feeling this way.

I start to lean forward to kiss him, but he lifts my hand to his lips and presses a gentle kiss to my knuckles, holding my eyes with those dark eyes of his. I can feel my blood pumping through my veins, begging me to ask for more. A kiss on the hand is a safe, slow step. This is good. Don't fall too far, too fast.

"Come on." He stands and pulls me up after him. "Tell me everything you know about butterflies."

CHAPTER EIGHTEEN

ELI

The scent of lilac fills the air from the large bushes that ring the small suburban home in front of us.

"I feel like such a stalker," Charlie says, and I don't disagree.

We parked around the corner. Even though we're planning to knock on the door, the car felt too conspicuous. A purple and yellow hearse is not exactly a "blend-in" type of vehicle. I'm still hoping this doesn't work out, and we decide we can't come forward about the show being rigged. I know it's the right thing to do, but my life doesn't feel stable enough to withstand the potential consequences.

Still, if Cornelia is willing to help, I'll do anything to help prove myself to Charlotte.

"What makes you say that?" I ask in a deadpan. "Was it the hour I spent trolling her social media for contacts, the unsolicited email, or the fact that we managed to find her address and show up at her house?"

"All of the above."

I put on my Bobby voice, "That is correct!"

She laughs. "He's still not British. It feels so brazen to just be standing on the sidewalk like this. Like we should be peering through some bushes with binoculars or something instead."

"We're here to talk to her, not spy on her."

"I didn't say we *should* do that, just that it *feels* like we should."

"We can still back out," I suggest, trying to sound casual.

"It took us an hour and a half to get here; we're not backing out."

Charlie jumps from toe to toe and flaps her arms like she's about to run the hundred-meter dash.

"You know we're planning to wait for her to answer, not playing ding-dong ditch, right?"

She glares at me. "I am aware. I'm nervous. I'm shaking out the nerves."

Palm up, I wave my hand in invitation. "Proceed."

"Thank you." She nods her head, then continues jumping about. "Okay, I'm ready."

We walk up the pavement to the brick bungalow, and up the two porch steps.

"This was a bad idea," she hisses.

I agree, but it's too late now. Wanting to avoid more jumping and flailing, I knock.

"Coming!" a muffled voice shouts.

We both go so rigid we probably look like we're straight out of *American Gothic*; we just need a pitchfork.

Cornelia swings the door open, and oh god. The hair. The screen somehow did not do it justice. It's everywhere, stuck at angles that defy the laws of physics. Her heavy makeup is full of glitter. There's an actual glare coming off her face.

"I don't want what you're selling unless it's Girl Scout cookies."

Charlie recovers first, with a forced laugh. "We're a little old for the Girl Scouts. You're Cornelia Debutant, right?"

"The one and only! Who's asking?" Before we can respond, she squints and leans toward me. "Wait a minute, I know you! You're the hottie on *Brain Battle*, right?"

I laugh and glance at Charlie.

"Oh, please don't." she says. "His ego is far too large already."

Cornelia moves to shamelessly grope my biceps, before I can dodge it. She licks her lips as she invites us inside, and behind her back, Charlie gags and mouths, "Sorry."

My feet dig into the porch. Charlie frowns, clearly worried about what we've gotten ourselves into. This is my chance to prove to her that I can do the right thing, that I can tell the truth, and that I can put her first. I follow Cornelia inside.

Her living room is full of kitschy knickknacks. A collection of Flamingo lamps perches on the bookshelf in one corner. Hot air balloon lamps, Christmas lights, and stained-glass light fixtures dot the ceiling. The seating consists of a pillowy pink loveseat and a neon-orange chair in the shape of a high-heeled shoe.

Cornelia waves me to sit on the loveseat. Charlie moves to follow, and Cornelia hurries over, the large purple sequins on her top rustling in her wake. Charlie doubles over with an "oof," as Cornelia elbows her way past. She deliberately wedges herself onto the loveseat in the small space between myself and the armrest, rather than the larger open space on my other side. Charlie frowns, then shuffles over to the shoe chair. I discreetly scoot away to put some space between Cornelia and me.

"Cookies?" Cornelia extends a small plate to me.

"Um, sure." I take a bite of one of the small chocolate chip cookies and chew slowly. It's completely stale. Never one to turn down a baked good, Charlie reaches out to accept one as well, but Cornelia pointedly ignores her and returns the plate to the table. Charlie's eyes fly to mine, and bug out as we commence a silent conversation.

"What the hell was that?"

I grimace at the cookies. *"I don't know, but I think you're better off—this thing tastes awful."*

Her eyes flick to the door.

"Leave me alone with this woman, and I'll kill you."

"To what do I owe the pleasure of this visit?" Cornelia asks.

Charlie and I exchange a glance, our silent conversation screeching to a halt. We didn't discuss what we were going to say.

"You have a . . . lovely home. Such unique decor. Where do you do your shopping?" That's my brilliant girl. An icebreaker, to get her talking first. The way Cornelia lights up at the praise, it's immediately clear that it's the perfect question.

"Oh! My friend Stella owns a boutique in town—you'd just love it, darling! So much of my stuff is from there. Like this, and this . . ." she twists in her seat, pointing to various pieces of furniture and decorations. "My favorite thing to do is watch for items that belonged to celebrities—like this cuckoo clock belonged to Carrot Top!"

"Wow, that's so fascinating," Charlie says.

Cornelia rounds on me, "I also have a pocket scarf of Wayne Newton's! It's in my bedroom, if you want to come see." She tugs on my arm.

I press my feet firmly against the ground. Cornelia's bedroom is the last place I want to be.

"You have such a wonderful, um, aesthetic going on out here, I'm sure Eli would hate to leave it." Charlie is still smiling politely as she says it, but there's a protective edge to her tone, and it's sexy as hell.

"Yes, the aesthetic. Wouldn't want to leave that," I agree.

"Very well." Cornelia frowns but relents. "I'm sure you didn't come here to talk about my trinkets."

Here we go.

"We were wondering if you could tell us about your time on *Brain Battle*," Charlie says.

"Fans, are you?"

"I guess, yeah." Charlie looks at me for help, like I've got any clue how to ask this.

"We were wondering if you have any advice for us?" I ask.

"Honey, you don't need my advice. You just keep flashing those stunning smiles of yours, and you'll bring in the fans. After I was on the show, the paparazzi were beating down my door."

I seriously doubt that. We're going to have to be more direct.

"Did anything strange happen to you while you were on the show?" Charlie asks.

"Whatever do you mean?" Her voice cracks, and her spine straightens.

"Any conversations with the producer? Clint?" I ask. The switch is instantaneous. All traces of flirtation are sucked out of the air like a partial vacuum, leaving only hostile matter behind.

"I believe this conversation is over. It's time for you to go." She stands and I swear the flamingo lights switch to Disney-villain lime green as the wild hair takes on an ominous spiky-crown look, she's so intense.

We're quickly shoved out the front door.

"You'll stay away from that man's bad side if you know what's good for you," Cornelia warns before slamming the door in our faces.

We trudge away in defeat, as if through quicksand.

"That was a bust," I say, one hand on the steering wheel. I reach out to pat her leg but pull my hand back at the last minute, afraid to overstep, and rest it on the gear shift.

Then she initiates contact, her palm grazing my knuckle. I turn my hand to hold hers, and rub my thumb over her skin, before returning my hand to the wheel.

"I'm sorry," I say. "I know this was important to you. We'll figure out another way."

Charlie nods absently. If I read her gaze correctly, she isn't concerned about our objectives at the moment. She's got other things on her mind.

CHAPTER NINETEEN
CHARLOTTE

When we get back from Cornelia's, we split off to our own rooms. Eli has a couple clients to do virtual sessions with, and I need to work on a mountain of emails. We both can sense the way things have been shifting, and neither of us quite knows what to do about it. Avoidance seems easiest for now.

I sift through email after email, constantly hitting "Refresh" on my inbox, looking for more word from former contestants. All the while, my ears strain to pick up stray sounds from Eli's room.

I stare at the closed door between us. The worries that history was bound to repeat itself are buried. I'm once again falling for Eli Collins, and I'm pretty sure he's falling for me too.

I try to get to sleep, but I toss and turn, thinking about how hard Eli is trying; how he tried to take a nonexistent bullet; how he saved me at the museum. And so many other things. As important as our mission is, just for now, it can go on the back burner. All I want is him.

My eyelids grow heavy. I think about the feel of Eli's hand in mine and how when he ran his thumb over my palm, it sent tingles up my arm and through my body. Sleep pulls me under, but Eli is still there. Those hands are still there.

His hands are everywhere, caressing my body, running over my curves, teasing the band of my panties. His lips meet mine, then dust their way down me in a trail of gentle kisses. His tongue glides over me in the same path his fingers just followed, before he sinks lower and breathes warm air through the cotton. I moan, and just as his tongue finds me, "Oh!" I wake with a gasp. Sweat coats my skin, and the sheets are tangled.

Sunlight peeks through the thin hmotel curtains that I can never quite get to stay all the way closed. A sex dream about Eli. I glance at the clock. It's seven AM, and if the past week and a half have been any indication, he'll be waking up soon. I rush to the bathroom and splash some water on my face and the back of my neck, to cool myself down. My body aches for him.

I check my phone while I brush my teeth. Still more notifications than usual, and a follow-up email from my absent grandfather. Nope, not prepared to read that one. I mark it read so the notification doesn't glare at me.

Knock, knock, knock.

"Come in." My morning voice catches on the words as I exit the bathroom. The door between our rooms, which is beginning to feel like the magic portal that brings Eli to me, swings open.

"Hey, stranger." His voice is deep and full of suggestion. Is that how he always talks, and it's my own mind, in the gutter, interpreting things differently? Maybe he heard me panting in my sleep or read my mind.

"Hi." I lean against the doorframe next to him. He props his arms on the frame on either side of me and leans in close. My knees wobble. *Kiss me, kiss me, kiss me.*

My neck tingles with the desire for his touch, and my lips part. Eli smiles and leans in. He purses his lips and . . . kisses me on the cheek. Damn it. I'm ready for more, I'm ready for him—I just need to say it.

He spins away into his room, digging through his suitcase. That was disappointing. Maybe I imaged the tension. I'd thought he'd been waiting on me to get there. He still seems interested, but more reserved than before. I'm tensed like a spring, desperate to be released.

"What do you want to do?" he asks.

"*Throw you on the bed and go for a ride,*" the devil on my shoulder purrs. The imaginary angel on the other shoulder doesn't even say anything, just lifts a "don't you dare" eyebrow. I sigh. "I don't know. Definitely not study."

"There's a pool."

Just what I need: an opportunity to see him shirtless and have to further restrain myself from jumping him. Given the state of the rest of the hmotel, I'm not sure I trust the pool to have the proper balance of total alkalinity, pH, and calcium hardness. "Do you have a swimsuit?"

"No, but there was a mall across the street we could walk to."

It's not the romp I wanted, but I haven't worked up the courage to confess my desires yet, so it's an acceptable alternative.

The stores at the half-empty, dying mall are seriously lacking, and we return a little later with the cheapest swimsuits and bottles of wine we can find. He's got a plain blue suit that is huge on him and—unfairly—does nothing to accentuate the junk in said trunks. Meanwhile, mine is made of so little fabric, I'm not sure it can even be classified as a swimsuit. Eli's eyes nearly fall out of his head when I step into his room after changing. I'm glad I opted to still be wrapping my towel around me when I walked into his room, so I could catch his reaction to my exposed skin.

We edge through the creaky gate and drop our towels on one of the sparse rusty chairs surrounding the small pool. We slip into the water and make the obligatory comments on the temperature—the typical cold, but you get used to it.

"Have you talked to your dad yet?" I ask. I'm on the phone with my family every night. I talk to them most days at home, but not quite so much as I have here. To say they're excited is the understatement of the epoch.

"Sort of."

I stare at him until he's uncomfortable enough to spill. It doesn't work. "Sharing is caring," I prompt.

"We've texted a bit about the house and about selling the car. He also texted the day of the last episode. It said 'Proud.'"

I beam and throw my arms around his shoulders. "Oh, Eli."

I pull back enough to see him, and he gives me a small smile. Yeah. He's proud of himself too—he just isn't about to admit it. He might be cocky sometimes, but I know that text meant a lot to him.

Slick with the water and with so much skin exposed, the hug was probably unwise. I'm dying to kiss him, but I'm not sure the moment is right. Maybe I'm putting too much pressure on our second first kiss. There's no way my drunken self imagined the chemistry between us on the plane, or the growing feelings since. It's there. We need to loosen up a bit, relax after the weird vibe that our visit with Cornelia yesterday brought.

Eli releases me and I drift away. We wade around for a bit, talking about the museum trip and the other things we want to do while we're here, in addition to both of us still having to get some work done at the hmotel.

"You know, I still have a few clients this week. Since we're practically sharing a room, I might have to pull you into my training sessions."

"Not happening." I splash him.

"Hey, I might need someone to help demonstrate." He splashes me back.

"Maybe that guy will," I say, pointing to the Hulk-like individual walking across the parking lot.

"Okay, I can demonstrate myself, but I don't have any of my usual equipment."

I briefly wonder about his favorite equipment, probably nothing so interesting as the electric camel in the gym on the *Titanic*. "I'm sure you'll figure out something. Be creative."

He grins, a wicked glint in his eyes. "I've already got it figured out. I'll just bench you!" He dives under the surface, and before I have a chance to register what he's doing or swim away, he erupts from the water, lifting me above his head.

I let out a scream that fizzles to laughter. "Put me down!"

"Okay." He drops me with a splash.

His arms find me again as I scramble upward, and he pulls me to him. We're again face to face, but this time the weirdness is gone. The spark is alive. I wrap my legs around his waist. Beads of water sparkle on his eyelashes. I cup his chin, running my hand along his stubble. We're nose to nose, a breath apart.

His throat moves as he swallows, and his eyes flick to my lips, then back up to look at me. *Yes,* I try to communicate telepathically.

"Charlotte," he whispers. "Can I kiss you?"

I want to scream with relief. "Yes, please," I whisper back.

Our lips meet, gentle and testing. He is a taste that in all these years I haven't forgotten. The kiss is every bit as sweet as it was in my memory, now with the benefit of confidence and experience behind it. What started as a tender kiss quickly slides into one desperate with needy pressure. It's wet and smooth in all the best ways. The warmth of his mouth on mine is a delicious contrast to the cold water. A pleasurable shiver courses through me, and I press against him, molding my body against his. The kiss is like breathing. I can't fathom how I've survived without it for all these years.

His hand runs up the back of my scalp and through my wet hair, then dips down to trace my shoulders, my chest, all the edges of my suit. It isn't enough. I want more. Need more. I've waited years to feel this again, even if I didn't know I was waiting until recently.

"It's a good thing the mall only had these huge swimsuits, or I'd have a fabric shortage issue here," he whispers, brushing my hair out of my face, tucking it behind my ear.

I nuzzle my nose against him, and his grin widens in response. "This isn't a private pool. We could end up with onlookers any minute. Heck, the curtains are so thin, there's probably people watching us already."

"Are you saying you want to get out of here?" he asks.

My hips move against his of their own volition, answering for me.

"Thank fuck for that," he says, and pulls me, floating along with him, to the edge of the pool. He nudges me ahead, probably so he can check out my ass.

He pinches my butt, and I yelp as I'm climbing out. We quickly towel off, and I knot mine over my waist so I don't wind up giving the whole hmotel a show in my barely there bikini. I cling to his hand as we cross the parking lot. A housekeeper with his cart barrels down the narrow cement walkway toward us, and we press against each other and the wall to clear the way. It's all I can do not to yank those loose trunks of his down and climb him then and there.

Holding Eli's hand, I tug him toward the stairs, my pace quickening. I want him so badly; I break into a run at the top of the stairs. Eli runs with me, laughing full out now. "Hold on—my swimsuit is falling down." He slows, fighting to hold up his swim trunks that keep threatening to fall to his knees.

"Don't bother. I'm about to pull them off anyway," I say.

"Who are you, and what have you done with Charlie?"

I smirk as I fumble to get the actual key in the door. This freaking hmotel. This must be the first time in my life I've stayed at a hotel that didn't have plastic key cards. It's like I've traveled back in time. "It's still me, but the Charlie you knew is all grown up now."

Back in high school, he hadn't been domineering, but I'd allowed him to control the relationship. I couldn't believe the hot bad boy of the school wanted me. Even though he'd been trying to protect me in the long run, my idolization of him put him in a position to completely crush me. When he turned away, I felt so helpless, like I had no say in how anything played out. I wasn't going to be a passive member of this relationship anymore. That started with the bedroom.

The door thuds shut behind us, and I jump him. Eli stumbles back, a surprised exhalation escaping him before he reacts, enthusiastic in his response. He throws the lock over the door and stops holding up the loose suit. As it falls to the ground, he pins me against the door, lifting me off the ground so our hips are at the same level. I wrap my legs around his waist and groan at the feel of him hardening against me. Our lips move together with the urgency that only years of pent-up desire can bring.

Then my skin starts to prickle, and not in an about-to-combust from pleasure way. I freeze as the prickles intensify, trying to ignore the sensation.

"What's wrong?" he asks.

He's going to think it's him. He's going to think I don't want this. But the itch. Suddenly it's everywhere. I can't resist it anymore, and I'm frantically scratching at my arms and legs.

Eli moves off me and watches in confusion. His eyes fix on a spot on my leg. I follow them and gasp in horror at the bumpy red blotches forming there. The mood is completely ruined as my skin is on fire.

"Shit, shit, shit, shit, shit." I can't stop scratching.

"What is happening?" he asks. His hands move, absently scratching at his own arm, and I don't know if it's a sympathetic impulse or if he's itchy too, and then he spins, and I can see a rash forming on his side.

"It's from the pool. It must be a chlorine rash or something. I knew we couldn't trust the water here." I scramble off the bed and toward the bathroom.

"Well, then why didn't you say something *before* we got in it?" He's frantically scratching now too.

"Stop scratching—you'll make it worse," I say.

"You're scratching too!"

"I know—I can't help it!" All the passion of the earlier moments has been swept away by the urgency of the current situation. Between the lost moment and the blotchy rashes rapidly spreading over my body, I'm suddenly self-conscious and desperately wishing I wasn't naked. I shuffle toward the bathroom, trying to keep as much of my bits and bobs hidden as possible while I walk. "Stop looking at me!"

"Where am I supposed to look?" His eyes fly to the ceiling as he writhes around, trying not to scratch. "We need to get this shit off us."

"Showers!" I shout. He spins on his heels toward his room, and I lunge for the valves to turn on the water. It groans ominously like it has every time I've turned it on, but nothing happens. Then, the shower head launches off its mount, like a rocket, and dents the wall. Like a busload of toddlers suddenly unleashed on a playground, water shoots out in every direction. I scream, and a naked and still writhing Eli comes rushing back, looking for the source of the screaming.

"Don't look at me!" I shriek.

"I'm not! What the hell happened?"

"It exploded!" I try to turn it off, and the valve falls off in my hand. "You've got to be kidding me."

Eli reaches around me for the broken valve and holds it in place to turn off the water. One crisis handled, the itching on my skin is becoming unbearable, and Eli has resorted to scratching again too.

"I'm so fucking itchy," I moan.

"I know. Come on, we're getting this shit off us now."

He side-scoots to his room, trying to hide himself. He turns on his water, which fortunately does not explode. I reluctantly follow him in, both of us still training our eyes on the ceiling. I can't believe we're seriously in an only-one-shower scenario.

"You can go first." There's pain in his voice. I know he can't wait to get in there any more than I can. Chivalry ain't dead, but we're going to squash it for now.

"You don't have to do that. Just keep your eyes and hands to yourself." The mood has fled the country, and I do not feel sexy or like I want to be seen with the red blotches cropping up all over my skin.

I reach around the curtain and test the water. Still freezing. Fuck it. "This shithole doesn't have hot water; we're going to freeze."

We both step into the freezing water, yelping. I scrub every inch of my body with soap to free myself of the chlorine. "You're not looking at me, are you?"

"No," he grunts through teeth gritted at the cold. "Are you?"

"No, I'm busy getting this Satan's synthetic off me."

We take turns under the water, avoiding touching each other like cat burglars trying to avoid a laser-beam alarm system. It's a task not easily accomplished with both our eyes on the ceiling.

I exit first and bundle myself in a fresh towel. He follows and does the same. Right, well, at least my room can lend the privacy to get dressed in.

"Right. I'm going to . . ." I trail off and point my thumb toward the door, then bolt before he can respond.

CHAPTER TWENTY
ELI

I speed-dress and leave Charlie to her own devices while I run some errands. First stop, the front desk to report her shower. I enter the small lobby, to find the desk empty. There isn't even a real sign. There's a mile-long pharmacy receipt for a single Snickers bar taped to the desk, with "Back eventually" scrawled on it. Not "In five minutes," not "Soon," but "eventually." What does that even mean? All faith lost, I decide to try again later.

I cross the street and enter the pharmacy in pursuit of my own novel-length receipt and rash relief. A half hour later, I've retrieved lotion and hydrocortisone cream and am back in my room. I find the door between our rooms tightly shut. The door feels like more than just a physical barrier. I intuit that it's an emotional one too. Whatever had been developing between us, and as close as we'd been to something more, the damn rash ruined it.

Perhaps it was for the best. A lot has happened over the last week and a half, and we both have a lot of pressure on us, with everything at home riding on us continuing to win on the show.

We were broken for so long, maybe we need more healing, but god-damn it, I want her so badly. I knock on the door, and when she doesn't open it immediately, I fear she's shutting me out entirely. She inches it open and peers around it, as if a horde of strangers have moved into the room, and it's not just me.

"Lotion?" I offer.

"Thanks." She accepts the bag, then disappears, the door clicking shut in her wake.

I sigh and sink back onto the bed, to apply lotion to my arms, legs, and chest. I always planned to seek her out when I finally got my shit together. I'd see if I could find out from social media if she'd found someone or was single; if the latter, I'd drop to my knees and beg for forgiveness. I thought about it at different milestones, like when Dad had been out for a year and things were going okay, or when I enrolled in school. It never felt like enough. I constantly wondered if it ever would be. If *I* ever would be.

Seeing her again, with her looking at me with eyes that have forgiven if not forgotten, and are no longer full of hate, I'm so thankful the universe brought us back together and gave me this shot. I stare at the door, which makes her feel miles away. I just need to figure out how not to fuck it up.

There's a quiet knock, so soft that it would've been easy to miss. I suspect she's not sure that she wanted to knock in the first place, and is secretly hoping I won't respond.

I try to channel the smolder I know she can't resist, then swing the door open. She's got a robe on backward, and her cheeks are pink with embarrassment.

"There's a patch on my back I can't reach. Do you mind?"

Let me think. Do I mind rubbing lotion on the beautiful woman that I fell in love with all those years ago and haven't stopped loving since? "Not at all."

I take the tube from her and rub the cream on the raised patch of irritated skin. It's far from the sexy type of lotioning I'd like to do with her, but her trust in asking for my assistance, despite her obvious embarrassment, feels like yet another olive branch to help me across the minefield of eggshells that is this relationship.

Her muscles tense at my touch.

"What is it?" I ask.

"Just cold."

It can't feel colder than that shower was. "You sure?"

I finish with the cream, and she turns to face me. A thick strand of hair falls forward in front of her face, and I brush it aside, tucking it behind her ear.

"Eli," she begins. My name on her lips, spoken softly and free from hostility, is a delicacy I hope to experience for years to come. "I need you to know where I stand."

"With what?" I ask.

"With us."

"Oh." My mind races, trying to predict the next words that will come out of her mouth so I can keep my disappointment from my face if they're bad.

"I want you to know, I don't hate you anymore."

"Gee, thanks," I say sarcastically. No longer hating isn't as much as I was hoping for, especially given what almost happened between us. That didn't feel like it was about to be hate fucking. I was hoping she felt a lot more positively than that, but I'll take what I can get.

"That came out wrong." She frowns, looking away from my eyes. "What I'm trying to say is, this is more than just a fun time for me, and I consider you more than just my teammate. My many studies in vocabulary haven't given me the words to say how I feel right now, but I care about you. What almost happened between us . . . maybe it shouldn't . . . yet. I was all for it, and I want it. Badly. But I don't want this to become something purely physical. I want to give it a real chance. Show or not, I want to see where this goes. I guess I thought you should know."

I stare at her, confounded, trying to formulate words. When I don't immediately respond, she leans into me, folding me in a hug, laying her head against my chest.

My heart pounds underneath her. Words flash in my mind like flickering neon lights, beating their way through the blackness in my brain. *"More . . . care . . . see where this goes."*

"Thanks," I say, trying to buy time. Once, she believed every word that came out of my mouth. She was so honest, she could never believe that anyone else wouldn't be straightforward with her, but I'd ruined that.

"You're welcome?" She frowns as she starts to pull away from me, but I gently tug her back.

"Hey, I wasn't done. I'm trying to figure out how to put my thoughts into words."

"If you have to think about it that much, your answer is too thought out. I want to know what's going on in your heart, what you're feeling."

"You sure?"

"Honesty is—"

"Always the best policy." I close my eyes, terrified of her reaction. I owe her this truth. "I'm wild about you, Charlie. I love your beautiful brain. Every time you kick my ass with how smart you are, I fall for you a little harder. You're kind, and gorgeous and perfect. I don't deserve you, but damn it, I'm going to try to. I want to be with you for a long time after the show ends. I wasn't lying when I said I thought about you. All the time. For years. I wanted to reach out so badly, but I—"

Her lips crash against mine, cutting off my speech. My hand lifts to her face, cupping it. She pulls back from the desperate kiss and meets my eyes. "You mean that?" she asks.

"Every word." I search her eyes for a question or a glimmer of mistrust, but find none. I see something more akin to acceptance and joy.

We order a pizza, and Charlie regales me with the tales of Peyton Manning's surprising business genius in buying up Papa Johns franchises in Colorado just before marijuana was legalized there, and how pizza sales went through the roof.

We spend the rest of the night talking and watching movies. At the end of the night, she gives me a chaste kiss that leaves me wanting more, but if it means I get to be with her, I'm more than willing to abide by her rules and take our time. She wishes me good night, then disappears behind that door.

I lie in bed, wishing to have her beside me, but for the first time in a long time, feeling hope. Maybe, for once, I won't fuck things up.

CHAPTER TWENTY-ONE
CHARLOTTE

The following morning, Eli takes a walk to give me privacy in his shower. I'd tried to report the issues with mine last night after dinner, only to find a sign in the lobby. "Lobby hours are seven AM to seven PM. If you need anything outside of those hours, please wait until seven AM." This place really needs to work on its customer service.

I primp in my room while he takes his turn in his. Eli steps through the adjoining door, looking sexy as ever in his dark blue jeans, which hug his ass in the best way, and a plain gray T-shirt; his five o'clock shadow lines his jaw.

"Didn't you just shave?" I ask, befuddled. I swear he'd had a razor out and ready to go before I'd interrupted to borrow his shower.

"Yeah, why?"

"Your facial hair is like Tim Allen in the Santa Claus, but with instantaneous rugged stubble instead of a Santa beard," I say.

He rubs at his chin and shrugs. "I guess so. Do you like it?"

"I very much do." I lean up to him for a tentative kiss, still feeling a bit self-conscious to be so brazen with him. Add permanent five o'clock shadow to my list of turn-ons. Although, I don't think I'd find it so alluring on anyone other than Eli.

Eli, who wants to be with me. Eli, who is mine. He ruffles my hair.

* * *

We spend the next few days off exploring the city. At the Getty Center, we hold hands and lean against each other as we admire van Gogh's *Irises*, and I tell Eli how it reminds me of the blue morpho butterfly.

I grin to myself as I hear him encouraging his clients through virtual workouts, and I miss him while I sort through emails for my own work, continuing to push that one unread email to the back of my mind. We agree to stick to our own rooms, to be productive when we need to get work done, but I slide him notes under the door, cheering him on with his clients, sending him random facts and even one dinosaur doodle.

At the TCL Chinese Theatre, we break from a kiss to notice someone taking our photo and find it on the *Brain Battle* chat boards the next morning. On the Venice Beach Boardwalk, we take selfies with the art and get ice cream, sampling each other's. Licking the cold dessert in front of him has an intimacy to it that sends my blood shooting through my veins and my heart thrumming fast in my chest.

Eli's eyes are trained on me in my cheap bikini from the mall the whole time we walk up and down the beach. I can barely keep my eyes off his muscled bare chest in the bright sun either, and giggle at his constant struggle to keep his suit from falling off. By the time we return to the hmotel, I'm burning with desire. The desperate ache from before our disastrous dip in the pool has returned, and after the previous days of getting to know each other more and spending hours with Eli, I can't wait any longer. If I do, I might just combust.

Our obnoxious car drags into the parking lot. The moment we've exited the car, we're on top of each other. We break through the door, clawing at each other in desperation.

His hands rove over my hips, sending a shiver down my spine. I crave the taste of him and press my mouth to his. I want to devour him. His tongue teases my lips.

I push him back just enough to gasp, "Bed."

He growls and lifts me against him to carry me there. He climbs atop me, bending in for another kiss.

My hand finds his cock, but he gently pulls away. "You first," he whispers against my mouth. "All you. I was the shithead that kept us from doing this for the last twelve years, and I've been regretting it for a long time. I want to make you feel so damn good, you forget what a jerk I was, so we can have another chance, and I can do things right this time."

I swallow hard at his intensity but nod and pull him back down for more kissing. A thumb grazes my nipple, and I see stars. His fingers trace the strings of my bikini bottoms, peeking out over the top of my jean shorts. The gentle touch, so close to where I want to feel him, makes me shudder. In tandem we pull the shorts down, and he tugs the suit to the side and runs a finger over me. I cry out at the brief contact exactly where I want it.

"Jesus, Charlotte, you're so wet," he says, sounding surprised. I'm sure I'll overthink that later, but for right now, of course I am, and he'd better start making use of that soon.

"More," I demand, because my brain can't possibly string together two words at a time. We are at strictly monosyllabic speech levels of turned on right now.

He wastes no time in acquiescing to my request, sitting up to pull my bottoms off. I reach back and tug at the strings of my top and toss it away. His eyes widen, and he licks his lips, feasting on the view. I wasn't so well developed last time we did this. He shakes off his visual consumption and steps off the bed to kneel on the ground. He hooks his arms around my knees and pulls me roughly to the edge of the bed, making me clench and spasm with anticipation.

I lift my head to take in the glorious sight of Eli between my legs, but then his mouth is on me, and his tongue is teasing, and my back arches so hard in response that my head grinds back into the mattress.

"Oh my god," I yell.

Encouraged, his teasing licks turn into sucking, and my thighs snap closed around his head as my core tightens. My chest heaves, my breathing quickening to meet the pace of his oral ministrations. My arousal builds. Every time I think I'm close, he brings me soaring to another level. The fizzy energy of pleasure is a mountain inside of me, reaching heights I didn't know existed. Tears of ecstasy form at the corners of my eyes.

"Eli," I cry out. He thrusts two fingers inside me, sucking hard on my clit, and I implode. Colors burst to life behind my eyelids. Sound is whisked away into a vacuum. For several long blissful seconds, I ride on waves of euphoria, on another plane of existence. My body convulses with its release, my legs shuddering against his shoulders.

When my muscles relax, I fall limp against the bed, my breathing gradually slowing, my legs continuing to tremble with the aftershocks of my orgasm.

"That. Was . . ." I give up on finishing the thought, closing my eyes and focusing on catching my breath.

"At a loss for words?" he asks. "I guess we'd better study some vocabulary before the next show."

"Shut up." I laugh. I struggle to pull myself up to sitting, my legs having finally stopped shuddering. "Come here. Your turn."

I kiss him hard, letting my hands explore the dips and curves of his body that I couldn't reach before. I bite his lip, and the sound he makes sends a rush of pleasure through me. It's so hot hearing the effect I have on him.

I shove him back against the bed and kiss my way down his chest to the pronounced V that unfairly tormented me the entire day at the Boardwalk. My tongue slides over his cock, wetting it. I grip the base with my hand and begin slow movements while I tease the tip with my tongue.

"Holy fuck," he groans.

I hum in pleasure, and he tilts his hips. I take him in my mouth, eliciting another satisfied groan from Eli. I lick and stroke him for another minute, until he's panting my name. I'm pulsing with my own desire, one orgasm not enough. He's so hard in my mouth, I want to feel him thrusting into me. I squeeze my thighs together to relieve the tingling sensation building between my legs while I suck.

"Charlie, wait—"

I hesitate and pull back to look at him.

"I want to be inside you."

"Oh, thank god," I gasp. "I need you. Now."

He twists away from me to grab a condom from the night-stand. My impatient hands rove over my own body, every nerve ending begging to be touched while he rolls the condom on.

"Sit up," I command, feeling a little self-conscious to take control in a way I never have before, but getting a rush from it all the same. Eli takes his cues from me, keeping his hands by his sides, waiting for permission. I climb over him and trail my hand slowly down my stomach, shuddering as it dances over my clit, and down to his cock. I stroke him a few times, before guiding him to my entrance. I move the tip in circles, teasing myself before I finally dip down onto him. My eyes slide closed, and I whimper at the incredible sensations as he fills me.

"Touch me."

He dips his head forward and takes my nipple into his mouth, squeezing my other breast with one hand and gripping my hip with the other. I grind against him, exquisite sensation building in my core.

"Eli," I gasp, quickening my pace. His other hand drops to my waist, and he helps me move when the waves of elation cause my pace to falter.

"Oh god, you feel so good," I pant, and pull him against my chest. I grind and buck until my head goes fuzzy, and pops of color cloud my vision as I cry out and shudder against him.

We tip to the side, allowing him to roll on top, and I want all of him. His strong arms prop him up on either side of me as he pounds into me, in rapid movements, to find his own release. Each thrust is fucking bliss.

He calls my name as he comes, then collapses on top of me. I curl my legs around him and hold tight as we both catch our breath. In a minute, I'll move so we can clean up, but I want to hold onto this for just a little longer.

No, I never want to stop feeling like I do in this moment. I want to hold on forever.

CHAPTER TWENTY-TWO

ELI

Charlie glances over at me from behind her laptop and adjusts her reading glasses on her nose. God, she's beautiful. A day later, and I still can hardly believe we're together as more than friends. The look on her face as I made her come apart in bed is permanently etched on my brain.

My inbox remains empty of anything other than junk mail. I close the lid on my ancient laptop. I should feel disappointed. I know I should. Instead, I feel relieved. I know how badly Charlie is hoping for evidence against the show, or someone else willing to share their story, but the possibility that our prize money will be lost if this comes to light is very real. With the growing expenses at home, it's a risk that is hard for me to take. I wish I wanted to take the high road here, but if it weren't for Charlie, this is one situation where the easy road is the clear choice. I hate that.

"Anything?" she asks hopefully.

I shake my head. Her frown of disappointment isn't as bad as I thought it'd be. "I really thought we'd hear from someone."

"It's a big deal. They probably need time to think about it."

"I know." Her shoulders slump. "But our next episode is tomorrow."

"So we proceed as planned, right? Refuse Clint's deal and keep competing honestly, and hope he hasn't decided to help our competitors instead. We keep looking. We move forward to buy time."

She nods. Thankfully, the stress of our conundrum has been somewhat on the back burner, in favor of relearning and enjoying each other this week. We'll have to think about it again next week as we continue our search for evidence. For now, we've just been burying ourselves in the pleasure of each other's presence.

"I'm exhausted." She tugs off her tight tank top, throws on an oversized T-shirt, and is wearing nothing else except her panties. She's got to be deliberately testing me. No way I'm making it through our planned dinner and a movie in bed. "You ordered our food, right?"

"I did." I wrap my hands around her waist and pull her to stand between my legs, where I sit on the edge of the bed. She makes a little happy squeak as she leans against me. "How exhausted?" I ask.

"Not exhausted enough to pass up an opportunity to have you inside me."

I grin. "I'm thrilled, but if you really are too tired, I plan to make sure you have that opportunity ev—as often as possible for a long time." I'd started to say "every day," but as the words fell out, it occurred to me that we couldn't drive back and forth every day. The distance is another problem we have to solve. I don't even have a car anymore, let alone the gas money to constantly travel back and forth. Nor a functioning roof. It's been incredible being with Charlie this week, but going back to reality after the show is going to be a nightmare. We need to win.

"Don't you dare try to deprive me tonight." She leans forward and presses a seductive kiss to my lips, quickly deepening it and sliding her tongue over mine.

Knock, knock.

"Dinner first." She stands and backs away, to hide her naked legs in the adjoining room while I grab our food. After retrieving our meal, I strip to my boxers and join her under the covers, to eat and watch movies.

"The best thing about us having two rooms is we don't have to worry about getting crumbs on the sheets, because we can just sleep in the other one," she says.

"This is a bonus I had not considered, but you make a wise point. French fry?" I offer.

"Please." She doesn't even bother with her hands and grabs it from me with her teeth. She's getting crumbs all over, yet she's so fucking sexy in this moment.

In the other room, her phone rings from its place on the charger. I watch her sashay to get it, the fabric of her shirt lifting just enough with each step to expose a hint of her bare bottom and tight lace thong.

"Hey, Gran," she says brightly into the phone. I text my dad periodically for a quick check-in, but Charlie has a nightly ritual of talking to her grandmother, if not her whole family. She slides into bed next to me and nods at the TV, indicating she wants me to pick a movie while she talks. I oblige. If nothing else, knowing she's talking to her grandma douses my budding arousal at her insistence on flaunting herself.

They talk for a few minutes, and she isn't shy about their conversation. She settles against me, and I wrap an arm around her. After ten minutes or so, she hangs up and nuzzles into me.

"Thanks for being patient. You could have started it." Usually, talking to her family puts her in a good mood. They have some rigid values, but they're good people, and Charlie loves them fiercely. Now, though, these words come out flatter than usual.

"Everything all right?" I ask.

"Yeah, no big changes with them. Everything is status quo—I just miss them. Gran was coughing a lot. She'll be all right, and she's getting the treatment she needs to keep her alive, I just know that once the prize money comes through, we'll be able to get her even better care and hopefully make her more comfortable. That's all I want from this, you know?"

I pull her closer and tug the comforter up, as if folding her in warmth could make her worries fade away and her grandma healthy again.

"I get it," I agree. I wish I could buy my dad a nice house and a car, and set him up to comfortably afford everything he needs for a long time. I know that he made his own choices, but I also know the risks he took in the things he did, and none of his crimes were ever violent. He never even owned a gun. What ultimately landed him in jail for a time was a sacrifice for me. He made the wrong choices for the right reasons and is trying to do better now.

She plants a gentle kiss on my chest and smiles up at me. "She's pretty awesome, my Gran."

I'd met her once or twice when coming and going from Charlie's house when we first dated, and of course there was the recent spaghetti night, but I hadn't interacted with her extensively.

"She seems like it. Tell me about her."

Charlie sits up, so I do too. She loves her family so much, and it's like her gran is too full of life for a horizontal Charlie's words to contain. She requires vertical story telling.

"Gran is full of spunk. She's sweet most of the time, but cross her at the Bingo Hall, and good luck." She laughs, and I adore the way the sides of her eyes crinkle. "But she never got over my grandfather, if you can call him that. That's why my family is so intense about the honesty thing, you know."

If I was going to understand just how badly I'd fucked up when we were younger, the whole story would help. "What happened with your grandfather?"

"Secret family. Gran was madly in love with him. She found out she was pregnant with my mom and thought they'd run away together. But when she told him, she found out that in the months they'd been seeing each other, virtually everything he'd told her was a lie. Even his name. He had a whole other family she didn't know about, and he chose them. He walked out of her life forever and shattered her heart."

"Ouch, that's rough."

"Unwed pregnancy back then, things were really rough for her for a while."

It's starting to come together why she'd have serious issues with liars, so I nod for her to continue. She shivers, and in reaction we both sink under the covers as smoothly as if choreographed.

"She's pretty level headed in general, but after that, I guess anytime anyone's honesty was called into question, she kind of lost it. If she caught you in a lie, even something like saying you liked a haircut you really thought was ugly, she'd freak out. She lived with us, so I grew up with that too. I once lied about stealing a cookie, and that was a mistake I never repeated. She's a wonderful woman, and knowing her history, I can't blame her, even if she's a bit extreme."

"And that didn't ever make you want to lash out? I think being so intense about it would have made me want to lie left and right."

I feel her mouth tug into a smile against my stomach as she runs her hands over my chest. "That's where we differ. I'm no rebel. All I ever wanted was Gran's approval. I'm not perfect, but I try really hard to always be honest, and with my family history, dishonesty is the one thing that's the hardest to overcome."

I hold my breath, afraid that any movement will remind her who she's with and what I did and why she doesn't want to be with me. "I'm sorry—"

"You don't need to keep apologizing for the same things. I'm not mad at you anymore. I'm madder at myself for the lies I told."

I wince. Somehow making her lie for me felt far worse than if I'd been the one. I need her to know that at least it wasn't for nothing. "If it weren't for you, I wouldn't have graduated. I might be getting my GED right now, instead of taking college courses. Hell, I probably would have struggled to get a job and wound up in jail alongside my dad if I'd gotten kicked out of school. I'm not advocating for lies in general, I'm just saying that one lie accomplished something great. You saved me."

She nods, but I feel a tear splash onto my skin. "I've spent a lot of time beating myself up over that. Thank you. I'm glad it did some good. And if you think I saved you, then we've both had a chance to save each other, though your saving me was a little more literal. I guess we're even now."

She shifts so her face is in line with mine. I kiss her and taste the salt of her fallen tears. Thinking about her family and dredging up her past has her upset, and that is not what I was going for, but I'm glad I understand her and her family's background better.

"I'm not keeping score," I whisper, and kiss her again.

"Me neither." Her returning smile is weak, not quite reaching her eyes.

"Something is still bothering you. What's wrong?"

She bites her lip, considering. "There's something I'm keeping from Gran."

"Do you want to talk about it?" I ask.

"My grandfather reached out to me," she whispers.

I work to control my expression. "Wow, when did that happen?"

"Just this week. Right after last week's episode. He sent an email saying he wanted a chance to get to know me."

"What did you say?" I ask.

"Nothing yet. He sent a follow-up two days later, but I never read that one."

I gently pull her hair out of her bun. "And how are you feeling about all this?" I run my fingers through her hair, massaging her scalp and twisting the strands.

"Mmm, that feels nice," she says before taking a quiet, pensive moment while I play with her hair. "I don't know . . . confused? I feel guilty about not telling my family, but also Gran's in bad enough shape right now without the shock of his sudden reappearance. The timing is a little weird too, with us being on the show. Like, why now, after all these years?"

"That is a little odd," I agree while continuing to twist and untwist her hair.

"I don't know what I'm going to do, so I'm just kind of . . . letting it sit until I feel ready to make a decision. I love my family so much. I don't want him to come in and throw a wrench in that. Maybe that makes me selfish, but I don't know. I might have felt differently if he'd done this when I was younger, but I'm thirty. He's had his chance. If I'm his afterthought, maybe I don't need to put myself through meeting him just to ease his conscience. Does that make me a terrible person?"

"Not at all. It's perfectly reasonable for you to do what you need to do to take care of yourself."

She nods and snuggles into me. "I just hate keeping it from Gran."

"I know. But you don't have to decide anything today, and whatever you decide, I'll support you any way I can."

She tips her head up to kiss me, then falls back against my chest with a yawn.

"Maybe we just call it a night? We've got the show tomorrow afternoon, and we want to be well rested." I'd have gladly stayed up the whole night with her, our bodies entwined, but there's time for that later. Sharing a bed with her and waking up next to her is good too.

"Please. I'm sorry," she says.

"Don't be." I click off the TV. In the dark, I gently wrap an arm around her waist. She scoots against me, and a chip crunches under us.

We both laugh. "Maybe we should switch to the other bed."

We get up, and I bang my knee on the doorframe, stumbling toward the other room. "Damn dark," I mutter.

"It's *Eigengrau*," she says.

We pull back the sheets and lie down on the bed. I grin and kiss her cheek, then whisper in her ear. "That's it. Talk nerdy to me."

"That's the name of the color when you open your eyes in the dark." She shifts and settles against me.

I love this woman, I think. *"Eigengrau,"* I repeat back to her before we drift off to sleep.

CHAPTER TWENTY-THREE
ELI

Good luck today.

Even though it's been over a year since my dad was in prison and without a phone, it's still nice to be able to get casual texts from him whenever. It's especially good to know he'll be watching.

"Find another funny cat video?" Charlie asks from the driver's seat, checking her mirror and wincing as the car lurches and pops over a bump on the way to the studio.

"Just a good luck text from my dad."

Her whole face lights up, and she reaches over to squeeze my hand. I didn't think I'd ever talk to anyone about what life was like while he was gone, or what it's like now that he's back. Having Charlie to open up to this week has been therapeutic in a way I could never have anticipated, and her understanding the significance of this for me . . . I take a deep breath to steady myself.

Charlie's been back in my life for only two weeks, and I already can't imagine a life without her in it.

Me: *Thanks. Everything good there?*
Dad: *Yeah.*

I frown. I didn't expect much from him, but more than a single word update would be nice. I roll my thumb over the screen, debating whether I should press for more, but ellipses appear, saving me from the decision.

Dad: *Call me after the show.*

Shit.

"That was a quick change in mood. What happened?" Charlie asks.

It appears my emotions are fully on-sleeve today. Either that or she can read me better than I expected. She always managed to see through my rebellious teen act to the nerd who loved his classes back in high school; I guess it isn't a surprise she can read me now, when I'm worried about Dad.

"I don't know. There's something my dad's not telling me. He wants to talk after the show."

"Shit," she says. "Something's up, but he's worried that telling you before the show will throw you off your game."

"Exactly." It's a lost cause now. I'm going to worry and conjure up worst-case scenarios, so either it's terrible and I'll be right, or I can find out and it won't be as bad as I'm imagining. Better get it over with.

Tuning out the never-ending cacophony of car horns, I call him.

"'lo?" His voice is gruff and low, worn with the kind of gravel that a life of hard choices and even harder consequences brings. He sounds tired and cautious.

"What's going on?" I skip pleasantries, because even in LA traffic it only takes so long to get to the studio. If I'm going to need to come to grips with whatever he tells me, I'm running low on time.

He sighs, and it's long and drawn out. I can picture him stretching his neck around wherever he is right now, buying himself time to respond. Charlie squeezes my hand before returning hers to the wheel. In the mirror, her brown eyes brim with concern.

"I didn't want to mention it until after the show. I don't want you to worry," he says.

"Too late. I'm worrying." I don't even know what to expect. I focus on the lingering sensation where Charlie's hand just squeezed mine, and the comfort the gentle heat brings. It calms me enough to rid my ears of the loud, panicked pulsing that has risen up.

"A bad storm came through last night. The roof was in bad condition before, with the hole in my room, but now it may as well not exist. There's leaks in two other spots. Some neighbors gave me tarp in the meantime, but it's going to need a fix faster than we can wait for the money from the show."

"Damn it," I whisper, doing mental calculations. I priced out the roof when it first started leaking, and again when he reached out about the hole. It isn't cheap. That alone will eat up nearly an entire episode's winnings, and we're going to have to make a deposit on it out of what little we have. We can't catch a fucking break.

Charlie's hand finds mine, squeezing reassuringly.

"Yup," Dad says, and there's an edge to his voice that tells me that isn't all. Double damn. They say bad things come in threes.

"What else?"

"Nothing. We'll worry about the roof when you get back. We'll figure something out. You just focus on the game."

"What?" I insist through gritted teeth.

Another long-suffering sigh, which I impatiently wait out. "I got a call from my parole officer, asking me to come by tomorrow."

"What di—" I begin, but he cuts me off.

"It's not time for a check-in so it struck me as odd, that's all. It's probably nothing. You focus on the show and that pretty girl of yours."

I glance over at Charlie, and she tilts her head at me, the edges of the worried line of her mouth just crinkling upward in an encouraging small smile. Pretty girl indeed, and finally, after all these years, we're together. I inhale deeply and gather myself. The news isn't good, but also probably isn't as bad as what I would have conjured up on my own, so I'm glad I called.

"Okay," I say, because I need to focus and don't have the mental energy to devote to roof problem-solving right now.

"Good luck," he says.

"Thanks," I reply, and the line clicks silent.

*   *   *

We spend the rest of the drive quizzing each other on trivia as part of our new warm-up ritual for the show, and before long, we've arrived. We walk into the building hand in hand, but it isn't long before Sarah finds us and directs us to separate rooms for hair and makeup.

"See you in a few." Charlie kisses me goodbye as if it's the most natural thing in the world. I wonder if I'll ever shake off the surprise that kissing her all the time is an option now. That she doesn't still hate me. That she's back in my life at all.

I try to stay focused on the game and run over random facts in my mind as the makeup artist smears my face, but I keep drifting back to the call with my dad. Rain seeping in through gaping holes is bad enough, but we can't go through a Michigan winter with the roof in bad shape. The first earnings check to come in is going to have to go straight toward the roof, and it's been patched so many times, it's unlikely that anything other than a new roof will do.

I think of Dad, trudging in from one job only to get ready for another, and I want to drive my fist into the table next to me. Every time I begin to climb out of the hole, the wall crumbles in my hands and avalanches down on me.

Behind me the door clicks open, and the rumble of activity outside filters in.

"Can you give us a minute?" an eely voice says, and I immediately recognize it as belonging to Clint.

The makeup artist's eyes widen in surprise, but they nod and step out of the room.

"This won't take long," Clint says.

I spin on my chair to see him looming like a vampire in a shadowy corner of the room, silently waiting for the door to click closed behind the exiting makeup artist.

I cross my arms and lean back in my chair, raising an eyebrow at him. It's a kinder greeting than the *What the fuck do you want,* I'd prefer to give him.

"Hello again, Eli." His voice drips with condescension.

"Clint." I tip my head.

"I trust Sarah told you about the show's ratings last week and the projections for this week?"

"She mentioned numbers were good," I say.

"Good is an understatement. Clever stunt at the museum this week, coming to Ms. Evans's rescue like that."

My blood boils. Charlotte could have died. She'd turned blue. That was one of the most terrifying moments of my life, and this asshole has the nerve to congratulate me like we'd planned it. "It wasn't a fucking stunt. She was choking."

"In that case I suppose I give you too much credit. It wasn't a brilliant scheme, but a stroke of good luck."

I seethe, clenching my fists. The woman I love almost dying is not a turn of good fortune. "What's your point?"

"You two are making us a lot of money. It's in the show's best interest to see that this continues. We made you an offer before." With each sentence he steps closer to me, leaving his shadowy corner and crossing the small room to look down on me in my chair. "I don't suffer delusions that Ms. Evans will see the mutual benefits involved here, but you are a different story."

"What makes you think that?" I stand to meet his eyes, because fuck letting him use height to shift the power dynamic further in his favor; he's already got the edge by running the show.

"I saw your face when we asked. If she hadn't been there, you'd have agreed. I'm giving you that opportunity now. I specifically asked for you two to be brought to separate rooms. She's not here. She never has to know."

My stomach drops. I should have known that's what he wanted. In retrospect it's obvious. I hate that he's right. I did waver. Even though Charlotte and I were already growing closer a week ago, we've spent nearly every moment together since then, for the last seven days. I've come to know her on a new level—and she, me. So much has changed. I'm not the same person I was a week ago. But the roof. The car. Dad.

"I'm asking again," he continues. "Let me give you the answers. You get your prize, and the show keeps making money. Everyone wins."

As much as I need the money, I won't do this to Charlie. I can't go behind her back and betray her like this, not when I've finally gotten a second chance. When *we've* finally gotten a second chance. "No deal." I turn my back on him and sit again in my chair, turning to face the mirror—as if I have anything to personally accomplish without the makeup artist here, but I'm done with Clint.

"Suit yourself," he says nonchalantly, but his reflection in the mirror has an oily, self-satisfied, canary-acquiring-cat smile that warns me he isn't through with me yet. "But it'd be a shame if there were to be a problem with your father's parole. He has a check-in coming up with his officer, doesn't he?"

The call Dad got. Clint could have easily made an anonymous tip-off call to the police. What else is he capable of? That motherfucker. I'm on my feet again and moving toward him, but he's already got the door open and is calling the makeup artist back inside. "Check your pocket, Mr. Collins. Good luck tonight."

CHAPTER TWENTY-FOUR
CHARLOTTE

"Ms. Evans." Clint tips his head as he steps past me out of Eli's ready room. I smile in acknowledgment, but a shiver runs down my spine. Dude still gives me the creeps.

"Knock, knock." I tap on the door to make my presence known. Eli's jaw is clenched, and his eyes are trained over my shoulder, where Clint has disappeared around a corner. "What was that about?" I ask.

"Nothing. He's just an asshole," Eli growls.

While I'd tend to agree, I don't like Eli's molten expression nor the implications of what they may have been talking about following our last discussion with Clint. I'm trying to trust Eli, so I nod and force cheer into my voice.

"Nervous?" I ask.

"Cool as a cucumber," he says, regaining some of his normal smooth charm. The makeup artist finishes with him and excuses themself, and Eli grabs the supplied jacket off the hanger in the corner. He hesitates over the pocket, his expression souring again.

Then, he shakes his head, and whatever it was passes as we dive back into grilling each other on trivia.

After some time, Sarah pops her head in. "You're up. Let's go."

My palms sweat as we follow her onto the set. The heat of the stage lights hasn't caught up to me yet; it's all nerves. One would think I'd be getting used to this by now, that it wouldn't be so intimidating, but I have a feeling we could make it through dozens of episodes, and I'd still feel anxious at this moment. I take deep measured breaths.

Eli notices, and his hand finds mine with a reassuring squeeze that I'm growing accustomed to. What did I ever do in tense moments without it?

I can do this. We can do this. *Do it for Gran.*

They count down to live, and there's Bobby, introducing us. I smile and wave, my other hand gripping Eli's as we approach our shared podium.

"You two have caused quite the stir lately. Some fans caught you on camera at the museum earlier this week," Bobby says.

With everything that passed between us, the museum feels so long ago. It's almost like we were entirely different people then. My pulse quickens and I'm not so sure I like being the center of everyone's attention. I wasn't just getting to know Eli this week. I was falling back in love with him. I always wanted to be on a TV game show, but I didn't think it would involve giving the world an audience to my love life, yet here we are.

"We both love museums, so it was at the top of our list of things to see while we're here in LA." I do my best to steer clear of mentioning the photos of Eli coming to my rescue, but my luck isn't good enough to avoid that conversation.

"It looked like you two did a little more than sightseeing," Bobby says suggestively in his over-the-top host voice.

I swallow past a lump in my throat and glance from camera to camera, unsure what to say.

"We signed some autographs for some fans," Eli says, redirecting. "It's been weird being suddenly launched to a sort of celebrity status."

I smile at him gratefully. Off set a crew member is waving frantically at Bobby, miming choking and giving himself the Heimlich maneuver. He looks so ridiculous, I let out a little laugh.

Bobby catches it and reads it incorrectly as my attitude softening toward his questioning.

"It seems like you've been reacquainting well. I believe Eli even came to your rescue this week, is that correct?"

Eli leans forward, probably ready to tell Bobby off, but I lay a hand on his arm. Forget it. People already have seen us together anyway. Might as well lean into it.

"Yes, I was choking, and Eli saved me. I was lucky he was there." I look up at Eli, and I know he's reliving those scary moments too. I can see the concern in his eyes and want to wash it all away.

I stand up on my tiptoes and kiss him. He's still for a moment of surprise, but when I don't step back, he takes my face in his hands and kisses me back like he means it. He pushes all his nervous energy into the kiss and his intense relief that I'm all right. I push my own right back into it as well, and the studio audience oohs and ahs. Bobby laughs, and having accomplished what he set out to with his questions, he turns away from us, moving toward his centered podium to start the teams portion of the game.

Behind the cameras Clint looms and nods appreciatively. I can practically see the dollar signs in his eyes. We're nothing but pawns for him. It makes me feel a little gross and cheap, but in the end I have Eli, and that's all that matters.

As usual, they give us a couple quick, easy questions first. We get our second question correct. I high-five Eli, and he grins widely back at me, but the smile doesn't spread to his eyes. Whatever he and his dad talked about must still be grating on him. I try not to worry. I need to focus.

The opposing team gets their questions right as well, with zero hesitation.

Bobby turns back to us for our third questions.

"Which dancer injures his knee in the musical *A Chorus Line*?"

I lean forward, ready to answer. I know this. The subject is right in my wheelhouse, and I'm certain I've heard the answer before. Eli knows this is my strong category, so he makes no attempt to stop me from answering. The answer is on the tip of my tongue, but as I open my mouth to speak, my mind goes blank.

The answer is right there—I know it is. I paw through mental filing cabinet after mental filing cabinet in a definite scramble for the answer as the clock ticks down, but no answer surfaces. My heart is pounding like a jackhammer. I turn to Eli and, eyes wide, shake my head. I have no idea. The answer is gone—just gone— and we can't afford to miss a question this early on.

Eli's jaw drops, realizing my panic, and he shakes his head too. No! My stomach drops. It's not his fault—this is supposed to be my category. We're supposed to be able to rely on me here, and I know that I know it, but the answer won't come in time.

The buzzer sounds, and with brows raised Bobby pivots to face the other team, and the young woman Renée leans forward without hesitation and says, "Paul!"

The second it's out of her mouth, I recognize it as the correct answer and swear under my breath, forgetting entirely that I'm miked, but with the tape delay they probably just mute it. Renée and Gregory, the elderly man she's paired with, high-five.

"I'm so sorry," I whisper to Eli. "I knew that, and I completely froze up. Damn it! I really knew it. It was right there on the tip of my tongue."

"It's all right," he says reassuringly. "It's just one question."

He's right—until he isn't. The next question is sports, and it's like we're reliving the previous question, only with our roles reversed, because this time Eli freezes up, and again the other team steals our points, putting us significantly behind. We're crashing and burning. I'm not sure we can afford to get any more wrong and still win. Missing a question isn't a death sentence, but if they then steal, it puts them double the points ahead. That happening twice in a row so early in the game is not good.

I look to Eli again, and his brows are furrowed. After that call with his dad today, he really needed this, and we're both screwing it up for ourselves.

It's our turn again, and Bobby asks, "What species is biologically immortal?"

I nearly collapse in relief that I know the answer. It's one of my favorite animal facts. It's so incredibly cool that a certain type of jellyfish is able to revert back to an earlier stage in its life cycle. While it can still be eaten by a predator or killed in some other way, if left unharmed, it's immortal. To my right Eli leans forward and also knows it. We confer and thankfully agree, so we turn to Bobby and say in unison, "Turritopsis dohrnii."

We're back on track, but the other team gets their next question right too. I'm starting to worry we might lose this. I'm still better off than I was before the show. The prize money from the first two episodes will go a long way toward helping with Gran's bills and getting her better care, but now that there's a very real chance we won't be moving on, I'm realizing how much I'd been hoping, even expecting, to win at least once more.

Eli's hands clench and unclench, and those dark brows are so sharply furrowed they look like they're trying to burrow straight into his face. He needs this money even more than I do.

Logically, I knew there was no guarantee we'd win tonight. I wasn't even consciously aware of my assuredness we wouldn't lose, and yet now I'm forced to grapple with that reality. I need to come to grips with it quick.

We answer our question correctly, and I clutch the podium tightly as Bobby poses the next question to Renée and Gregory.

"What album became the first CD pressed in the United States?"

The two of them argue for a moment in hushed tones, and when they turn to face Bobby, it doesn't look like either one of them wants to put forward the answer they're clearly not confident in.

"*Living Eyes* by the Bee Gees."

Bobby checks his card and wrinkles his face like he's been punched in the gut. He always seems genuinely supportive of all the contestants. It's one of the reasons he's so beloved, and why finding a replacement for him is so difficult for the show. The idea that someone like Clint might take his place is sickening. "I'm sorry, that is incorrect. Let's check in with Charlotte and Eli, with an opportunity to steal."

With them not gaining points here, we're already closer in score to them than we were before, but they aren't likely to miss many questions. This steal opportunity is critical, but I'm again unsure of the answer.

"I've got nothing," I whisper to Eli.

He frowns. "I have a guess, but I'm not confident in it."

"Go for it," I say, "because I don't even have that much."

"*The Visitors* by Abba?" Eli ventures his guess, and his voice cracks with his lack of confidence.

Bobby's face dramatically sours again, and my heart sinks. "I'm sorry, the correct answer is *Born in the U.S.A.* by Bruce Springsteen."

Behind the cameras, the crew signals, and Bobby cuts us to commercial.

"Four minutes, people!"

"I'm grabbing water." Eli heads to the small water station behind the set.

I'm about to follow, but the makeup artist who helped me earlier rushes over. "You've got to stop wiping your face," she scolds.

I don't mean to, but between the stage lights, and the stress, I'm sweating buckets, and my natural reaction is to wipe it away.

"Smile so I can redo your cheeks."

I try to oblige, but it feels like my skin is covered in plaster. The edges of my mouth don't want to curve. We're going to lose.

CHAPTER TWENTY-FIVE
ELI

Before they called commercial, I caught Clint talking to one of the makeup artists and nodding in our direction. The moment commercial is called, the makeup artist Clint spoke to makes a beeline for Charlotte. He set me up with the perfect distraction. I tell Charlotte I'm getting a drink and duck backstage near the watercooler.

I can't believe we're losing. It was easy to talk a big game to Clint before. After the week Charlie and I had, we felt unstoppable. I imagine being at home. We'll freeze our asses off all winter because the heater won't be able to keep up, and if we let it try, our bill will be so high, the heat will end up getting shut off anyway.

We need a roof and a car. Dad needs a break. We need this money. Clint's parting words echo in my ears. *"It'd be a shame if something were to happen with his parole."* Cornelia warned that he was not someone to cross. I'd thought it was possible that Charlie was right, and his threats were a bluff, but Dad's parole officer had already called him, and Clint knew about it. I suspect Clint has resources at his disposal that I can't imagine. I don't doubt for one second that he could somehow make good on that threat, just to keep me here.

I glance up as the crew calls people back to their places. Across the room, Clint stands tall, his dark eyes locked on me. He points to his pocket.

I can't do this to Charlie. But I can't do this to Dad either. I'm trapped.

"Places!" Sarah shouts.

I'm a teenager again, coming home to an empty house, only finding out when he called me later that he'd been taken away. Sinking to the floor, I stared around realizing for the first time how truly alone I was. Seeing Dad return home, a husk of the man he'd once been, with haunted eyes, taking months to reach a semblance of normality. Freezing in place, looking lost in our home after so long behind bars.

I'm being shredded apart by a decision I don't want to make, but there's no time. I'm going to have to play by Clint's rules. I'm going to have to cheat.

Charlie's a ball of stress next to me. I just got her back. If she ever finds out I cheated—especially after she was so horrified by the idea of it when it was offered to us, and after she told me about her grandfather and why honesty is so important to her family—it'll be the end of us.

She is all I ever wanted. With her, I'm never starved for good conversation. She keeps me on my toes. She's a one-woman adventure, stunning and intelligent. The only way to keep her is to lie. About lying. The one thing she hates most.

I'm doomed. If we lose, it's all over for my dad. If we win, at least there is the small chance that she may never find out.

I gamble on low odds over no odds. My gut wrenches because it feels so wrong. The decision clicks into place, solidifying in my brain. In response, I'm immediately affronted with Charlotte's face, age seventeen, mouth slightly parted and eyes sallow with horror and disappointment. Even as I know with a dreadful certainty that I'm destined to see that face again if I continue down this path, it's the choice I have to make.

I take a quick glance around, but most people are on the other side of the set or are busy. No one is watching.

Resigned, I pull the card from my pocket. I can't risk getting caught, so I only have seconds. I quick scan the list, then read through it once more, trying to commit the answers on the second half of the list to memory.

I grab a quick glass of water and down it in an attempt to wash away the acrid taste of my own betrayal, then hurry back onto the set.

"You okay?" Her eyes flicker with light as she searches my face for real answers.

I nod and my stomach lurches. I can't even look her in the eye without getting sick anymore. She trusted me again with her heart. She believed I wouldn't lie or betray her again, and I've done it in the first week. I'm disgusted with myself, but I'm doing what's necessary to protect my dad.

"It's all right. If we lose, we'll figure something out. I'll help you. We'll figure it out together."

Together. The word ricochets off the walls of my mind like a lost hiker's desperate plea for help in an empty cavern. Could we really stay together? Is there a world in which I could forgive myself for this lie enough to face her again? Could I ever move past it and give us a real chance? I don't know, but we'd damned well better win this game so this isn't for nothing.

Bobby asks the next question, and I'm relieved to realize that I would have known the answer, even without the card. Is it cheating to have seen the answers if I already knew them? It seems like a gray area, and gray isn't all that far from silver. This could be my silver lining.

Our opponents get their next question wrong, and hope springs to life, a little firefly in my soul. We've got a chance to gain more ground. I'm again spared from my guilt when Charlie is ready with the answer.

The game continues, and we further lessen the gap, with one or both of us knowing the answers. I'm still brimming with guilt, but with each question that one of us would have known without help, that fades little by little. Until the final question.

"What company used the slogan 'Refreshes the parts other beers cannot reach'?" Bobby asks the other team. They watch us nervously, probably trying to decide if we have the answer and how critical this question is. They don't know it, or at least they're not sure if they do. If we both answer wrong, there will be a tie, and the game goes to sudden death. If they get it wrong and we get it right, we'll overtake them in points. We'll win the game, win the prize money, and advance to the next episode.

I would have one more week to spend exploring a new city with Charlotte. A whole week to somehow work out how to tell her what I've done and convince her that it was an extreme situation and won't happen again. One question, and I knew the answer before it was asked.

One question, and my tongue suddenly feels like a cinder block in my mouth. Heavy and rough edged. When the question was posed, although the answer sprang to mind, I know it is only because of my watercooler studies. I would not have known it on my own. Charlotte looks at me with inquisitive hope. She doesn't know it either.

The answer clock winds down, and Gregory finally answers. He's wrong. The queasy feeling is back with a vengeance. Any small measure of relief I'd felt over the last few questions is wiped away in a moment. If we win this, it won't have been through honest means.

But I have to.

I'm sorry. I silently will her to understand.

I trip over the word and have to clear the lump out of my throat before I try again. "Heineken." I croak out. The word tastes foul and chalky as it falls from my lips. It boomerangs out and swings back to hit me where it hurts. *What have I done?*

"That is correct!" Bobby says. "Charlotte and Eli have won again for the third week in a row! We'll see you all next week, when our unlikely lovers return to take on a new set of challengers on *Brain Battle!*"

A cannon sounds, bursting loud in my ear, and confetti falls around me for the third time in as many weeks. Charlotte leaps into my arms, and my body moves reflexively, catching her and spinning her around. Her lips move, but I can't catch the words. They come out low and distorted. The whole room looks fuzzy, like everything is underwater.

*   *   *

A half hour later, we've received our congratulations and instructions for the coming week and are back in our attention-grabbing vehicle, on our way to the hotel. Less than an hour, and this secret is eating me alive. It feels like an entire horde of angry insects is living inside me and scraping away at my flesh. Devouring me. This is not a secret I can survive.

When I tell her about the threat, she'll understand. She'll see that I had to, for my dad. I know cheating was wrong. I know it was a dishonest thing, but I won't move forward in this relationship lying to her. My hands flex on the steering wheel as I try to drum up courage.

I'm silent because if I open my mouth, this secret that cannot be contained will come pouring out of me like a tidal wave. Charlotte doesn't seem to notice yet. She's riding the thrill from our win.

"Three in a row—can you believe it?" she squeaks.

I nod, and the small movement makes me dizzy, the world tilting on its axis and spinning me around. Maybe I shouldn't be driving. Not that we're going far. We're at a dead stop in bumper-to-bumper traffic.

"I'm going to call my family now, so we can celebrate when we get to the hotel." She winks at me exaggeratedly, then grins down at her phone as she dials. I'm going to break her goddamn heart. Again.

CHAPTER TWENTY-SIX
CHARLOTTE

We finally pull up to the hmotel and check in. I don't even bother with my room, following him straight into his. I toss my suitcase aside and flop onto the bed with a giggle, my arms thrown wide.

"Three weeks! Three weeks!" I shout into the comforter. It comes out as something muffled and probably indiscernible. I roll over onto my bed and grin up at Eli, ready for him to celebrate with me. I'm ready to tempt him into some seriously mind-blowing celebrations, when I realize he isn't smiling. In fact, he looks downright miserable.

I feel my own smile fall and my stomach twist.

"Eli?" I whisper, suddenly afraid.

"Sorry," he shakes his head. "We did it. Three weeks. Great job." He smiles but it's weak, and fake.

"What's going on? Why aren't you more excited?"

"It's nothing. I am excited. I'm just tired, that's all."

He's definitely not alright. My mind is reeling. I'm playing out the night over and over in fast succession, looking for what set this off. Trying to figure out where everything went wrong, because this is not the face of someone for whom everything is going right.

His phone buzzes, and he pulls it out. His lips part, and he looks relieved. "Someone responded. Marcus. He was on for five episodes last year—remember him?"

I nod, still trying to puzzle out the changes in Eli's mood.

"He says he'll meet!" Eli shouts, then his face falls. "Oh. But he's going on vacation this week. He can't meet until next week."

The nudge about our investigation loops my brain back to Clint's offer. Then, I remember how angry Eli looked when Clint was walking out of his dressing room earlier, and suddenly I'm filled with dread.

"Eli, what did Clint say to you before the show?"

I watch as he considers his options. The fact that he has to think about it and doesn't answer immediately rips apart the fragile sprouts of trust I'd been nurturing. He folds in, as if he's taken a blow to the stomach, and I know he's made his decision.

He walks forward and sinks to his knees in front of the bed. I hurriedly scoot to the edge to face him.

"I'm sorry," he says. "I'm sorry, I'm sorry, I'm sorry."

I'm afraid I already know what he has to tell me. I can't think of anything else it would be, but we both agreed not to take the answers. We were looking for evidence to expose them. He knows what this means to me. He has to know. He wouldn't do this. He couldn't.

He looks up at me, and I watch his face crumple. Lines I hadn't known existed mar his forehead, and his mouth turns down with a line taut with agony.

"Clint threatened to fuck with my dad's parole if we lost. I took the answers." He turns his head aside as he says it, unable to meet my eyes.

I must have misheard him.

He bows his head, the picture of pure defeat.

I didn't mishear him.

Emotion swells in me, a tangled mess of rage and disappointment. Heartache. I know what this means. He's just pulled us right back to where we were in high school, and while I appreciate him telling me about it, he waited to tell me until now, and I just don't think it's something I can accept. I feel so betrayed.

"When?" I ask, because I have to know. Was any of the last week real? I thought I loved him and that he loved me too. When he'd apologized for our past, I'd thought he meant it. That I could forgive and forget, and we could move on. While I was falling straight into his arms, was he lying all along? Am I that big of a fool?

"Today. While you were getting your makeup done before the show. I told him no. I swear I did. I was telling him to fuck off with his offer, but then he threatened my dad. You don't know what it was like, Charlie. I can't see him go through that again. I can't."

It stings a little less to know he wasn't planning this all along, but it isn't the relief I was hoping for. I feel like I'm going to vomit. I can't believe he cheated so we could win the game.

He's trying to protect his dad. There is a part of me that acknowledges this, but all it feels like is an excuse, one I'm not really in a place to process right now.

We could have figured it out. He just said that a former contestant was willing to talk to us. With their information, we might have been able to come forward. There must have been another way. I could have tried to help, but he didn't give me that chance. He's forced me into a position, once again, where I have to throw him to the wolves or become a liar myself, and I hate him for it. I've seen this show before, and I know how the story ends. Eli getting what he needs. Me, alone and abandoned by him. I can't go through it all again.

I can't even just walk away now. Even if the money we've won so far was enough, I'm invested in everything going on, and I signed a contract. I have to be here next week. I feel backed into a corner; trapped, with all my options stolen away. Maybe he'll see this is wrong. He clearly feels guilty. Maybe we can spend the week trying to figure out a solution. It's frail, but it's the last hope I have to hang onto.

"And next week?" I ask, feeling tears well up in my eyes. "You know he'll ask you to cheat again."

"I'll have to take the answers," he mutters, looking down at the ground. My single ray of hope extinguishes, the flame gone out entirely.

"No." My chest constricts, and suddenly the room is too small. I spin around, my panicked brain struggling to remember where the exit is, even though it's in the same place it is in every hotel. "I can't. I won't. No. I'm not going to lie for you again. I've done it before, and I felt low and dirty, and I've seen what your gratitude looks like. You'll take your money, and I'll never hear from you again. Well, you don't get to be the one to leave this time. It's *my* turn," I spit.

I finally get a grip on my location and fling my suitcase into my own room. I can't breathe in here. I need space. I spring the door to the hallway open wide, practically kicking it off the hinges in my desperation to drink in some air from a room that doesn't have Eli in it.

I'm so mad but being near him only makes me want to draw closer. His gravitational pull and my own foolish, unrequited love for him will suck me in until I unravel and implode.

I run down the hall and set my sights on the door to the stairwell.

Behind me, Eli shouts my name.

I don't look back.

* .* *

As soon as I calm down, I retreat to my room, checking the hallway to make sure it's clear before I do. Once inside, I dash straight to the adjoining door and lock it tight, my heart sinking a little further in my chest as I do.

It's for my own good, but damn it, the pain. It's cruel that an emotional loss can have such a physical impact.

I shoot Sarah a text that I need to get out of here.

Are you sure? she replies. I'm not, but I need to try to be, so I reply in the affirmative, and she gets me a ticket on a flight home early tomorrow morning.

I get almost no sleep, tossing and turning. He's only feet away; only one door separates us. If my heart could bear it, I could open that door and crawl into his bed and into his arms in a matter of seconds. Every fiber of my being wants to, but the more I give in, the harder it will be. If I let him force me into lying, I'll hate myself. I'll end up telling Gran, and it will ruin my relationship with her, and whatever time we have left together. If I cave, it will ruin me when he looks past me like I don't even exist and like everything we ever shared meant nothing.

When I get to the lobby in the morning, eyes bloodshot and sore from lack of sleep, Eli is waiting.

"I knew you wouldn't hear me out if I knocked," he says.

"Go away."

"Please, I'm so sorry. I'm so, so sorry. I need the money bad, but I would have said no anyway. I really was going to. If it weren't for the parole, I'd have said no. I swear it. Charlie, please believe me."

"No," my voice cracks on the single word, and tears don't even bother welling this time. They spill out in thick, heavy drops. "You don't get to make it out like I'm the one being the jerk. You're trying to protect your family, and I get that. But if I do this with you, or even if I just go along with you doing it, the guilt will eat me alive. You don't get to reel me back in so I can do you a favor, and then leave me again. It took me way too long to get over you the first time. I'm not sure I ever did. I'm not letting you ruin me again."

I storm past the baffled clerk and straight to the waiting car, flinging my luggage into the seat next to mine and slamming the door behind me.

"Did he follow?" I ask the driver in a small voice that I don't like for myself.

"No, but he looks a lot like someone kicked his puppy. Faces don't get much sadder than that," he says.

"Please drive." My lip quivers as I try to hold back more tears. The driver hands back a box of tissues, and I shatter.

CHAPTER TWENTY-SEVEN
ELI

Once she left, there wasn't much point in staying. Touring the city without her would have felt wrong, so I called up Sarah and got myself on a flight to spend the week at home before the next taping.

If it still happens.

We signed a contract that obligates us to be there, but surely there have been times in the past where people have had emergencies come up that have prevented them from reappearing on the show. Charlie is a brilliant woman. If there is a way out of it, I have no doubt she'll find it, and I also know she isn't going to cave and lie.

I manage to get back some of the clients that I'd canceled on for the week, who hadn't wanted to do virtual sessions. I work out alongside nearly everyone. When I can't face myself, it feels good to funnel all my energy into physical activity, and lots of it.

"Sorry about the girl," Dave says as I'm checking out with him at the front desk before leaving work.

My head shoots up. "How do you know about that?"

"Seriously? You two and the meme were so huge last week, and then some girl posts a video of you two shouting at each other in the lobby. It's everywhere, man."

The damn clerk. If she followed what we were arguing about, or if people can hear it in the video, I may have fucked this up even worse than I thought. What exactly did both of us say? Did we out the show?

"Show me," I demand.

"Really?" he asks.

"Yes, really. Now. Please."

"Damn. Masochist." He pulls his phone out of his pocket and taps around on it for a minute before handing it over. I turn the volume all the way up.

Dave isn't wrong. It hurts to watch this, but I need to know just how much trouble I'm in. I hold my breath as I watch and listen. You can make out a muffled shout here and there, but we're just far enough away that you can't hear or understand the conversation.

I sag in relief. "Is this the only video?"

"Yeah, the only one I've seen."

After finishing up with Dave, I drive home, ready to collapse in relief over my narrow escape.

*   *   *

I scoop a spoonful of the sauce I made for dinner and taste it. Bland, but I can't even tell if that's really the case or it's just my mood. Everything seems devoid of color and flavor without her.

Outside the window, I hear raised voices but can't make out what they say. I run to the door and fling it open, almost running into Dad storming into the house, another man with his back turned walking away.

"What was that?" I ask.

"Don't worry about it," he grumbles, kicking off his shoes.

"You were just in a shouting match. How am I supposed to not worry about it?"

"It's Lucky."

My eyes widen at the mention of Dad's former friend that he'd run into and brushed off weeks ago.

"He's been hanging around this week, trying to talk to me. I keep telling him to piss off, but he's not listening."

"What's he want?" I ask.

"Don't know, don't care."

It's strange for Lucky to be insistent on hanging around all of a sudden, and it's worrying given the terms of Dad's parole. "Dad," I begin cautiously, knowing he's not in the mood to talk about this, but worried all the same, "how did your meeting with the parole officer go?"

He grunts. "Not much to say. Same shit as always, making sure I'm following the rules. Asked too many times if I was in contact with other known criminals, which is why Lucky needs to stay the hell away from me."

He disappears to his room, to get cleaned up for dinner and his second job, slamming the door behind him. It's clear he considers the discussion over, but I can't stop thinking about Clint's threat.

When he comes out of his room, he's calmed down and back to himself.

"Smells good," he says on a yawn. I try to push my worry over Lucky aside. Dad is already frustrated and exhausted. I don't need to worry him further with my own paranoia.

I shove a forkful of pasta in my mouth, and the tomato sauce and heavy hand of garlic melt there. "Tastes good too," I say.

We eat in silence, Dad stewing in his issues, me stewing in mine. Between worrying about Charlie and Dad, I'm in a mood, and not primed for conversation. We make quite the pair. I stomp over to the sink to clean up my plate.

"Are you going to tell me what happened with you?" my dad finally asks. He shuts off the sink so I can't wash any more dishes and am forced to give him my attention. "I'm barely home at the same time as you, and I can still tell you've been moping."

Knowing my pain is written all over my face for anyone around me to see only makes my mood worse. I'm so angry, and it's all directed straight inward. Well, inward and at Clint. I have a right to be mad at him, but the blame with Charlie still falls on me.

"I'm fine," I mutter.

"Bullshit you're fine." He holds my gaze for a moment and then shakes his head. "It's something with Charlotte, right? You've got to talk to her about it."

"I can't."

He shakes his head, and I bite back a defense of her. He doesn't know what things were like between Charlie and me in high school because he wasn't there. I never told him. He carries enough guilt without knowing every detail. I haven't told him much about Charlie this time either. All he knows is what he saw alongside the rest of the world on live TV, and what he can gather from my moping. I doubt he's seen the video Dave showed me.

"If you want to talk about it sometime, I'm here," he says. "But right now, I've got to get to work. See you tomorrow."

I nod and take his plate. Dad walks out the door, and I move to resume cleaning, when suddenly the last sound I want to hear rings out: the blip of a police siren. I sprint to the door and run outside, not bothering with shoes.

An officer jumps out of the car and walks over to Dad. My heart rate spikes to peak cardio levels, and I feel sick to my stomach. This has to be a nightmare. It can't be happening again. "Are you Keith Collins?" he asks.

Dad shakes his head, eyes on the ground, and lets out a long sigh. "Yes, I am."

"Mr. Collins, we have a warrant for your arrest," the officer said.

"That's bullshit!" I shout, jogging over. "He didn't even do anything!"

"Sir, I need you to stay back," the officer yells.

"Listen to him, Eli."

"But Dad you didn't—"

"I know I didn't do anything wrong, but they've got a warrant, son. You're not going to accomplish anything here. The lawyers will have to sort it out."

"What's the warrant for?" I demand. My body is in panic mode. If I don't calm down, I'm going to wind up in shock. My mind is frantic with repetitions of *This is Clint's doing. This is my fault. He's going to jail again, and it's all my fault.*

"Associating with a known felon, in violation of his parole." Dad cooperates while they put him in cuffs, so the officers give us a minute before bringing him to their car.

"Eli, I want nothing to do with Lucky or any of them, I swear to you. I've stayed away from all that. I'm never going back to it."

He's trying to reassure me of his innocence, but I'm pretty sure I'm the one to blame. If Clint is as powerful as Cornelia implied, it wouldn't have been hard to find Dad's known associates and track them down. He already implied he knew about the parole meeting. He could have bribed Lucky into sticking to Dad and tipped off the officer. It would explain why Lucky's been clinging to him for seemingly no reason.

"I know, Dad. But I have a suspicion as to what happened."

He sighs, sounding resigned. "I thought I was done with these places."

"Hang in there. I'll figure it out. Just give me a little time."

"Don't go trying to do something heroic like take the blame and get yourself in here," he says.

If I could, I probably would, but I don't think I'd get far with that, given he was seen with Lucky. I don't have a plan yet, and I can't make any promises. I'm the one who got him into this situation. I'm the one who cheated at the game and allowed myself to be manipulated by Clint.

I'm the one who deserves to end up behind bars, just like I always knew I would.

CHAPTER TWENTY-EIGHT
CHARLOTTE

"Are you sure you don't want to come over for dinner, honey?" Ma asks over the phone, which I have set to speaker. I've stopped by their house once since I've been back to visit with them and Gran, but I'm limiting my time there until after the show.

"I don't think so." I glance down at my sweats. Far too much effort to change, and I don't want them to see me like this.

"Or I could come there?"

My usually clean house screams post-breakup. One look at any of the trash bins, and there's enough tissues and empty tubs of ice cream to erase any doubt of my current mental state. I've spent most of the week at my house, sobbing.

"No, Ma. Not today. Sorry."

I know the state I'm in is just an excuse for not seeing them. I also feel too guilty not seeing them, with Kenneth's email still in my inbox.

"Alright, if you're sure," she says, and we hang up.

I finally opened it when I got home.

Dear Charlotte,

I'm not sure if you received my previous email or not. If you didn't, you probably won't receive this one either. If you are reading this and you need some time, I understand, but please call me. Give me a chance.

Everyone wants me to just give them a chance. Eli wanted a chance too. I gave it to him, and he threw it away. With a little distance from his confession, I can even understand why. I'm not sure he had much of a choice. I'd have been pissed he went through with it regardless, but I might have been able to get past it if he'd been honest about it from the start. Instead, he chose to do this behind my back and take away any choice I had to go along with it, and any chance I might have had to be understanding. It feels too much like history repeating itself.

I still haven't decided what to do about Eli. I scoured my contract and couldn't find a way out of it that wouldn't have felt sketchy in its own right. I'm legally bound to one more episode before I can be free.

It's laughable. I spent my whole life dreaming of being on a game show. For years I've studied, taken tests, and gone to live auditions. Finally, I make it there and wind up trying to find a way out of it.

It's so frustrating that there's nothing I can do right now. All my agency has been ripped away from me. A small voice nags at the back of my brain, itching like the mosquito bite that you tell yourself not to think about, and only end up thinking about more. There is one thing I can do.

I pull up my inbox and dial the phone number in the signature. I'm going to confront my grandfather.

* * *

An enormous light fixture, like a chandelier if all the pieces were spread out, spans the ceiling of the restaurant. Quiet jazz plays in the background, and the air is filled with the smell of smoked hickory.

"Hello, I'm here to meet Kenneth Stuckey," I tell the host.

"Ah yes, miss. Right this way." The tables are covered in white linens, and the menu on the website didn't list any prices. It's going to be expensive. Either I'll be eating a single bean, or he better be planning on paying. Seventeen percent of diners' meals might go uneaten in restaurants, but that will not be the case here. I'll be sure to get every penny's worth.

He'd suggested the restaurant. I'd contemplated pushing back and suggesting somewhere else, but if things didn't go well, I didn't want him at my place, and I didn't like the power that going to his would grant him. Some place public enough to help with my comfort, but where we could have a conversation without having everything we say overheard, was just what we needed. So, while the restaurant isn't one I would have picked, it's a good choice for this.

I give a discreet flap of my arms to cool my sweaty pits and try to calm my fidgety nerves as we approach the table.

An old, but relatively spry-looking man in a tailored gray suit and with a stringy gray comb-over stands up to greet me.

"Oh, Charlotte. It's you!" he says.

I nod my acknowledgment and smile awkwardly. Yup, it's me. The granddaughter you waited thirty years to give the time of day.

He extends a wrinkled hand. I glance at it, and then at him. A simple handshake seems such a strange introduction for your estranged grandfather, but I'm not sure what would be less weird.

I finally shake his hand, and we both sit. My throat feels tight and dry. I take a sip of water from the goblet in front of me.

"Hi," I manage.

"Hello. I'm so glad you came."

I'm not sure yet that I am, but so much of my life was feeling out of my control, deciding to see him was something I could choose, so here I am. "I'm not sure what to call you," I admit.

"Whatever you're comfortable with is fine," he says rather unhelpfully. *Grandpa* feels far too familiar, but *Mr. Stuckey* or *Kenneth* both feel wrong too. I guess I don't have to decide now, but I'm not sure what else to do with the conversation either, so I drag my finger across my glass, drawing patterns in the condensation.

"Why don't we figure out what to order," he suggests. "My treat."

Thank goodness for that.

"Alright." I scan the menu, and when the server comes by, we put in our orders.

That done, we're once again left in an uncomfortable silence, and the nerves start my leg bouncing under the table. He's the one that reached out. He's the one who sent a follow-up email, so eager for me to respond and meet him. It doesn't feel like it should be on me to start the conversation.

Unable to stand the silence any longer, I blurt, "So, you wanted to meet?"

"I did." A series of expressions pass over his face, but none that I'm able to categorize.

Some of the most mysterious items in the world have baffled humans for decades. There was the almost certainly artificially made tooth wheel, similar to those used in modern gears, discovered in Russia. It was dated at over three hundred million years old, but the lightness of the material lead some to suspect alien origins. For objects like these, while their origins remain unknown, to those who study them, they've become as familiar as the back of one's own hand.

This man is the opposite to me. I know our origins. I know he's my grandfather by birth, and I know Gran's side of the story, but who he is and his expressions are as alien to me as the origins of that tooth wheel. He's a total stranger.

"Why?" It feels rude to ask, and maybe I should grant him a bit more grace, but I don't feel wrong in expecting an explanation.

"Is it so hard to imagine I might want to get to know my granddaughter?"

I do my best to keep my tone earnest. I'm here, after all. I'm giving him a chance and trying to withhold judgment. I just want to understand. "A little bit, yeah. It's been thirty years. Why now?"

He taps the table as he considers his answer. "I've always regretted how I treated your grandmother and not having a relationship with your mother or you. It was finally time to remedy that."

"So you mentioned in your email. And I can understand that much. What I don't understand is what made it finally time. I don't know when you reached out to my mom, but if it was recently, you've had a good fifty odd years to do this. Even if it was a long time ago, you've had thirty years with me, or at least once I turned eighteen if Ma wouldn't let you talk to me when I was younger. After all these years, I'm having a hard time believing you woke up one day and said, 'Today is the day,' unprompted. I'm not trying to be pushy, but if you want a relationship of any kind, I need the full picture, and it feels like I'm missing something."

He chuckles a little. "You don't pull your punches, do you?"

"When the time is right to, sure. But all I'm asking for here is a little honesty."

"Very well. In the sake of . . . honesty"—he meets my eyes—"my wife left me. Divorced at eighty-five. I haven't heard from my kids or grandkids in months—"

"Your *other* grandkids," I correct.

"I . . . yes. My other grandkids. You're right. I'm sorry."

The server arrives with our food, giving me a much-needed moment to process this information, and I'm grateful for the distraction that covers an awkward silence. He's reaching out because he's lonely and because I'm his last resort.

"Why did she leave?" I ask after we've both had a chance to eat a few bites.

"We were downsizing to a smaller house. While packing up, she found some letters from your grandmother from around the time your mother was born. She was angry, but she still wanted me to be a part of your lives, so she tried reaching out a few times. I kept the letters. I'm not sure why."

"You never told your wife about her, in all that time?"

He shakes his head.

"Just like you told Gran you were single. Failed to mention that you had a whole family."

When he looks down this time, he looks ashamed. It's a glimpse of remorse that humanizes him to me, but the fact that it took the rest of his family leaving to get him to reach out is not exactly winning him points.

"I don't know what you want me to say, Charlotte. I've made a lot of mistakes. I can't change that. I'm trying to do better now."

I hear the words, but they feel flat. He gave me his truth, or at least what he, on the surface, thinks to be true. It's time to give him a truth of my own.

"Because you were forced to. You're trying to reconcile with us, but only as a stand-in for the family you lost, not because you actually care about me, my mother, or my grandmother."

His eyes widen, and his wrinkled face crinkles further in hurt. It wasn't my goal to hurt him, but I'm trying to protect my family. My life is full of people appearing out of nowhere, trying to make amends. I gave it a shot once, and I didn't want to let my experience with Eli ruin who I am, a generally trusting and forgiving person. I heard Kenneth out, and I might even still be willing to let him into my life, but I need him to know it will take more than a flimsy hello.

"I can understand why you'd feel that way, but that's not what this is. I do care. I do want to know you. I'm an old man. I want to fix my mistakes to the best of my ability while I still can."

The room has started to feel too small, and my chest is tight with anxiety. It's time for me to make my exit.

"Then I hope you can also understand that this is a lot to take in. I need some time to sit with it. There's . . . I don't know if you've seen, but I've been on a TV show recently, and things have gotten a little out of hand with that."

"I saw. I've kept tabs on you at a distance, for what little it's worth." These words surprise me. Maybe he has cared, on some small level, even if he's never acted on that. I can't think about it now, though. My heart is thundering in my chest, and it feels like we're dining at Pike's Peak. The air is too thin.

"Right . . . so, there's been a lot going on lately, and I just need some space to process this. Thank you for reaching out."

"Better late than never," he says sheepishly.

"That's true," I agree, feeling like I'm not getting enough air. "You can keep emailing me for now. I'll let you know if and when I'm ready to meet again."

His disappointment is evident in his shrunken posture, but he nods. "That's fair."

"I'm sorry, but I need to go." I stand, gathering my purse, and force out my parting words. "Thank you for lunch . . . er, Kenneth."

He stands respectfully for my departure, and I bolt for the door. I gasp in the fresh air outside the restaurant.

Eli. Kenneth. Ma. Pop. Gran. Clint. My head throbs, and for once in my life I have no plan. I have absolutely no idea what I'm going to do.

I spend the rest of my week hiding at home. At least, attempting to. My family has never been great at the whole alone time thing.

My parents might not have all the latest apps, but they aren't digitally illiterate either. While Eli and I are not exactly gracing the covers of the magazines at the checkout counters, if you're a fan of the game show world and know where to look, news of our blowout is hard to miss.

Brain Battle fans have been following our ups and downs since we appeared on screen together in that first episode. The staff at the hmotel knew we were on the show, and of *course* someone managed to capture our fight in the lobby on camera.

We went from a passionate kiss on live TV to a public screaming match in under twenty-four hours. I wonder if I'll ever live it down. I know my parents have seen the video and know that Eli and I have fallen out, but they tiptoe.

Gran knows something is up too. We're so close, she could spot a problem a mile away. Still, they're all giving me space to tell them in my own time. I'm not sure if I love them for it or wish they'd pry.

Eli is only the half of it. Now I'm hiding having met Kenneth from them as well. It's going to take me some time to figure out what I want to do, but after meeting him, there is one thing that became very clear to me. Gran has always stressed the importance of honesty because of the lie he told her that led us down that path. I've always had a vague understanding and respect of that. But seeing this old man who lost his family because his lies finally caught up to him, I saw just how destructive a lie could be.

I can't lie. I just can't do it. And yet, there's Eli and his dad. There is so much on the line. The last two weeks with him were something I wasn't sure I'd get to feel again.

I've dated on and off. Some of the men have been alright, and some have been horror stories for the books, but no one felt quite right, like the perfect fit to my jigsaw puzzle that Eli was.

Honesty should be cut and dry. A simple decision, and yet in this case, even though I know what I should do, and my revelations from meeting with my grandfather enforce that, it breaks my heart to make that choice. I'm so hurt by Eli, but it hurts all the more that I understand his actions and still struggle to forgive them. Even if I could forgive them, but I couldn't go along with them, for him that could mean losing his father again. I'm not sure he'd be able to forgive me.

When it finally comes time to fly back to LA, Ma offers to drive me to the airport. Three hours before my flight, she stands on my doorstep, a sympathetic frown in place.

"You ready?" she asks.

"You're a little early. It's a small airport. We probably don't have to leave for another hour," I say.

"I know; I thought we could grab some ice cream."

My mouth thins into a line, and I bite back my sigh. Here comes the talk, but it's not like I'm going to turn her away when she's already here. Also, ice cream. Who has the power to resist the all-powerful allure of deliciousness? Not I, despite having consumed it in mass quantities over the course of the week.

Everyone knows the healing properties of ice cream. It's not just me; it's science. MRIs have proven it lights up the same happy centers as winning money and listening to your favorite music.

We hit the nearby ice-cream stand in its final weeks of serving before they shut down for fall. It's a small building with walk-up windows, surrounded by a slew of picnic tables, and is almost always packed. We order our cones and camp out at one of the tables.

"Do you want to talk about it?" she asks before crunching into the chocolate shell.

"Is not talking about it an option?" I ask, and maybe a bit of sarcasm reminiscent of my teenage years slips in.

"Sure. We can just sit here and eat in silence, or we can talk about the latest in your father's vendetta against the squirrels in our yard."

I laugh but don't give any further direction on where I want the conversation to go, so silence it seems to be.

"Ma, did you ever resent feeling like you had to be honest all the time?" I ask.

She barks out a laugh, as if anything else would be completely ridiculous. "Of course."

She tips her head, waiting for me to continue.

"I could never stand the idea of letting her down," I say.

She nods. "My mother is a good woman, but the way she constantly harps on about honesty has always gotten on my nerves. I understand it, and I appreciate it as a value, so I never deterred her efforts to instill it in you, but I've always found little opportunities to sneak in lies. Small ones with little to no effect on anything, just to spite her." A wicked grin spreads across her face, and she takes another lick of her cone before turning to me. "But we're not talking about me here, are we?"

I crunch down the remnants of my cone and wipe my face with a napkin.

"Why does everything have to be so hard?" I ask.

"Oh, sweet girl." Ma's voice trembles and she pulls me into a hug. "Life is rarely easy. You just have to figure out the path to walk on that makes you happy."

I was happy with Eli, but now I'm not sure any decision I make could lead to that kind of happiness again. I'll either be racked with guilt over cheating on the show and accepting money I didn't deserve that another contestant may have needed just as badly, or guilt over choosing my morals over Eli and leaving him and his father to their very real struggles.

I'm not sure I'm ready to talk about Eli or Kenneth and face her judgment. I just want to get through this next day. Thankfully, she's true to her word and lets it slide.

Twenty minutes later, we're at the airport drop-off, and she leans over the center console to give me another hug.

"Knock 'em dead, sweetie," she says. I cringe, weighed down by all the truths I'm currently omitting. It's only for another day. Whatever I do, with Eli and the show at least, it ends tomorrow. I'll tell them when they can't talk me out of it, or into him. "I love you," Ma says.

"Love you too," I say. Then, I walk away, turning my back on her and my morals.

CHAPTER TWENTY-NINE
ELI

I pace the set and check the time again on my watch. I've been a wreck since they took Dad away. I need to talk to Charlotte. We're not up until the second half of the show, but taping is about to start, and I haven't seen her. Not that I have any idea what I'll say to her when I do. Every line I've come up with sounds wrong, so I've decided to wing it and speak from the heart. I'm sure I'll regret that decision later, but fuck it—I don't have any better ideas.

With each minute the clock ticks closer to go-time, I'm beginning to think Charlie asked Sarah to run interference. Every time I try to look for her, Sarah appears, telling makeup to touch me up, or running through stage instructions that I've been through several times by now. If this is going to be my last chance to ever see Charlie, I'm selfishly hoping to get as much time with her as possible, even if that time is tense.

As the new contestants take their places at their individual podiums for the first portion of the show, Clint swoops down on me from I'm not even sure where, and it takes all my self-restraint not to clock him immediately.

"I trust you received my package." The clerk at the motel's front desk handed me an envelope when I'd checked in late last night. I'd tried not to open it, but then I'd gotten a text from an unknown number.

Tough week? Remember what we talked about. We wouldn't want anything else unfortunate to happen.

The son of a bitch had carried out his threat before I'd even done anything wrong and was continuing to blackmail me. I hated it, but a vague text from an unknown number wasn't proof enough of anything. I'd have to come up with a lot more evidence if I was going to do anything about it, so for now I had to play Clint's game. I couldn't let Dad down. I opened it; A tidy list of all the answers for today's questions. I read it, memorized it, and couldn't eat dinner for feeling sick to my stomach over it. Or breakfast. Now I feel even more sick for the empty stomach, twisting with guilt.

"What the hell did you do?" I seethe. "I took your damn answers. We won the episode."

"And yet, I seem to remember telling you that you were not to tell a soul. Ms. Evans seemed awfully upset after last week. Strange, I would have thought she'd have been happy to have won another week." He taps his chin. "I wonder what could have set her off?"

I'm struggling with a reply when he leans forward, and his eyes burn with all the same anger that I feel, and he snarls, "Don't toy with me, Mr. Collins. Did you receive the package or not?"

"Yes." It's as much as I'm willing to say. I'm not a generally violent person, but my muscles are twitching with the itch to destroy this man.

"Win, or there will be further consequences," he says.

"I read your goddamn note. Leave me the fuck alone," I growl.

He grins the self-satisfied smile of a man who is very used to getting what he wants, and I wonder just how many other lives he's ruined, and how men like him, the ones who are most likely to abuse their power, always seem to be the ones who end up with it.

He slinks off as the crew rushes around, calling for places. At this point I ought to be in a side room, warming up with Charlotte, but clearly she doesn't plan to let that be the case this time. I'm not surprised, but a small part of me is hopeful. I have to be. I'm falling apart with worry over my dad. I need her. I decide to stay off set, watch the opening questions, and keep an eye out for her. Even a minute or two more with her would be more than I deserve, but I would drink those minutes in greedily.

A few players get knocked out; the questions proceed; and much like our first episode, it comes down to three for a final question, where their times will determine their slots if they're all correct. Still no sign of Charlie. One more question and a commercial break until we're due onstage. The question passes, and commercial is called.

As the commercial break winds down, and Bobby is preparing to interview this week's new team, Sarah appears, escorting Charlie, as beautiful as ever despite her current expression. Her purple slacks swish as she marches over. Once in place, she adjusts her bun, making it messier, and then crosses her arms over her white shirt and yellow vest. She looks at me for the briefest of moments, doe-eyed with terror. Her lip trembles as it shifts between a frown and a scowl. Then, she fixates on a point to the right; a bit of stage with nothing on it. She doesn't say hello, doesn't acknowledge my presence beyond that glance. I guess that's how we're playing it.

And then her hand flies to cover her microphone.

"Eli, I know you feel like you have to do this, but you don't. It's not just about a lie. It's illegal. Your dad wouldn't want you putting yourself at that kind of risk for him."

My heart seizes. She's not wrong, but she doesn't understand. He put himself at that risk for me when I was a teen, and now he's been doing things the right way, and I've already somehow managed to put him back in jail. It's my fault he's there. I have to keep things from getting worse for him. I don't even know what Clint is capable of, but I'm terrified to imagine it.

Besides, the ship has sailed. "I've already looked. It's too late."

Her face crumples before her lips purse in a stormy resolve. "So, pretend you didn't. If it's an answer you don't think you would have known, don't answer."

Except that cognitive bias is a thing. "You know about the curse of knowledge. Even if I tried to do that, there's no saying what I would and would not have come up with."

"It'd be better than nothing," she hisses, and her eyes are watery. She presses her lips together in a way I know to mean she's fighting hard to keep tears from falling. "Please, Eli."

Bobby winds down his interview with our new challengers. He'll soon be throwing to us, so we have to be quiet. Our hands both drop from our mics down to our sides. My mind spins and my stomach is knotted so badly, I could vomit. Charlie and I paste on fake smiles and jog out to meet him, waving enthusiastically at the crowd.

Bobby skips the interview and settles straight in for questions. Someone must have given him a heads-up that the lovers are quarreling, and they don't want a repeat of the first episode.

As the returning champions, Bobby comes to us first.

"The name for the game Jenga is derived from a word meaning 'build' in which language?" he asks. It's a Charlie comfort-zone question, and an easy one at that. She fumbles over her words and puts her fingers to her chin in thought. It's nothing like the sheer panic in her eyes last week when she froze up and couldn't wrap her mind around the answer. That was genuine. This is acting. I raise an eyebrow at her, and her nose twitches. I recognize the action as her questioning herself.

Her internal compass must be rioting. Let me cheat or lie herself about knowing the answer. I lean forward to answer it, a question I would have known without help, and finally she leans in herself.

"Swahili," she says.

"That is correct!" Bobby says, and the crowd cheers out around him.

The show proceeds with much of the same. She answers some and lets me take a few. She's smiling for the camera and the viewers at home, but with the exception of her parents and Gran, who are definitely watching from their living room, no one knows her like I do. I can see, in the slight tremble of her lip and the way she keeps stepping on her own toes as a nervous fidget, she's about to break. Clint watches us like a hawk, or maybe more of a vulture.

They call for commercial at the standard time, and she clicks off her mic and marches toward the watercooler. I follow.

"We could end this right here." She whispers.

"Except it wouldn't be the end of it for me. Or for my dad," I say. "Clint knows from that damn video the clerk took that I told you. He already acted on his threats. My dad's in jail right now. I can't take the chance that he could do more.

She pulls down the spigot for the water jug so hard it snaps right off in her hand. "He got *arrested*?"

"Yes. Clint wasn't bluffing."

"Shit," she mutters, frowning at her cup.

"So, I have to take the answers. I have to win."

"I'll answer the ones that I can. I hope you know what you're doing."

Do I know what I'm doing? I've thought it out, looked at it from every angle I could possibly think of. There's no way out of this corner that doesn't end poorly for one reason or another. I hate it, but cheating feels like the only real choice here.

"One minute!" Sarah shouts, shooting us a pointed look.

Sarah walks over, lightly, as though she's walking on eggshells. Her eyes keep flicking to Clint. It worries me that she'll face repercussions for Charlie's and my struggles.

"We going to be all right here?" she asks, laughing nervously.

"Peachy." Charlie grips the edge of the podium.

"Great," Sarah says in a way that conveys she knows it's anything but. She backs away as a stagehand shouts out a countdown. "Hello, everyone, we're back!" Bobby says, and he definitely stresses the *everyone* and gives us a "keep your shit together" glare. Once again, we have rattled the lovable host.

Bobby flings us a question, and Charlie answers it, seemingly without thought.

Bobby looks at her with distrust but admits that she's correct and turns to the other team. Charlie turns on me the moment the cameras are likely to have flicked over to them.

Her eyes are pleading, and I want so badly to give her what she wants, but I can't stop thinking about my Dad behind bars.

Does she honestly not see how trapped I am?

"That's correct!" Bobby says. He glances over his shoulder at us, to make sure it's safe to pan back to us. Finding us still standing apart, even with silent conversations clearly happening, he walks toward us and flings another question our way. Another I would have known, and she seems to know I would have. I lean over and answer.

"Correct again!" Bobby walks back toward our competitors.

"What would you have me do?" I repeat.

Her face, which thus far has remained stoic, suddenly crumples. I know immediately that asking again was a mistake. "Don't lie. Don't put yourself at risk. Trust that we can find a way to fix this for your dad. Choose yourself and choose me," she whispers, so quietly I'm almost unsure I heard it, but that's wishful thinking. I heard it. The blow of it folds me over. I lay my palms flat on our podium, arms outstretched. I take a step back and double over, head between my arms and take in deep steady breaths.

Choose me. Those words are going to haunt me for the rest of my life. If anything else was on the line—my house, my car, my degree, my job—I would have. But my dad has lost too much time. He's fought too hard to come back and sacrificed too much to try to do right by me. He never did it right before, and now that he is, I can't be the one to send him back to the bottom.

I want to choose her. I want to choose her so badly, but I just can't. Another round of questions happens while my head is down, and Charlotte answers. Finally, I catch my breath enough to straighten. I take another hit to my gut when I see the shine in her eyes, watery but glinting with the faintest flicker of hope. I give the smallest shake of my head in answer to her demand and watch as it burns out.

I don't know how I'm going to live with that. Extinguishing that hope feels like extinguishing her soul.

Charlie closes her eyes and lets out a resigned sigh. She's done with me. We continue the game, and it comes down to the final question. All we have to do is get it right and we win.

In true *Brain Battle* form, they throw to one final commercial. Charlie tenses up and turns to me for one last try.

"You told me you were afraid of ending up like your dad. I know I already said it, but what you're doing is illegal. You're so afraid of ending up like him, you're doing it to yourself."

Self-fulfilling prophecy. Is that really what I'm doing? My mind races, replaying her words, and examining all my actions over the last two weeks . . . and over the course of my life, really.

"What country served as the set for Tatooine in *Star Wars*?" Bobby asks.

My heart drops. It isn't one I would have known. *Self-fulfilling prophecy.* I'm so thrown by the perspective Charlotte has placed on things and her insistence, I reconsider, I've given myself a mental block. The correct answer hovers in my peripheral. A mental snapshot that's just out of my grasp. I reach and reach into the depths of mind, and I can't get my fingers around it. My pulse quickens, and I look to Charlie in desperation, begging her with everything I have to help. She looks at me blankly, and I verbalize it.

"Please," I say.

Her eyes widen at the realization that I don't have the answer. Her mouth hangs open, and she shakes her head sadly. "I don't know it." I believe her, even if I don't know what she would have done if she had.

My eyes scan the room, as if an audience member will be holding up a sign with the answer printed on it. Clint's stare is murderous.

My hands start to shake. How could I possibly have forgotten the answer, even with the question to trigger the memory.

Bobby clears his throat. "We're going to need an answer."

I can't even come up with a guess. I'm completely frozen. I look once more to Charlotte for help. Any answer is better than no answer.

"Ethiopia?" Charlotte asks rather than answers.

"Final answer?" Bobby asks.

Charlotte looks to me, and I still can't move, can't think, can't breathe.

"Yes," she says.

And then, like a damn burst, my brain clicks into gear, and the answer finally comes to me a second too late.

"No!" I shout. "That's not our answer!"

Bobby hesitates, looking truly nervous for the first time I can ever recall in the many years I've watched the show. He glances at the off-stage judges, who both shake their heads.

"I'm sorry, Eli. Charlotte said final answer, and her answer *is* final."

Time slows, and my jaw drops. The decision to cheat was hard, but I hadn't worried about actually doing it once I'd decided, because I knew all the answers. It wasn't complicated. The possibility that I'd forget an answer—I never saw it coming.

Bobby recovers, frowning his usual wrong answer frown. "I'm sorry, that is incorrect. Kyle and Andrew, the game is all tied up. Steal the points, and you win the game!"

My stomach drops further as I take in the smiles on their faces. They know it, and we've already lost.

Kyle leans forward. "The republic of Tunisia."

Andrew starts leaping in celebration before Bobby has even told him it's correct. Confetti falls from the ceiling above them, and for the first time, I feel the awkwardness of standing to the side, watching it happen for someone else. It isn't the prize money I care about anymore. My father's arrest made my financial concerns secondary.

I haven't even made it off set when I see Clint looming. He's staring at me, anger rolling off him in waves.

Charlie has turned her back to me and is being escorted away by Sarah. Clint pivots on his heels as well. I glance between Charlie and Clint. I need to talk to them both, try to salvage something, but I've only got time to talk to one of them.

I run after Clint, and I doubt it's the right decision, but I have to try. I catch him and skid to a stop blocking his path. His eye twitches.

"What?" he demands.

"I tried. I memorized the answers. I tried and I drew a blank. I couldn't remember the answer."

"The deal was, if you wanted to avoid further consequences, you win the game. Did you win?" he asks.

"No, but I tried to follow your rules. You can't take it out on him. Please. Leave my father alone. Take it out on me. Please, leave him out of it."

"Tsk, tsk, tsk." Clint shakes his head. "I don't believe that taking it out on you will get my message across quite as effectively."

With those ominous words, he turns and walks away, leaving me alone in an empty hallway.

CHAPTER THIRTY

ELI

A sea of voices, and tinny PA announcements do nothing to dull the throbbing behind my eyes. A traveler in a hurry runs into me and bounces right off as he tries to weave through the stream of people making their way to and from their gates.

I'd wasted no time in finding Sarah after the show and getting a ride straight to the airport to catch the next flight home. I was eager to leave LA, where life had teased me with a perfect week with her, only to then blow everything up in my face. I was not in any hurry to get back to Michigan, where I'd continue work and school, not making enough money in a house that was falling apart and that would feel too empty with Dad gone.

How could everything go so drastically wrong in the course of a week?

I make it to my gate, and I see light brown hair pulled into a messy bun, sticking out above one of the seats facing away from me. I should have known she'd end up on the same flight, but in the fog of dread over what Clint would do next, it hadn't occurred to me.

I wait for the anticipatory flutter that I usually get around her, or anger that her insistence on getting in my head during the game caused me to forget the answer, making us lose, but I'm stuck in neutral. I don't know how to feel toward Charlotte right now. I'm terrified to see what will happen to my dad, but I'm also relieved that the show is over, and I no longer have to make the decision whether or not to cheat with every episode. The scales are balancing, but the term *happy medium* doesn't apply. I feel more like an unseasoned bowl of mushy oatmeal.

This could be the last time I see her. If nothing else, I think we both need closure.

"This seat taken?" I ask, pointing at the seat next to her.

She hesitates, eyeing me over the rims of her glasses before reluctantly moving her purse.

"No, go ahead."

I need a minute to decide what to say to her, and I think we're both wondering just how awkward this flight is going to be. "Where are you sitting?"

"27B," she says, without needing to check her ticket. "You?"

I pull my boarding pass out of the front pocket of my back-pack. "32C."

Her body relaxes, and I do too.

"I'm sorry about your dad," she says.

"Me too."

"What . . . Eli, what happened on the show?"

"You got in my head, and I forgot the answer," I snap, a little more harshly than I intend to.

Her mouth opens like she's about to speak, then closes in a frown. She fish-mouths a few more times before saying, "I see."

No apology for it, and thinly veiled disappointment that I hadn't decided not to lie.

"What does that mean for us?" I ask.

She shifts in her seat before meeting my eyes. "What do you want it to mean?"

"That's not an answer," I point out.

"No, it isn't," she admits.

What *do* I want? I look at her and think about the flight to LA for our second episode; the accidental touches, and how badly I wanted her to let me in and give me another chance. I remember holding her hand in the gardens and the way she kissed me in the pool; Snuggling with her while we watched TV and talked about our families. What I want is to go back to that. Things may have been complicated still—we had a past—but it felt simpler than it does now. I still want her and believe her to be right for me, but how does she get past my lies, and how do I get past my own guilt that my dad is in jail now because of me, and that I cheated on the show?

The gap between us feels like a chasm.

"I want you, Charlie. But I'm not sure what I want matters, does it?"

A tear leaks out and trails down her cheek. "I want you too, but knowing what happened with this show, and staying with you? I'm not sure I can handle it. This is no small lie. This is the kind of lie that could put both of us behind bars with your father. I've seen what big lies can do; how they have the power to twist and ruin a family and come back to bite even years down the line. I love you, Eli. I love you so much, but I can't see a world in which this works."

Each word hits me like I'm her own personal punching bag, no matter how gentle she's trying to be. It's strange and fucked up. I'm upset with her for distracting me and trying so hard to talk me out of using the answers that I forgot them. But I also know I'll be able to forgive her for that, and I just want to be with her.

"Then, I guess this is goodbye." We're both in Michigan, but far enough away that it's unlikely for our paths to cross if we don't engineer it.

Tears fall freely on her face, and my stomach twists with my own hurt and the pain of seeing hers. I can't stand it and fold her in my arms. She sinks into them willingly and heaves a deep sob. We've caught the attention of several eyes, but fuck them. Thankfully, I don't see anyone recording.

The gate agent calls for boarding, and those in the first groups to board stand around us and form a line.

"I'm going to get cleaned up before we have to get on the plane." She gives me one more squeeze before darting off toward the bathrooms. Having said our piece, I join the line and board the plane.

A red-eyed Charlotte boards shortly after and takes her seat a few rows ahead of me. I scan through movie options, a pang in my chest as I scroll past *Sweet Home Alabama*. Ultimately, I settle on an action movie that I mostly zone out for, barely processing a single minute of it.

My eyes keep drifting up to her. I hear an occasional quiet sniffle and see her hand move toward her face, armed with a tissue. Eventually she shifts so I can't see any part of her from my seat, and when I get up for a bathroom run as an excuse to check on her, she's sound asleep.

The plane bumps to a landing, and I lean to get a view around the people in the rows between us. If this is it, I want one last look at her as she walks away.

She disappears down the aisle without a glance back at me, and I follow the procession when my row's turn comes. Out in the terminal, it's a mass of unfamiliar faces, moving in all directions, until my eyes land on her. Two gates away, she stands watching me. We both freeze, just staring at each other, before eventually she lifts her hand in a wave and mouths goodbye.

The connecting flight to Lansing is in one direction, Grand Rapids in another. My heart shatters as I once again watch the love of my life walk away from me. This time probably forever.

CHAPTER THIRTY-ONE
CHARLOTTE

I take a bite of the snack mix and grimace, fighting the temptation to spit it out.

"Pop, what did you buy? This is disgusting!"

"I thought I was grabbing the usual stuff," he says sheepishly. "I didn't notice until I got home that it was bonfire and pickle."

I shake my head. "Why is that even an option?" My otherwise competent father's snack kryptonite strikes again. It's truly incredible how often he messes them up.

I've been home for a couple days, but this is the first time since returning that I've seen my parents. I needed some time to decompress and readjust to work and my normal life. I agreed to a game-watching night, but only if it wasn't *Brain Battle*. The harsh memories are too fresh, and I have no desire to watch a show that is rigged.

After seeing how late in life Kenneth's lies came back to bite him, I can't let this linger over me, or I'll spend the rest of my life waiting for the other shoe to drop. I still plan to come forward with what I know eventually, but I don't have the mental energy to continue my search for evidence just yet. When I do, I'll do my best to keep Eli out of it, without any further lies.

We all settle into our chairs, and the show begins. I call out answers as normal, and my family shares their usual bafflement at my ability to get the questions correct, but something is missing. There's tension in the air, because they don't know it, but I'm keeping a secret.

Gran breaks into a coughing fit, and it's a knife to my chest. The check from my first episode hasn't come in yet. If I'd only gone along with Clint's deal, I could have won more money and used it for Gran's care. But I can't second-guess myself. I tried to do what was right and follow the morals they instilled in me. Everything is so twisted.

One episode in, the tension only grows thicker. The guilt over meeting with Kenneth and not telling them what happened on the show is eating away at me. I have no idea how they'll react if I tell them. Not only did I lose the show, but I've lost Eli, and now it feels like I'm losing my family too.

A new episode starts, and the answers are there in my mind, but it feels like so much energy even to open my mouth and call them out.

A few questions blow by, and I can feel everyone's eyes on me. Maybe I should just go home. How is it possible that achieving a lifelong dream has ruined everything? I search my soul, trying to find the words to make my family understand; to begin some sort of healing process, whatever that might look like.

Finally, I open my mouth and the words pour out. I start with telling them about meeting Kenneth.

The three of them sit quietly, patiently listening to me without interrupting. They let me talk and talk until I've gotten it all out. Finally, when they're sure I've finished, Mom moves to speak.

That's when Gran starts coughing again. Violent wheezes rack her small frame, and she waves for her oxygen tank. I leap up and grab the mask from where it hangs, cover her mouth, and turn the tank on. She takes a deep breath, but her coughing continues, and her eyes lose focus.

My parents hover behind me.

"Do something," I shout.

"Do what?" Ma asks. "She's coughing."

She isn't just coughing. Her eyes spin around like marbles in their sockets, rolling upward, then falling shut as she slumps back in her chair, unconscious.

"I'm calling," Dad says, holding his cell phone to his ear.

"We need an ambulance at—"

I tune him out, staring helplessly at Gran. My eyes roam over her body, as though a sign will appear with detailed instructions on how to help her, but I'm clueless. I hold the mask to her face. A brain full of knowledge, but I can't triage my grandmother when I need to. After my experience at the museum, I even considered looking into some basic first aid. I haven't had time to follow through. It should have been my first priority. I should have known.

My hand starts to shake. I'm so anxious, the energy is seeping out of my pores, making my body quiver. *Keep it together.*

"Take a deep breath, Charlotte," Ma says, her voice gentle. She puts her hand on the oxygen mask, gently nudging my hand away. "We don't need you going into shock as well."

I try to do as she says. *Think. What's next?* I take her fragile wrist in my hand and feel for a pulse. She's got one, though it feels alarmingly feeble.

"Here, I've got a stopwatch on my phone," Ma says. I count beats, quickly confirming that it's too slow.

Sirens sound outside the door, and Pop is there opening it and shouting, "In here!" Everything is a blur as my eyes flick from

Gran to Ma, to the paramedics marching toward us. Ma takes my hand and tugs me backward, away from Gran, and my heart is pounding so hard my head aches. I watch the paramedics work, and my brain stops processing what is going on around me. I can't follow anything anymore. I blink, and she's on a stretcher, and they're wheeling her out the door.

"I'll go," Ma says, and follows them out to the ambulance.

Then it's quiet. Too quiet.

There's nothing external to drown out the persistent thoughts in my head, telling me I shouldn't have told her all of that. I got her worked up. I caused this. It's my fault, my fault, my fault. I'm vaguely aware of Pop guiding me to a chair and easing me into it. Him moving around, gathering things, and clearing away our discarded snacks. I shake my head, and time snaps into focus as he steps back into the room from the kitchen.

"Charlotte? Are you back with me?" he asks.

"Y—" my voice catches, and I clear my throat and try again. "Yes."

"Okay, good. Do you want to go up to the hospital? I grabbed some things. Phone chargers, snacks, in case we're there for a while."

"Yeah," I say.

"Are you okay to drive? We should probably take two cars so we can come home and take shifts if we need to." I'm so thankful for Pop's organization in this moment, though I hate that he's so prepared for this particular event. It isn't the first time we've held vigil in a hospital for Gran.

"Yes, I can drive." I'm still panicking, but my head is clear. The initial foggy reaction has worn off, and I feel safe to get myself there.

Pop nods, and we head out the door.

*   *   *

"Any update?" Pop asks.

Ma shakes her head. "Not yet. They've got her back in a room."

We all silently acknowledge this, hovering awkwardly in the middle of the room, and then in synch we move toward a cluster of chairs and settle in to wait. Pop is in his chair for about three seconds before he springs back out of it. He is the worst person to be at a hospital with. He can never sit still. He's a pacer, and it makes everyone around him twice as anxious. At least, that's what it does to me.

"Ned," Ma prods.

He glances over, then winces at the look Ma gives him. "Right, I'll just . . ." And he trails off and disappears from the ER waiting room, out into the main hospital.

I pull out my phone and thumb through my contacts. I've found it hard to make friends as an adult and have trouble converting the casual friendships into anything beyond that. That's not the real problem, though. The real problem is, I know exactly who I want to talk to right now.

When my heart is aching and scared for my grandmother, the person I want to talk to is Eli. The arms I want around me are his. The hands I want to hold belong to him.

It isn't fair. Life keeps standing in our way, but my heart keeps calling to him.

He hasn't so much as sent a text.

Neither have I, and I probably never will.

Eli is gone. Gran is in the hospital. My heart hurts. My head hurts. Even my skin aches, like it's stretched too tight, like I'm about to be ripped apart at the seams.

It's all more than I can bear. I collapse into my mother's arms and sob.

CHAPTER THIRTY-TWO
ELI

I shut the door to the house behind me, and the door to Dad's room on the way to my own, so the leak can't stress me out. I flop onto my bed after another day of work, knowing it isn't enough. Without Dad home working his jobs, we're completely screwed. If those checks don't come in way earlier than expected, there's going to be no home for him to come back to.

I shower, but the warm water does nothing to soothe the ache in my muscles. They're still too tense with anxiety to relax post-workout.

I've got a couple hours before my classes start for the evening, so I throw on a pair of fresh clothes and head to the jail for a visit with Dad.

"You look like shit," he says.

"Thanks a lot."

"I'm all right. Stop worrying about me. It's not so bad. I'll serve out my sentence, and we can start fresh again afterward."

"It's not all right. It's my fault," I say.

"Don't say that." He glances around. He knows the charge he's been hit with but has no idea the real reason he's in there right now: because I brought Clint's wrath down upon him. He's never even heard of Clint. But he's still trying to protect me, as if I could somehow be implicated for who he spends his time with. That's Dad, always trying to do his best, often with the wrong resources and information.

"You don't understand," I begin, ready to finally tell him the whole story about Charlie, and high school, about the show and what I did. How the moment things got hard and I was faced with a difficult choice, I chose the wrong path. That no matter how hard he tried to tell me to do better, I followed in his footsteps after all.

He holds up a hand to stop me before I can get the words out. "You've been looking over your shoulder, afraid to end up in here alongside me as long as I can remember. I don't know what happened, and I don't need to. What I do know is that you've got a good head on your shoulders, and a good heart."

"No, Dad," I say. "You don't understand. The first chance I got, I—"

"Whatever you did, whatever this is, it's that . . . what do they call it? Self-fulfilling prophecy. You're so convinced you're not good enough that you don't believe yourself capable of making the right decisions, so you make the wrong ones and think you had no choice."

He's making the same exact arguments as Charlie. The more I hear it, the more it sounds uncomfortably logical.

"Give yourself the chance to do the right thing. You don't deserve to be here. You never did. If you end up here, make sure you really know why, and that it isn't just because you can't imagine anything different for yourself," he says.

I reel. I thought I was doing what was right by protecting my father and trying to make the money we needed to have a good life. Clint saw me waver and latched right onto my weakness. Charlie begged me to see and do what was right. I weighed the options, already assuming I would go the illegal route.

"Time's up," the guard nearby says.

Dad nods and stands to go, but before he does, he turns back to me one last time.

"I love you son."

I lift my hand and wave. "I love you too, Dad."

I've got an email to respond to.

CHAPTER THIRTY-THREE
ELI

I may have blown my chance with Charlotte already, but that doesn't mean it's too late to do the right thing. I'll give myself some peace of mind and maybe her too if I take down Clint. If he gets caught, it could also have the side effect of getting my dad out of jail. If it doesn't, I have to accept that even if Lucky's presence was my fault, his original sentence wasn't. I won't abandon him while he's gone. When he gets out, whether it's sooner or later, I'll be there.

I watch the clock tick down to my scheduled meeting with former *Brain Battle* contestant Marcus and adjust my laptop in front of me, ready to take notes. Time to make the call.

"Hello?"

"Hey, is this Marcus?" I ask.

"Yeah, that's me."

"This is Eli Collins. Thanks for agreeing to meet with me."

"I'd say no problem, but I feel like it might be," he says.

"I know what you mean. Look, I'm going to be direct. There was some shady shit going down when we were on the show, and I want to report it. I suspect this has been going on for a long time, but I don't have much proof, and I'm hoping you can help."

Marcus is silent on the other end of the line.

"Were you ever approached to throw a match, or provided the answers to win, or anything else like that?"

"I wasn't." My hope is crushed. He was my only lead. I still hadn't heard back from anyone else Charlie and I reached out to. I could still go forward with my story, but lacking evidence, it's likely to get brushed off.

"But I think I can still help," he suddenly adds.

My heart skips a beat and I straighten in my chair. "How?"

"The guy I was up against in my third episode was staying at the same hotel as me. I met him at the lobby bar the night before the episode, and he recognized me. We shared a few drinks and talked, and he ended up making it through to the final round." Clearly, back when Marcus was a competitor, the show invested a bit more money into contestant accommodations than they had for the motel we'd stayed at.

"What happened?" I ask.

"I was going to lose. I saw that creep Clint talk to him on the break, and next thing I knew, the guy was missing all his questions. I saw him at the hotel again after the show, and he looked shaken up. He said, 'Be careful,' and then left."

"What was his name?" I ask, frantically typing out notes on Marcus's story.

"Roy Heath. But that's not all."

My hands freeze over the keyboard. "What else?"

"It didn't sit right with me, so I kept tabs on things, even once I was off the show. Around that time, one of the crew got fired. I looked her up, and she wrote a blog post saying the show was rigged."

"No shit," I said, already pulling up a fresh browser window to try and find it. How had we never come across it before?

"Yeah, man, but I went to show it to someone the next day, and it was gone. I followed her socials for a while, but never came across anything like it again."

Damn it. So much for that.

"Her name was Martha Craig. That's all I've got. I hope it helps, but look, don't use my name. Something was off with that guy, and I don't want to be dragged into it."

"Understood. I'll keep you out of it. Thank you. This helps a lot."

I disconnect from Marcus and immediately get to work.

*   *   *

"May I speak to Janice Trout please?" I ask from the small kitchen table in our quiet home.

"One moment please," the receptionist says. I researched reporters, and based on some of the stories she's covered in the past, I've decided Janice is who I want to go to with my story and the information I got from Marcus.

There are formal methods for reporting gameshow fraud, and I intend to fill out that paperwork as well, but knowing the lengths he's gone to with my family, I know that Clint wouldn't hesitate to bribe people, or do who knows what else, to block any legal action or loss of his position with this coming to light. I have to spread it far and wide, so it's too late to put the genie back in the bottle.

"This is Janice," she answers.

I tell her my story. She listens quietly, with murmurs and clarifying questions here and there. When I've told her about everything, including the carried-out threats against my father, the speaker crackles as she blows out a breath.

"I haven't come across anything like this. There's news about reality shows being fake all the time, but no one expects those to actually be reality, and it isn't illegal to stage things on those, but a game show could be big. Depending on how many people are involved, there could be some serious court cases."

"I know," I say.

"Do you have any evidence of this?" she asks.

"I have the two cards I was given. I took pictures of them on my phone for the time stamp, and I put them in bags after the show, just in case, so it's possible fingerprints could be pulled off that," I say.

"Fingerprints would be for a formal, legal investigation. I'm a reporter. I'll take the photos of the answer cards, but a recorded conversation would have been better. Is there anyone else that might be able to comment on this?"

Charlie was there the first time Clint made his offer, but there's no way in hell I'm dragging her into this now. Every step of the way I will make it abundantly clear she had no part in this. I don't want her implicated when she's done nothing wrong. This is where Marcus's info comes in handy.

"I did some digging of my own. Nothing concrete, but I've got some leads. I'd be surprised if we were the first people they'd offered this to, but I can't say with certainty." I tell her about our visit with Cornelia—though I don't share her name—and our attempts to reach out to others. I tell her what Marcus said as well—again excluding his name—and give her all the information I was able to find on the other former contestant and crew member.

"I'll reach out to them and see what I can come up with," she says. "I guess that leaves one question. Do you want to remain anonymous in all this, or are we putting your name out there?"

I hesitate, drumming my fingers on the worn edges of our kitchen table. I hadn't thought about anonymity as an option for myself, even if I'd protected it for Cornelia and Marcus. I was more than happy for my fifteen minutes of fame to be over and to drift back into being a no one. Fame is not a factor here. I want to forgive myself for this and the things I've done in the past. To accept that I can be a good person, move on, and give myself a real chance at a decent life, I have to own my part in this and accept the responsibility for my actions.

"You can put my name in," I say.

"You're sure? Naming my source will give credibility to the report, so that's good with me, but you should know you're probably going to get dragged through the mud and could very well end up getting charged right alongside the director and producers."

I take a deep breath. One step at a time. Take a note from *Frozen II* and do the next right thing. I smile and think of Charlie, snuggled against my chest, talking me into watching Disney movies at the hotel. Yes, I'll do the right thing for her, and for myself.

"I'm sure."

"All right, sit tight for a few days while I do some digging and see if I can get any more evidence or confirmed sources. I'll let you know once I've got the green light and have it ready to publish."

I end the call and stare at the phone, fingers once again betraying me by hovering over the address book icon. I'm not sure that forgetting about Charlie forever is realistic. Even with everything else I've had to deal with, I still haven't been able to push her out of my mind for more than a few minutes at a time. She's always there, smiling and laughing. Lighting up when she learns something new or stumbles into an opportunity to tell you about something amazing she knows. Should I tell her? She'd probably say, "Good for you—now lose my number."

I don't know if it's selfish to contact her or if I'm holding myself back from a chance to do the right thing. I can't trust my own judgment anymore, and I have a feeling it's going to take a lot of time, and probably some therapy, before I get there.

Nothing needs to be decided tonight. I've got a few more weeks left in this semester, and I've got studying to get to. For now, I'll focus on making it through the night. I'll worry about forever another time.

*   *   *

As it turns out, forever takes about three days to force me into decision-making. I'm at the gym, on a break between training sessions, when my phone rings with a text from Janice.

That former employee panned out, and I've got two other former contestants willing to comment. The story goes live on Tuesday, but per your request, I've emailed you a copy. Buckle up, kid.

Tuesday. A few more days before everything changes, once again. I still haven't decided if I should talk to Charlie. I don't want her to come across this out of the blue with no warning. Janice promised she'd make it explicitly clear that Charlotte was not involved, but there's a good chance someone will reach out to her.

I want her to know why I did it, and that I don't have any expectations that it will mean anything for us. I want her to know how I feel, without feeling pressured to do anything. Texting, calling, or showing up all feel too pushy. I need to figure out how to respect her boundaries and accomplish everything else at the same time.

I connect to my ancient printer and print out a copy of the article. Or begin to. The thing runs off one little line at a time, and it moves as if the printhead is being pulled by a harnessed snail.

I growl and pull out some blank paper to handwrite a note to go with the article. I fold up the article and my note and press them into an envelope, feeling like I'm sealing my fate rather than a letter.

CHAPTER THIRTY-FOUR
CHARLOTTE

"We brought food since clearly you're not eating whatever they're serving in the cafeteria," Dad says.

I couldn't take off work after having taken time for the show, but I've spent every moment I could at the hospital, and Dad's right: I haven't had much more than one small meal a day.

"Thanks." I accept the bag from him. My stomach churns at the thought of food. Gran isn't doing well, and it feels wrong to do mundane things like work and eat. I set the bag on the side table next to my visitor's chair and resume holding Gran's hand.

Mom puts her hand on my shoulder. "Sweetie, you need to eat. Your grandmother wouldn't want you doing this to yourself. What is she going to say if she wakes up to find you all skin and bones, and exhausted at her side?"

I stretch out, sigh, and grab a fry out of the bag. "She'd ask what I was doing sitting there like a fossil, and tell me that I ought to go do something," I admit.

"Exactly," Ma says.

"I just don't want her to wake up alone. I got the okay to stay here again tonight," I say.

My parents exchange a look.

"I'll spend the night at home tomorrow."

Mom hesitates, "All right. But eat your dinner, and then at least get some rest while we're here. Those bags under your eyes, you've been staying awake with her all night, haven't you?"

I shrug because the truth will only get me a longer lecture, and a lie will get me a TED talk.

"We stopped by your house to bring in your mail," Dad says.

"Thank you."

"We left most of it on the counter, but this one looked like something you might want to see." He hands me a standard-size envelope, stuffed thick with folded-up paper. I scan the front. Return address: Eli Collins.

My stomach flips seeing his name, even though I've been thinking about him constantly since we last saw each other. Part of me wants to drop the letter straight into the recycling, but I already know I'll read it, especially with how thick it is.

My parents both watch me expectantly, and I slowly slip it into my purse. I project my odds of ugly crying after reading to be roughly ninety percent, and I don't need them to see that.

After eating, Pop heads home, but Ma says she'll stay a little longer. I cave to her demands, curl up in my chair, and fall asleep.

*　*　*

A shuffling sound wakes me up, and I blink, disoriented, trying to remember my surroundings. A nurse glances up from where she stands at Gran's side. That's right, the hospital. No one else is in the room. Ma must have left while I was asleep.

"Sorry to wake you. Just checking up on your grandma."

"Any change?" I ask.

She shakes her head. "About the same, I'm afraid."

I nod and sit up in my chair, stretching to relieve some of the discomfort of too many nights spent in a stiff chair, as if *one* wasn't too many. The nurse finishes, makes a quick note on her chart, and exits the room, leaving me alone with an unconscious Gran.

"Let's see what he says, shall we?" I say.

My nervous fingers fumble with the seal, and I'm left with a handful of envelope shreds, and the contents.

Dear Charlie,

Upon seeing my name on this letter, you might be tempted to pitch this straight into the fire, but I hope you'll keep reading because I need to warn you about something. There's going to be an article in the New York Times *on Tuesday about* Brain Battle *and influencing outcomes. I did my best to make sure it's clear you weren't involved and wouldn't have any insights, but I wanted to give you a heads-up, just in case. A copy of the article is enclosed.*

I pause my reading to flip to the next page, and glance at the title of the article: *"Quiz Show 'Brain Battle' caught red-handed in prearranged outcome scandal; Eli Collins of recent 'Brainy Beaus' fame speaks out."*

He really did it. I don't know whether to be enraged or relieved. Eli is finally being honest, but everyone is going to assume I was involved too. I flip back to his letter to see what he has to say for himself.

I promise that unless I hear from you first, this will be the last time you hear from me. I heard what you said, and I'll respect your wishes to be left alone, but I hope you'll forgive me for this goodbye. I spoke to the reporter because I realized you were right all along. Clint was going to do what he wanted, no matter what. I was using his threats as an excuse for myself and taking the wrong path again.

I'm finally seeing that I've used things, like my dad, as justification for my actions for a lot of years. I didn't realize I was doing it, but I was a fool, and you were the one who got hurt because of it. I guess what I'm saying is, I'm not perfect. I've got some work to do on myself, and I'm going to try. In the meantime, I want you to know I'm sorry.

I love you, Charlie. I should have told you every day while I had the chance. You're the smartest person I've ever met, and I love every beautiful piece of you.

I won't ask for your forgiveness or hold out hope for the future. In making my statement, I have zero expectations for what that means for us. When we were younger, after I ruined everything, I left you thinking I hadn't cared. I know I messed everything up again, so I figured the least I could do is make sure I didn't do that to you again. You are everything.

I have always and will always care about you and wish you all the best life has to offer.

—Eli

My traitorous heart flips. I'm disappointed, but I'm not actually sure if it's because I don't want him reaching out at all or because deep down I was hoping for more than a letter. Part of me doesn't want him to leave me alone; wants him to keep fighting and for me to find a way to forgive him. I've been pining over him for years. It didn't go away the first time he hurt me, and it was unlikely to go away immediately this time either.

He loves me. At least, he says he does.

And I believe it.

Damn it, but I really do, because as much as I've tried not to, I love him too.

I flip back to the article.

Several former contestants of the popular live trivia show "Brain Battle" have come forward with accusations that the show's producer, Clint Mariano, approached them with answers for the show's questions to keep them on the show longer in an attempt to impact ratings.

Several contestants. That gets my eyebrow jumping. I guess I shouldn't be surprised he managed to get a hold of others who corroborated. Experiences like that are rarely unique to one person. Still, given Cornelia's reaction, I'm surprised that Eli or this reporter were able to find someone else willing to come forward so quickly. Then again, the day of our last episode, he mentioned that someone else had been willing to meet with us. Eli must have kept the meeting.

Eli Collins, a recent contestant who appeared on four consecutive episodes of the show, was the first to speak out. "He approached me about taking the answers, and I said no, but when I came in for the next episode, he brought it up again. He slipped me the card without me agreeing to it, and then made threats against my family. I was worried for my relatives, so I did what he told me, and memorized the answers."

It continues to outline Eli's story in detail, only leaving out the specifics of the threats that Clint made, likely to protect Eli's father.

Four of the latest episodes of the popular live trivia show "Brain Battle" received a little extra attention when two contestants were paired together and were found to have history.

I roll my eyes. A predetermined outcome conspiracy and they're playing up the romantic angle between us. The article wastes a couple paragraphs on speculations about our brief love affair before meandering back to the scandal.

An inside staff member stated, "Clint tried to keep those conversations secret, but there's people everywhere on set. Word gets around. I left the show years ago, but even then, I'd heard of it happening. I know Clint sometimes had interns drop off envelopes to contestants and warned the interns they'd be fired if they looked inside them."

Clint wasn't so wily after all if the staff picked up on it.

The article goes on to give brief comments from the other two former contestants and speculates on the potential legal ramifications, promising to follow up with an update once more is known.

I lower the letter to my lap. Even after reading the article, I can't decide how to feel. The ambient noises of the hospital around me and the slow thrum of my heart count out the minutes of my silence.

The show will get what they deserve and be unable to cheat innocent competitors out of the prize money they ought to have won. I won't have to live with the guilt of not saying anything, and I feel less foolish for having fallen for Eli again, now that he's doing the right thing.

Damn it, Eli.

He admitted he cheated. At the very least, they'll take away his prize money for the third episode, and probably mine too. That sucks, because Gran is racking up some serious medical bills, but we didn't deserve the money in the first place, so I'm at peace with that. We'll make it work.

What I'm not sure I can come to terms with is Eli. All those years ago, I lied for him. I got in trouble, and he never said a word in my defense. He never even bothered to say thank you. Then, he ghosted me. I tried to talk to him, to ask why, and nothing. Just a year of wandering the high school hallways with a broken heart, and him acting like I didn't exist.

This Eli, who calmly spoke with me at the airport and then sent a letter to respect my space, was someone different. He explained that he'd only accepted the answers under threat and begged me to understand. He'd come clean and been careful in his phrasing to make it clear that I wasn't involved. He may have hurt me again, but I can't keep pretending that he hasn't changed or isn't trying. He's risking major repercussions going public with this.

And he loves me.

Cough, cough, cough.

I jerk my attention to the bed, where Gran lies, her eyes wide open.

"Not the hospital again," she mutters.

I laugh, a tear springing from my eye, and rush to her side, taking her hand. "Gran?"

"I'm all right," she says. "Help me sit up. Am I allowed to have water?"

I help steady her hand with mine and use the other to raise the back of her bed, then run to grab her some water.

"What's the verdict?" she asks.

"They were worried that you hadn't woken up yet, but here you are. They said so long as you woke up and seemed normal when you did, then you should be fine. They had to do another surgery, and they've got you on some new medications."

"So, I'm not dying," she says.

I grin back, so relieved. Gran is back and she's going to be okay. "No, you're not dying."

"Then what on earth are you doing here, and why do you look so tired?" she asks.

I laugh again and wipe away the tears from my cheeks. "Just keeping you company."

Even all gowned and IV'ed up, Gran isn't taking any shit. She gives me a knowing stare. "What else?"

I tell her everything. About past-Charlotte and Eli, present-Charlotte and Eli, the game show, the article—everything. When I'm finished, Gran nods slowly. Letting it stew. She reaches for the water with a shaky hand, and I help guide it to her lips.

"You've had a lot on your plate, with all of this and with meeting Kenny. No wonder you seemed stressed."

"I'm sorry for going behind your back. I just wanted . . . I don't know what I wanted. But I shouldn't have kept it from you. Or given that you're here, maybe I shouldn't have told you. I don't know."

"Charlotte, darling, stop. You did the right thing. I owe you an apology."

My jaw drops, horrified. "What do you have to apologize for?"

"My vendetta against your grandfather has really done a number on you."

"No, honesty is a good thing! Check the children's aisle at the bookstore. It's a virtue every parent tries to instill in their children."

Gran nods. "Of course, it is, but I was extreme. It's also a parent's or grandparent's or whatever caregiver's responsibility to help teach that life is about balance. Sometimes the circumstances necessitate the lie. Do you really think I like your father's mustache?"

I laugh. "I was surprised you'd been so enthusiastic. It's very . . . caterpillar-like."

"It made him happy, and I couldn't see the harm in letting him have that. I'm an old woman, and it's taken me a lot of years, but I'm finally learning."

I frown. "I don't understand."

Gran shifts in her bed, and I help adjust her blankets. "Do you know what my greatest regret in life is?"

I do a quick mental scan of my life and my time with Gran. It's seemed pretty good. "Being turned away by my grandfather?"

She shakes her head. "No. I didn't have any control over that, and even if I did, I wouldn't change it. Being with him brought me your mother, and you, and I wouldn't change that for the world. But it does have to do with him. I regret not forgiving him."

Gran, who has spent more than forty years cursing his name and devoted her life to making sure no one in her family ever acted like he did, wishes she'd forgiven him? "Why?"

"Think of all the time I wasted. I put so much energy into hating him that there was never any room to fall for anyone else. I didn't realize how much time and energy I'd given up to hatred until I got sick. He reached out to your mother too, you know. She decided not to meet with him, and that's her choice. She told me about it a few weeks ago, and I've been thinking about it ever since. I decided I've finally forgiven him now, but it feels like it's too late."

"It's not too late. If you want to talk to him, you could."

She chuckles, which turns into a cough. "No, sweetheart. When I say it's too late, I don't mean too late to see Kenny, though I don't think I'll do that either. We'll see. What I mean is that I should have forgiven him a long time ago. I missed out on so much living because I was hung up on an old wrong. It's too late to get that time back.

I try to apply what Gran is telling me to my situation. I thought I'd forgiven Eli, but I'm still clinging to the past deep down; otherwise, I'd be with him right now. I couldn't stay, but I'm not sure I want to move on from him either. Gran knows me all too well.

"It isn't for me to say if you belong with Eli. Maybe you do, maybe you don't. But don't waste your energy holding the past against him. Time is precious. From what you're telling me about this article and his letter, he's trying. Go to him or set him free."

The more I think about him, the more I miss him. The more I miss him, the surer I am that he's right for me. I just have to take that leap.

"And quit holding vigil over me like it's my death bed. Go take a shower—you stink." She winks.

Eli's made his move, whether it was for me or not. Now it's time for me to make mine.

"Thanks, Gran."

"Off to woo your man?" she asks.

"Something like that."

CHAPTER THIRTY-FIVE
CHARLOTTE

I pull into Eli's driveway, exit my car, and my fantasy arrival has already failed to account for a scenario in which Eli doesn't see me arrive. No bother. Slightly less dramatic, but I'll just have to knock on the door instead.

It really unravels when no one answers the door. Time for plan B. I have to either sit around for who knows how long and wait for him to return, or figure out where else to find him. Work is the most likely place. I pull out my phone, look up the gym, and head out.

On the way, new mental images develop in my mind. I'll pretend to be one of his clients, and he'll come over, ready to train someone, and then he'll realize it's me. His jaw will fall to the floor in surprise. *"I love you too,"* I'll say, and he'll sweep me in his arms and take me right there on the weights bench. Maybe not the last part. Fantasy-Charlotte got a little carried away. We'll definitely hug and cry and agree to meet back at his place as soon as he's off work, where we can talk things out and decide to move forward together.

I check that he isn't in sight of the gym's sign-in desk, then walk up to the employee there.

"I need to talk to Eli Collins, please. But if possible, could we pretend I'm one of his clients instead of telling him who I am?"

The teenage ponytailed employee looks at me quizzically.

"One, that sounds super sketchy," she says.

That's a fair assessment without further explanation.

"I'm here for my 'you had me at hello' moment." I grin, confident. What woman wouldn't be ready to help me out after that?

Except she clearly has no idea what I'm talking about.

"My grand gesture," I clarify. "He grand-gestured me, and now I want to grand-gesture him, so if you could help me surprise him, that'd be great."

Her nose crinkles and her brow furrows, as though I've handed her a page full of hieroglyphs to decipher and not spoken plain English.

"I'm living a second-chance romance with a thirteen-year time gap. We broke up, and he did something big, and then told me he loves me, and I need to tell him I love him back," I deadpan, trying to hand her a form of Rosetta stone, having thoroughly lost all my momentum for plan B.

"Oh!" She lights up, but then her face falls again. "I wish I could help. He isn't here."

Could have led with that—I check her name tag—Stacy. I close my eyes and take a patience-regaining breath.

"Do you have any idea where he might be?" She shrugs, and a tall man in shorts and a muscle shirt and a name tag that reads "Dave" comes around the corner.

"Thanks, Stace, I'm back." His eyes lock on me and widen in recognition. "You're the girl from the show!"

"I am," I begin, ready to go into my whole spiel again.

"He isn't here, but we've got to get you to him! Holy shit, I can't believe you came. This is just like a movie."

I give Stacy a look. See? It's a thing. Dave is in the know. "Do you have any idea where I might be able to find him?"

"The investigators asked him to come up to the police station for his interview."

The police station. Are they going to charge him after all? Since he hadn't gotten his money yet, and he's the one who finally came forward, I thought they'd take away the prize money and leave it at that. I have to get to him. I won't take the fall again for something I didn't do, and I don't think he'd want me to, but maybe I can help.

"Thank you," I call over my shoulder.

"Sure. Go get your man. Good luck!"

* * *

Back in the car, I envision a scenario in which I race to the station and peel into the lot, park at an "it was an emergency" hurried angle, and burst through the doors, yelling, "I object!" Then I remember it's a police station, and peeling into the lot would not be smart; and it's an interview, not a trial, so the *I object* wouldn't make a whole lot of sense and would probably win me some stares.

I really should have thought all this through better. I'm normally more organized than this.

In an entirely undramatic manner, I walk up to the counter.

"Hello. I'm looking for Eli Collins."

CHAPTER THIRTY-SIX

ELI

My ass is numb from the metal of the folding chair. I guess that's part of the confession strategy. Subtly make people as uncomfortable as possible so they're anxious to talk and get out of there. I've been sitting in the small, stuffy room for way too long, and I've gone over everything that happened several times.

I'm beginning to wonder if they're ever going to let me out of here. I lodged a formal report the day before the article ran, and I imagine the attention from the media likely caused them to expedite their investigation, which included a very long and uncomfortable interview with me.

The door opens, and one of the officers interviewing me pops his head in. "You have a visitor."

"What?" I ask, but the door has already closed again. This doesn't make any sense for two reasons. I'm not a prisoner, and I'm not sure why I'd be receiving visitors. Only my work knows I'm here. Somehow, I doubt there is a personal training emergency that requires my immediate attention.

When the door opens again, I must be hallucinating, because Charlie is standing here. She's posed like Wonder Woman, there to save the day.

"Surprise?" she says. Or maybe asks. Her confidence withers as her shoulders droop, and she shifts her feet anxiously.

"Charlie?" I ask.

"Yes," she says.

"Charlie!" I run forward, ready to lift her up and fold her in my arms and kiss her lips off, but I slide to a stop just short, suddenly fearing she's here relevant to the case, and not me.

Before I can start toward her again, she erases any doubt and launches herself at me. I stumble backward but regain my balance when I land against the table in the middle of the room. I catch her and pull her in close.

She's warm and smooth and smells vaguely of popcorn—perfectly Charlie. I squeeze her tight, afraid this might not be real, and if I let go, she'll vanish.

"Surprise wasn't what I was supposed to say," she says against my chest.

I pull back, and she tilts her chin up, to meet my eyes.

I smile back at her. "What were you supposed to say?"

"I love you too," she whispers, and my body lurches, after my heart does a quick shutdown and reboot, in shock and elation over hearing those words on her lips, directed at me, and not in a context where she's saying goodbye. Whatever she sees on my face makes her small smile spread to a wide grin. "Can I have a do-over? I really wanted to get this moment right." She pulls back and makes a move toward the door to redo her entry, but I give her arm a gentle tug, and she spins back into my arms.

Her eyes shimmer as she looks up at me.

"Please don't go anywhere," I say.

"Fine. I'll have my do-over right here. I love you too, Eli."

"One more time," I whisper, because maybe the third time is the charm that will convince me it's real. If I hear it once more, I'll believe that I didn't screw up my chance with her forever, and she still feels the same way that I feel about her.

She lifts her head up, pressing her lips to mine. I inhale a surprised breath around her, then lean into it, kissing her back. She lets out a little giggle, and then her hand slides up my chest, and I completely forget where we are, losing myself in the moment and her. My tongue tangles with hers, and my pulse quickens. She whimpers and presses her palm harder into my chest. All I see is stars. The kiss convinces me as much as the words would have, if not more.

Then, one or both of us pulls back, and I'm so dazed I'm not even sure who, but one of us realizes that an interview room at the police department is not the best place to get it on, and we need to stop before things go any further. Not that my dick is getting the message.

"I love you," she repeats, "in case it wasn't clear."

I laugh. "I got the message that time."

A knock sounds at the door before a detective pops his head in.

"I think they're done for the day. You're good to go," he says.

I take Charlie's hand in mine, and her smooth, thin fingers curled around mine is a slice of heaven, that, as much as I'd hoped, I never thought I'd get to have again. It still feels like we have a lot to work out between us, but she came back. We can talk about it and figure it out.

We get to the lot, and my face falls. Now that she's here, I don't want to leave her side for even a moment, but we've got separate cars.

"Well, that sucks," she says, apparently realizing the same thing as me.

I squeeze her hand a little tighter. I know I'll see her again in all of five minutes, but after being so afraid I'd lost her forever, it feels like I need to absorb enough of this to hold me over for that five-minute drive. A little flame of Charlie that can keep me whole until we get there.

"Meet me at my house?" I ask.

"See you there."

CHAPTER THIRTY-SEVEN
CHARLOTTE

Eli lets us into the house, and we wind up side by side on the couch. I'm probably more on top of him than by his side, if we're being specific.

Eli's fingers dance up and down my back, gently rubbing it and teasing my spine. I'm tempted to swing a leg over him, skip all preamble and settle myself on his lap.

"We should talk first," he says.

"Must we?" I ask, even though I know he's right.

He just gives me a look.

I sigh. "Okay."

"I fucked up," he says.

"Yep," I agree. "But you were in an impossible position, and you made it right. I forgive you. Just don't do it again."

"I won't."

"I was hard on you," I say. "I see that now. My whole family has been living in the past, holding onto old grudges and coming down on anyone that even hinted at opening those wounds. I cemented it so hard in my brain, I didn't know how to react any other way. Even though I said I did, I never really let go of what happened in high school. When I thought I saw the same thing happening again, I bolted."

He nods, his brows drawn together worriedly. "That all makes sense, but what's changed?"

"Us." I shrug. "The circumstances weren't as similar as I was making them out to be in my head. You didn't blow me off; you tried to apologize and explain from the start. It took me some time, but I realized that you are different. I had a little help from Gran."

"Oh?"

"I was holding her grudges for her, and as it turns out, failing to forgive is her biggest regret." I lie on his shoulder, and he rests his chin on my head, clasping me in his arms. "I almost called you before she told me that. Gran got worse. I went to meet my grandfather, and I told her about it, and the next thing I knew she was in the hospital again. It felt like my fault. It still kind of does. I really needed someone to talk to, and the person my heart was aching to call was you."

"Is she okay?" His eyes flick to mine, concerned, and my heart flutters.

"She's going to be. She's been at the hospital for a few days. She had to have surgery, and didn't wake up until this morning, but she's back to being Gran."

"I'm glad she's doing better, but I'm so sorry I wasn't there for you," he says. "I wish I could have held your hand through it."

"I was being stubborn. In a way, it was like you were. I knew that if I needed you, you'd be there."

He gently nudges my chin, and I turn and look at him. He presses a soft kiss to my lips. "I would have. How did it go with your grandfather?"

I shrug. "That one is a work in progress. I think I'll see him again, but we're taking it slowly, and I don't think the rest of my family has an interest in getting to know him, which is fine with me. How have you been with everything that's been going on?" The article may have only come out today, but if they had time to find and interview other sources, and he was able to get it to me ahead of time by snail mail, he must have been working on this since the day we left.

"Honestly, it hasn't been great," he admits, and I wince. It sounds like he could have used someone to talk to as well.

"I'm so sorry. Your dad?"

He looks away and down at the floor, no longer meeting my eyes. "I'm trying to figure out how to get him out of there. I've been trying to track down Lucky, the guy he got in trouble for being around, to get him to admit he was there against Dad's wishes, but haven't been able to yet. It's just our word against Clint's at this point. I'm hoping it won't hold."

My stomach lurches like I'm going to throw up. It's my fault. I'm the one who made us lose. I was following the rules and being honest, trying to do what I thought was right, but it may have cost Eli his family.

"It's my fault," he says, and I can't help but let out an exasperated laugh at the similarity in our thoughts. "He was doing so well, and now he's back in there because of me."

"Don't beat yourself up over this. You tried. I'm the one who distracted you into forgetting the answer. We lost because of me."

He smiles and shakes his head. "Maybe we should both stop taking the blame for things that we shouldn't. Clint is the only one to blame here, and we were both just doing the best we could."

"I'm beginning to realize there's a lot more gray area in the world than I'd ever thought."

"Agreed."

"What do we do?" I ask.

His thumbs, which had taken to slowly running back and forth over my knuckles, grow still.

"What do you mean?" he says.

"What do we do to help him?" I ask.

"Charlie, this isn't your responsibility; you don't have to do anything."

"When I said, 'I love you,' I meant it. We're a team, and not just for a TV show. I want to help."

"I forced you into taking the fall for me once. I'm not going to ask you to again," he says. I appreciate so much that he wants to do this on his own and doesn't jump right to involving me.

"I know. And thank you. But you aren't asking. I'm offering. Tell me what you need."

He kisses the top of my head, trailing his hands over my body. "I've talked to the reporters, the formal report is filed, and I've talked to the police about Dad's situation. All there's left to do now is hope for the best. But thank you. If anything does come up, I appreciate the offer. But for now . . ." He leaves that sentence unfinished and adjusts himself underneath me.

"For now?" I ask innocently, knowing full well where he's going with this.

"I have been miserable, wondering if I was ever going to see you again. Now that I am, I want to see all of you and take my time memorizing every inch of you."

"That could be arranged," I say, sitting up on top of him. I grind my hips over him and feel him hardening beneath me.

"Not here," he says, and carries me to his bedroom. He lays me gently on the sheets, and I breathe in the scent of him.

"Eli," I whisper, tugging him toward me. He holds himself over me, his muscles taut. Our kisses become frantic as we tug each other's clothes off. It's not enough. Desperate for more sensation, my own hand moves over my stomach, and then down to the slick heat between my thighs.

Eli's eyes widen as he watches me, taking in every inch as he promised.

"Are you going to join me?" I ask.

"Join. Definitely join." He lunges, taking my nipple into his mouth, and teasing it with his tongue. I wrap my hand around him as his fingers find my clit with gentle teasing strokes that drive me wild.

"More," I gasp. "I need you."

He grabs a condom from the nightstand, and I writhe in anticipation as he tears it open and rolls it on.

He groans as he thrusts inside me, and I lift my hips to meet him, on a gasp. He rocks back and forth inside me with slow exquisite movements, adjusting his position, until my breaths hitch.

"There," I cry.

He follows my cues, quickening his pace to match my breaths, and I claw at his back, wrapping my legs tight around him, pulling him closer. We almost lost each other. No amount of closeness can be enough.

He plunges deeper into me, hitting just the right spot, and I scream as I fall apart under his rapid movements until he shudders, then stills on top of me. Sated tears spring to my eyes, and I start to laugh.

"Laughter is not the reaction I was going for," he says.

"I'm sorry—it's just a continued release," I manage through my laughter. "You found the Whipple Tickle."

"I found the what?" he asks, settling beside me.

"The Whipple Tickle. It's what they almost called the G-spot after Beverly Whipple discovered it was a thing."

"They did not."

"Oh, they did, when it was finally discovered in—get this—1982."

His fingers pause their absentminded trailing over my skin. "You're kidding me."

"Nope." I say slowly, popping the P.

He laughs and kisses me again, before I regretfully pull away for a bathroom break.

When I step back into the room, Eli is still on the bed, bare chested and looking like a total snack. "Come here, you," he says.

I oblige, crawling onto the bed, and laying my head on his chest.

I "hmm," with quiet pleasure when he takes me into his arms, and everything feels like it's going to be alright. Here in his embrace, it feels like I'm home.

EPILOGUE
ELI

One Year Later

A host of top executives at Game Show TV, including producer, Clint Mariano, were convicted of a laundry list of crimes for their involvement in, attempted cover-up of, and threats toward contestants in the rigging scandal on the popular live trivia show "Brain Battle" as the trial came to a close yesterday.

The executives were charged to varying degrees, based on their level of involvement. Mariano was found to have been the mastermind, facilitating most of the fixed answers, and was charged with a ten-thousand-dollar fine and a one-year prison sentence. He was also found guilty of charges including blackmail and bribery.

Witnesses included recent "Brain Battle" team turned couple, "Brainy beaus Charlotte Evans and Eli Collins of Michigan. While Eli Collins was the original whistleblower on this case, both he and Evans testified. The couple have been seen together frequently and are rumored to have continued a romantic relationship beyond the show."

I glance up from my phone screen. "There appears to be speculation about an untoward relationship between us, m'lady."

"Romantic relationship confirmed." Charlotte gives me an over-the-top eyelash batting, then leans in and kisses me. I melt into it. I could kiss her all day and all night if life didn't require me to do things like work, eat, and sleep. I love her soft lips, delicate but also so capable of a frantic roughness that drives me wild. I love *her*.

"You two ready?" Dad walks out from behind a stack of boxes. Two more days until the big move. When Dad got out, he'd insisted it was time I live my own life and stop spending it supporting him. He said he needed to stand on his own feet, and I needed to find mine, so we sold the house. Between the sale and my prize winnings from the first two shows, we've managed to pay off our debts. He's got a lease on a small apartment near his one job, which he got back after they heard what really happened. He now can afford not to have two jobs.

"All these boxes." Charlotte runs her hand over one of them and flashes me a teasing grin. "I don't know. I might have to rethink things. I'm not sure I've got room if you're bringing all this stuff."

"Too late—you're stuck with me." I wrap my arms around her and feel the vibration in her chest as she laughs.

"That is one kind of stuck I'm happy to be."

I kiss her again. She kisses me back, then swats me away.

"We'd better go, or you'll be late," she says.

I check the time on my phone screen and jump to action. We're cutting it a little close. The three of us pile into Charlotte's car.

* * *

Charlotte

"Charlotte!" Eli's dad, Keith, shouts from an aisle over and a few rows down. "There's some open seats here."

I nudge my way through the crowd of people over to him.

"I can't believe you convinced him to do this," he says.

"I didn't," I respond as the college president steps onto the stage. "I think he realized he's not 'too cool for school' when half the country saw him nerding out on TV with me. He worked hard. I think he wanted this moment to celebrate it," I say.

After some brief speeches, the students begin to file on stage. I scan row after row of square-capped heads and wonder which one is Eli. That's when I see it: A hat painted in brilliant white letters. "You're my final answer."

I emit a high-pitched squeal of swoony delight.

"Saw the hat?" Keith asks.

"Yes! Did you know?"

"Swore me to secrecy. Caught him crafting a few nights ago. Muttering something about his girl being Pinterest worthy and 'hashtag nailed it.'"

"I'm going to give him so much crap for that later," I say.

"I don't think he'll care. He's been spending tons of time on there. He keeps talking about pinned recipes and shit. He's hooked."

On stage, they finally finish off the B's and move on to the early C's. My feet do a little tap dance on the floor, ready to cheer my face off for him. He worked so hard, and I'm so damn proud of him, it feels like my heart might just burst. I scoot to the very edge of my seat.

"Clark . . . Collard . . . Eli Collins," the college president calls his name, and there he is, walking across the stage, looking smug. And who'd have known a graduation robe would do it for me, but dang, that's my man.

I scream and cheer, clap and stamp my feet, proud tears bursting from my eyes.

After enough time for me to mentally recount all of the last several months with Eli and to have Daydream-Eli go rogue and start suggesting naughty things, and then my face flushing, the ceremony finally comes to an end. Everyone pours from the auditorium and outside.

Families stand in little clumps, groups of nicely dressed people circled around individual graduates. I'm so proud to be part of Eli's support system. A part of his family. My own family is doing well. Gran is still sick, but Kenneth has chipped in for her care, so she's getting the best that money can buy. We originally refused Kenneth's offer; I wasn't about to let him buy his way back into the family. But after I met with him a few more times and things were going alright, he still seemed to genuinely want to help. He said he had a lot of lost time to make up for. He's not on visiting terms with the rest of the family yet, but I think they're coming around.

Eli walks over, the side of his mouth quirked up in a smirk.

"You did it!" I screech and leap at him. He grins wide as he catches me, still holding tight to his fake diploma. I know he called the office twice to make sure they had my address on file for them to mail the real one.

I take a picture of him with his father. Then it's our turn. I nestle up next to him, and he drapes one arm around me and holds the diploma up proudly with the other hand. I peer up at his elated expression, his dimples showing.

As Keith takes the picture, I take a mental snapshot of my own. This is a moment I want to carry with me forever.

In this moment, it feels like we can accomplish anything. The brainy beaus are ready to conquer the world.

ACKNOWLEDGMENTS

To my husband, Jeff, you are my final answer, even if you never let me live that one trivia question down. Thank you to my daughters for inspiring me every day and making me want to be the mom that shows you if you work hard, dreams can come true.

Thank you to my whole family, once again, for all of your love and for cheering me on, and to grandma for your guerilla-marketing tactics gone viral!

It takes a whole lot of effort from a whole lot of hardworking individuals to get a book into readers' hands. Thank you to my agent, Emmy Nordstrom-Higdom, and the rest of the Westwood Creative Artists team for everything you do. Much love to my brilliant editor, Melissa Rechter, for your continued faith in me and my work, and your feedback that helps it really shine.

Sarah Horgan, I'm in awe of your talented artistry on so many outstanding covers and am lucky to have had you work on mine. It's adorable. Thank you to Rebecca Nelson, Madeline Rathle, Dulce Botello, and Thai Fantauzzi for your hard work on this book and for putting up with my ceaseless questions. Thank you to the rest of the Alcove Press team, including Matthew Martz, Doug White, Stephanie Manova, Holly Ingraham, Jess Verdi, and Laura Apperson.

I didn't get a chance to thank the incredible narrators for my previous book, *To Get to the Other Side,* in those acknowledgments, but they did such an amazing job, I want to put my appreciation in words for Stephanie Kay and Paul Heitsch.

They say that writing is a solitary art, but I've found that to be entirely untrue. I'm incredibly grateful for the friendship and support I've found from so many other writers. I'm so lucky to have debuted in 2023. You all were wonderful to collaborate with and learn alongside, especially my fellow romance debuts.

Thank you to Meika Usher and Lyssa Kay Adams for your wisdom, friendship, and all the hours in coffee shops to keep me accountable and to chat and vent with me when that's what was needed. And for not judging my obscene reaction to Panera's broccoli cheddar mac 'n' cheese.

To the writers of The Forge, I'm so appreciative for all the ups and downs we've shared, and all the writing sprints. My dear Write Squad, you've become the truest of friends, and I don't know where I'd be without you. From flying across the country to celebrate with me, to beta reads, mental health talks, and daily chitchat, I am unendingly grateful to have each and every one of you. Thank you to both groups, including but not limited to Shannon Balloon, Joel Brigham, Audrey Burges, Chinelo Chidebe, Jen Ciesla, Amber Clement, Laura Chilibeck, Kelly Kates, Kiera Niels, L. Nygren, Michael Nelmark, Rachael Peery, Christy Swift, Ruth Singer, Esme Symes-Smith, Megan Verhalen, and Kyra Whitton.

With the launch of my debut, I had the pleasure of meeting so many incredible librarians and booksellers. You are a wonderful bunch of people. Thank you for your support of my books and for everything you do for books and readers everywhere.

If you'd asked me a year ago where some of my biggest support would have come from, I would not have thought that answer would have been my dentist. For privacy, I'm not naming you, but you know who you are. Thank you so, so much for your excitement over my books and everything you've done to help share them.

Dear readers! Reading a book means taking the author's hand and trusting them to take you on a journey. Thank you for adventuring with me. I hope that Charlie's fun facts kept you entertained and that I managed to make you smile. Every time I hear from one of you, telling me you've enjoyed my words, it absolutely makes my day. Never stop! Please come say hi on any of my socials or join us in my reader group (links in all my social media bios).

To anyone I may have forgotten or who works on the book after I wrote this, I'm sorry, and I thank you with my whole heart.

Lastly, banned and challenged books include important topics. Representation matters. Fight for your libraries. Read banned books. Follow diverse creators. Be kind.

Thank you all.